LATERAL MOVES

THIA FINN

Lateral Moves
Thia Finn

WARNING: This is a work of fiction. Names, characters, businesses, places, events and incidents are either the products of the author's imagination or used in a fictitious manner. Any resemblance to actual persons, living or dead, or actual events is purely coincidental.

Disclaimer: The material in this book contains graphic language and sexual content and is intended for mature audiences, ages 18 and older.

Edited by Nicki Kuzn Swish Design & Editing
Proofreading by Kaylene Osborn Swish Design & Editing
Book designed and formatted by Swish Design & Editing
Cover design by Jason's Photography
Cover photo model: Jonny James
Cover photographer: Wander Aguiar Photography
Cover image Copyright 2017

DEDICATION

To college football players everywhere
who entertain their fans.
And make our weekends exciting!

TIMMS

"The PT said I'm good to go, Coach. Doc signed my Return to Work forms this morning." I handed over the coveted papers. Sitting around in the coaching office without a uniform on was going to take some getting used to.

His eyes scanned over the forms. "What are you standing around here for then? Go over to the central office and show HR the paperwork. You'll officially start Monday morning."

My former coach glanced back at the paperwork, but this time when he looked up, he gave me a long, hard stare. "Timms, you did a damn fine job during spring training, and I expect you to continue working with the new recruits as much as you do with Crew. We can't have you playing favorites out there. We pulled in several top choices from high schools for the QB position. Make sure you give them each an opportunity to prove themselves. You know what I'm looking for. He's gotta be the perfect fit to lead this team. And another thing..."

"What's that, Coach?"

"I spoke to the registrar this morning, and your classes for your Master's program are all set up for the fall. Make that your second priority. You're one of my interns for the fall and probably the spring semester, but you've gotta do the coursework, too. Getting your education is important for your future so get it done."

"Sure thing. I can handle it. Hey, Coach, thank you for giving me a chance." I smiled at him, and he rolled his eyes at me. I knew he still had doubts about my ability to coach, but I'd played quarterback since I started flag football at the age of five. I can read a defense, find an open player at fifty yards, and know how to get the ball where it needs to be. That's what I have to teach that puffed-up dumbass who thinks he waltzed in and won on his own last season. He better be ready to listen because I have a lot to say between now and opening weekend.

I sure as hell never expected my life to work out like this. When I tore my ACL during my senior year at Texas Agriculture University, I figured my football days ended on that third down. The problem was, I couldn't sit around watching some green shithead fresh off the bench take over my QB position. He wouldn't make a mockery of my Rams against the best teams in the conference. I might've left the field on a stretcher, but I didn't leave my guys to hit the turf and fail. We still had a season to win. I started it, and Crew finished it with my help, of course. Now, I had to get him ready to bring his A-game this season as well. Those were still my guys he needed to lead to the National Championships. I'd do all I could, short of killing him, to make him ready, so he better get his big head out of his ass fast, or I'll find another who will.

Walking out to my car, I glanced around the campus of TAU. The love for this university went way back in my family since both of my parents graduated from here. My dad played baseball in his college days, so our family came to see baseball and sometimes football when I was a kid. My mom preferred football, so she bought the season tickets to those games. Dad wanted me to follow in his footsteps, but I never liked baseball as much as football. I needed action, lots of action.

I heard a car door slam in the parking spot next to mine and looked up to see something I'd like to have a little action with. She was tall and built, something that usually didn't land a spot on my radar, but damn, this woman looked good in a skirt and a button-down shirt. They both fit her tight in all the right places, every seam sewn with her body in mind. She glanced at me over the top of my roof telling me she had height. I liked tall women. Hell, who was I kidding, I liked them any size.

"Oh, excuse me." The lightest blue eyes I'd ever seen stared at me. "I'm looking for Coach Jefferies. His office is in this building, right?"

"Yes, ma'am, sure is." I punched the button to unlock my car.

She gave a little laugh. "Don't call me ma'am. I don't work here, yet."

"I say ma'am to all pretty women." I gave her my panty-dropping smile and winked. "You say that like you're going to be working here soon. You Coach's new secretary or something?"

Her outraged laugh caught me off guard as she started up the sidewalk to the double doors. "Oh, hell no," she called over her shoulder as she pulled one open disappearing from sight.

It doesn't matter what she'll be doing in the men's athletics building, it'll be an improvement. I can think of a few things I'd like to do with her in there—like on a weight bench or in the showers. My own joke caused me to smile as I climbed in.

HR was the last roadblock to getting back in the game, only this time, on the other side of those white-chalked sidelines. I viewed it as a lateral move, but one I knew would work in my favor.

INDIA

What the fuck was I thinking?" I slammed the door behind me to my new apartment. Since I'd lived alone for almost a year now, I found myself holding a lot of one-sided conversations—another strange habit I'd developed. Fred Flintstone's feet sound came from my phone announcing an incoming call.

"Yeah?" My younger sister, Chyna, knew when I needed to talk. Even with her being five years younger than me, she could sense it.

"Hey, bitch. What's going on down in Nowhere, Texas?"

"Chyna, really? Why must you call me that? You know it's debasing to women everywhere."

"Quit being such a prude, India. I say it with love, sister."

Yes, our parents had the audacity to name us after their favorite countries. Our mother was weird enough to follow through with my dad's idea when they were backpacking around the world before we were born. I still wonder how he ever got her to be so adventurous back then.

"Back to my original question, what's happening in your little hellhole?"

"I met with the coach this morning, but he didn't have time for me even though I'd made an appointment with him a month ago. I've gotta go back tomorrow at four."

"Sucks for you. You should've known he would be the one to dictate your life for the next year. Isn't that what an internship is all about?"

"I'm not exactly sure what all this position is going to entail yet. I do know they've never had a woman as an intern to the coach, but hey, what's new about that in the football world?"

"What enticed you to go to Texas for a damn internship then? I thought you knew what the fuck you were getting into."

"They're allowing me to be an intern with the head coach this fall while I work on my Master's, and I can coach the kicking team. I'm hoping my skills will pay off, and I'll land a job with the University or at the very least get an offer from another one."

"So, you're going to dazzle them with your footwork and pray they even notice? That's a big leap, don't you think India, or is this how shit works in sportslandia?"

"I know you don't agree with my choices, but I don't want to give up football. It's still important to me. I want it to be part of my life, Chyna."

"Okay, don't get all butt hurt, beyotch. I'm only saying you know breaking into the dick domain is going to be hard, and I'm not talking about a boner here, either."

Ignoring her crazy euphemisms... "I've fought it for years. I know what it's going to take. I'll show them, though. I'm the best at what I do, and if I can teach just one guy to be the best in the conference, then I'll be a shoo-in for a job somewhere."

"I believe in you, India. You know that, right? I'll support your strange needs no matter what, but I fucking hate the idea of you getting knocked down if it doesn't work out. That's all."

I knew she tried to fill in where my dad would have jumped to bolster my spirits about playing in a man's world. He'd have been on the phone offering constant support from the time I moved here.

"Yeah, I know and thanks. I love you for it, too, among other things you're good at."

She yawned in the phone. "I'm exhausted. This whole sorority thing is killing me. I can't imagine how shitty it's going to be next week when that suck-ass alarm goes off at some ungodly, predawn hour."

"You have to go to school, Chy. That's why you're there, remember?" Our parents didn't give us a chance to do anything else between high school and college. They preached at us to attend college as if it was grades thirteen to sixteen.

"Yeah, yeah, I hear you. I have my schedule all lined out. The sorority planned an event just to introduce us to the campus like we were too damn stupid to do this shit on our own."

"They're trying to help you acclimate to your new surroundings. Take advantage of it. I was lost the first month I was at Cal U."

"So, tell me how many hot guys with massive schlongs were in towels running around in the athletic building when you were there? Wait, let me guess, you purposely went in knowing when they wouldn't be there."

"*Chyna*," I yelled into the phone. "It's not like that. I need for those guys in towels to respect me when I finally get hired as a coach."

"Then you better get used to seeing massive amounts of dick if that's where you plan to have an office. I just can't figure out why the hell you can't coach a female sport like all the other females? You know you could coach soccer with your eyes closed."

"You know why." I took a deep breath. We'd had this conversation a million times in our house. Chyna heard it at least some of the time before I left to play for CU. I loved football more than life. I played as long as I could, but since I couldn't get an NFL position as a kicker, it didn't mean I couldn't continue to be involved with the sport.

I love football—everything about it from the fans cheering in the stands to the final whistle of the game. My dad and I had that in common. He wanted a boy to play so badly, but instead, he got two daughters to raise. He never complained, but I could see it in his eyes when we watched a game together.

First, it was little league football—they wouldn't let me play. All I could do was be on the cheer squad, and I refused to even think about something so ridiculous. Why would I want to stand on the sideline in a skirt, no less, and scream and yell when I could be adding to the score every chance I had? My mom let Dad have his way, and he continued to take me to games. Thank God Chyna came along and was the epitome of lace, curls, and all things feminine.

I started soccer as soon as I could, though. Dad took me down and bought all the equipment sporting a huge smile with everything the athletic store offered. He didn't know much about soccer, but he did know they would let me play with the boys. I was big for my age when I was five, and I could kick harder and run faster than most of the boys, and my coordination matured much faster than boys did at that age.

By the second year, the teams fought over who would draft me first. I could kick harder and more accurately than most of the dad coaches, and they loved me. I was tough, too. They would never find me crying over a little kick here and there. My mom would come unglued when I came home with new bruises, but Dad always managed to calm her down.

When school sports finally started, my dad had to petition the school board to allow me to play on the boys' football team. My kicks split the uprights from thirty-five yards out with perfect accuracy over and over in seventh grade. If the team could get the ball down there, I could score at least three for our team. We won many games on my kicks alone.

High school proved to be more of a challenge, so I had to up my game with a lot of hard work which only made me more determined to do it. I put up with a lot of shit, too. In the beginning, the guys gave me hell every day on the field. When I beat out the upperclassmen for the kicking position, I gained a little respect but not completely—that ended when I kicked the field goal that was the winning score for district champs. The real respect came when I kicked a forty-three yard—my personal best—at semi-finals. With three seconds on the clock, Coach gave me the nod, and I went for it. I prayed, and then I told the guys in the huddle to pray. I'd never had to kick one that far in a game.

The quarterback caught the snap and held it just like I liked it, and I launched that ball off my foot sending it down the field. My life stood in slow motion for the seconds it took, but when that ball cleared the bar by two feet landing in the end zone, the team carried me off the field to a stadium full of screaming fans. Best day of my life.

By my junior year, college inquiry letters came in daily. Small colleges wanted me, but I wanted Division One schools. When my distance became so accurate, other schools hated playing us because of me. Scouts turned up to take notes while I dazzled them with my spot-on kicks. Between my coach and Dad sending off videos of my performance, offers poured in from everywhere.

"Tell the truth, India. You want to be out there with the guys in those tight, white uniform pants because you know they're freeballing under them and that gets you all horny," Chyna said and did whatever she could to make me either blush or be angry, but I wasn't falling for it this time.

"Yeah, skankadoo, keep thinking about guys in tight pants, and you'll be back home with Mom in no time." I knew she hated when I called her that.

"Fuck off, cockblocker." My least favorite name had me groaning and her laughing.

"Why would you call me that? I've never cockblocked you a single time."

"Because you cockblock all those hot guys who would like to get in your pants every time you put that football uniform on, and you know it. You block them from thinking of you as a girl, and you take their spot on the team."

"Shut up, twat-waffle. You know that's not true." I smiled. I could play her name game.

"Stop talking, ho bag."

"Bitch face."

"Cum muncher."

"Vagina breath."

"Oh, God, India. Just call it what it is, you dirty cunt."

"*Chyna*! That's so wrong."

"You started it." After a pause, we both started laughing. Only my sister and I can call each other names of this caliber and get away with it.

We both caught our breath, and the phone got quiet. "Have you spoken to Mom today?" Chyna broached the unavoidable question.

"No. You?" Guilt poured out in my tone.

"Not yet, but I might call her later."

"We can't avoid Mom forever." I could try, but I would still feel bad for it.

"Okay, I'll call her after dinner." She let out a deep breath.

We both loved our mother, but our relationships with her were complicated. After my dad died during my freshman year, Mom wanted me to come home.

She begged me to leave at midterm. That would mean giving up football, and I would be back under her control. The older I got, the more controlling my mom wanted to be with me which seemed backward.

We fought often, but with my dad around, he could always make her understand why I should go off to college and why I needed to play ball. She hated every minute of it. When I left for CU, she shifted her feelings toward making Chyna the perfect princess. She'd already started the day she delivered Chyna, but again, my dad kept her reigned in somewhat. After he passed away, Chyna's years at home would have been hell, but my sister was a force to be reckoned with by her teenage years.

She revolted at every turn to being the prim and proper lady my mom wanted all along. The girl loved being female, but the style my mom sought was never going to fly. Chyna stood up to her at every turn starting with her colorful language that could embarrass a hardcore sailor. I sometimes cringed when she went places with me, especially if something made her angry.

"Okay, anal muffin, later."

"My God, where do you come up these words, Chyna?"

"Oh, you know, from the internet. Isn't that where all things are found these days?" I could hear her laughing as she ended the call.

"She's going to be the death of Mom and me one day." I smiled thinking about how great it would be never to give a thought about how I appeared to others.

Pulling out my laptop to check my classes starting next week, my phone lit up again.

"Wonder what she forgot to tell me." Without looking at the phone, I answered. "Hey, ho, what'd you forget?"

"Uh, this is Coach Jefferies. I'm looking for India Durham. This is the number she gave me."

Well, shit. Just the person who didn't need to hear that.

"Oh, sorry, Coach Jefferies, I thought you were someone else." I could feel the blood rising in my face.

A *harrumph* sound came over the phone. "I wanted to see if you had time to come down to the coaching offices first thing in the morning? The other intern will be here, and I'd like to go over the information only one time. Is that possible?"

"Sure, I'd be happy to. What time?"

"Eight. I've got some family things to do, and I can tick this meeting off my list if you can be here."

"Absolutely, Coach. I'll see you then."

"Right." The phone went dead.

Just what I wanted to do on my last Saturday off, get out of bed that early.

I closed my computer and looked around my apartment at boxes still waiting to be unpacked. Guess

I knew how I'd be spending this evening. I had a feeling my time was about to belong to the coach after this meeting.

As I pulled open the door to the offices, I heard female laughter. Hmm, a girl in the coaching offices, that's new. I turned the corner in the hall to Coach Jefferies', and the first thing I saw was dark blonde hair pulled into a tight bun at the nape of her neck. He must have picked another female for a secretary. This woman looked too uptight to be the same girl from the parking lot.

Coach saw me coming through the glass windows and waved me in. I walked over and looked down into the same sky-blue eyes as before. Damn, she was beautiful. Her lightly tanned skin only enhanced her eyes. She was dressed in a tight black skirt and another form-fitting shirt. Her tits looked amazing even covered up.

I heard the coach make a noise as he leaned back in his chair, and it drew my attention from her. I wanted to drink in her entire body, but I moved my eyes immediately back to her face.

"Timms, this is the other intern who'll be working with us this fall, India Durham."

"India, this is Timms. He's going to be working with our quarterbacks while you work with special teams."

I watched her unfold from the chair, so her perfect body stretched to a tall height. I remembered this from yesterday, but now that she stood by me, I knew she was close to five-nine or ten. At six-foot-three, I hardly had to look down at her which was a first for me when looking at a woman. I liked it. Immediately. Hell, I liked her immediately.

"Hello." I took her hand gently to shake, but she came back with a hold on mine that rivaled a lot of guys' handshakes.

"Hi. Nice to meet you this time." She looked over at Coach. "We spoke in the parking lot yesterday when I came to meet with you."

"Right. I didn't realize I was talking to a famous kicker. I've read about your kicking ability for the last four years. It's a pleasure to meet you." Coach J gave me a strange look and then glanced at our still-joined hands. I dropped hers immediately.

"So, now you two are through playing handsy, let's get down to business. I want to cover the information about the positions you've both agreed to take." He handed us a sheet with a list on it.

"Your lists are basically the same. India will be working with the kickers, both the old and new recruits, just like Timms will do the same with the quarterbacks. You'll be expected to show up for any assigned classes you have other than this one, and I expect you to provide me with a schedule for those asap." He stopped and looked up at us both.

"You'll be working on the field a lot. I expect you to be here whenever you're not in class. You both understand that? You are being paid a stipend for the time you're here, and I expect you to be here all the time."

We both nodded our heads.

"The University is allowing me to keep you both for the full year if you should choose to stay in the program after the fall semester. If not, we'll find someone else to take your places. If you fail to commit one hundred percent to this program, you'll be asked to leave at the end of the fall semester. Not doing your job is grounds for me to kick you out of the football program sooner. Y'all got that?"

We both nodded but stayed quiet.

"Do what's expected, and there's not a problem. I'm here to teach you to do your jobs better and not babysit you. I'm not your momma so don't expect me to treat you that way. If you miss classes, miss practice, miss being in here, you're gone. Got it?" He only waited a beat before adding, "But if there's a problem I need to be made aware of, come to me immediately. I expect you to act as coaches to these kids and not their friends. I also expect you both to conduct yourself professionally at all times." He glared over the top of his reading glasses when he said this. "What you two do on your own time is between you, but when you're with this team, you are representing the University and this coaching staff. Do y'all understand what I'm talking about here?"

We both responded with, "Yes, sir."

India spoke up quickly. "That will not be a problem, Coach." She looked at me and gave me a strange look. Did she expect me to jump her bones or something when we got out of this office? That was not my style. If, and I'm talking a big if, we got together outside of a friendly conversation, she would be coming on to me not me luring her into my bed. She had a lot to learn about Theo Timms.

"So we're all clear on the expectations of the athletic department?"

Again, we responded with, "Yes, sir."

I knew he was a tough coach, but he also cared about his players. He wanted what was best for them. He agreed to take me on even though I'd never coached before my football career ended with my injury. After my surgery, he found me and asked me to work with the kid who replaced me. Because of this man, I graduated from college and got into the Master's program.

"Okay, so go do whatever it is you do on a Saturday, and we'll see you both Monday. Be sure to send me your schedules, so I'll know when to expect to see your happy faces."

We stood at the same time and said our goodbyes.

"You want to grab some breakfast?" India asked when we moved through the doors out of the athletics offices. "I didn't get up in time to have any, and I'm starving."

"Sure, that'll be fine." *See, she's already coming to me.* "Where you want to meet?"

"I'm new here, so you choose. I haven't had a chance to get out and explore."

"Then let me drive, and I'll show you around. It's a college town so it won't take long."

Her stomach chose that moment to make a loud rumble, and she turned the cutest shade of pink placing her hand on her stomach. "Oops, yeah, that's embarrassing."

"I think I better feed you first. Don't want you passing out from hunger." I smiled at her, and she turned even redder.

"I've never fainted in my life, but I guess my stomach is saying I could." She laughed at herself as she rubbed the flat surface. This time I followed her hands in the circle wondering exactly how that would look without that tight shirt over it. Damn, I have to get my mind off her body. We're going to be working and probably traveling together.

I opened the passenger door for her, and the look she gave me as she sat down puzzled me. "What?"

"Oh, I don't find many guys who open doors anymore. It's nice. Thank you."

I gave her a brief smile. Yeah, I'm that guy. My momma taught me to use good manners with females. She had a lot to learn about being in the south.

After a short drive, we arrived at The Big Horn Diner, the only place in town worth going to for breakfast. Being a little way out of town, it was far enough from campus that we could escape students everywhere.

She looked around as we sat in the red vinyl booth. "They have the whole vintage thing going on here."

I glanced around the place. "I guess. Never really thought about it. The breakfast is supposed to be good. Never been awake early enough to have it. I've had breakfast at a few places in town around three or four in the morning but never around nine."

"Oh, yeah. I forget you went to school here. Is this a big party school?" She looked over the top of the menu at me with an eyebrow raised.

"I guess it's as much as any other place where you put twenty thousand eighteen to twenty-two-year-olds in one small town with beer sold on every corner."

Thia Finn

"Yeah, I suppose that's true. Never thought about it that way before." The waitress came over and smiled at me and ignored India with her back turned away from her.

"What can I get for you, Timms?" She beamed a smile at me. I glanced over at India who had the funniest look on her face. I couldn't decide if she was shocked or pissed off.

"Well, I think it would be better if you took Coach Durham's order while I figure out what I'll have."

The pretty blonde turned and eyed India up and down which only added to India's obviously angry stare.

"Oh, you're a new coach at the University?"

"Yeah... yes, I am," India replied without looking up.

"That's cool. What'll you have?"

"I'll have the number seven with orange juice and coffee, please. I would like the eggs sunny side up and two whole-wheat pancakes." After a beat, she added, "Please." The coolness in India's tone made it clear she was not having the young woman treat her as though she was invisible.

"Sure thing." The waitress took India's menu and turned back to me. "And you?"

"I'll have the same thing the same way, please."

"No problem." The girl snagged my menu and backed away continuing to look at me until she hit the counter with her hip.

"Do you get this treatment all over town?" India asked when the girl finally turned away.

"What treatment is that?"

"The females you're seen with are treated like they're invisible because the girls can't get their eyes off you?"

I laughed a little. "No, not always. Now that I've graduated and am not the quarterback, they'll latch onto the young pup who's taking my place."

"So you're going to be coaching him to the next national championship?"

"Yep, Coach let me start during last season and in spring training."

"Does he have any potential? To replace the great Theo Timms, I mean."

I got the feeling she was trying to categorize me as being the enemy here.

"He's good. Really good. He came with a lot of high school experience, but that's not Division One college play. He's still a little too cocky for me, so I spend a lot of time deflating his ego."

India laughed out loud when I said it. The sound made me smile. It was a genuine laugh that captured all my attention. She obviously didn't hold back much which was rare for a lot of women. The smile that accompanied it was off-the-charts beautiful, and I couldn't take my eyes off her lips as they turned up in such a gorgeous way.

She calmed down quickly when the waitress returned with our drinks.

As the girl walked away, she looked up at me. "Sorry. I didn't mean to laugh so hard at what you said, but you have to admit, it was pretty funny."

"Why do you think that? I was being honest."

"It's funny because I can just imagine you being the same way when you were the quarterback. You know, all cocky and supporting a big, inflated ego that females like the waitress were all too eager to help with."

I took a sip of my coffee and looked at her. I knew she was right, but she didn't have to know that right away. I ruled the campus when I was a student.

India's face sobered quickly. "Hey, I'm only joking. I didn't know you back then so I could be wrong."

It was my turn to laugh, good old Chi Omicron Chi always came back to haunt me. "No, you got it pretty much right, I guess. As president of XOX and quarterback of the team, I didn't have a problem dictating lots of things that went on."

"And I'm sure that included who and how often, too." It was her turn to glare over the rim of her cup.

"Now, I didn't say that." I never took my eyes off hers. "But since you mentioned it, you're right. I had my pick of the litter anytime I wanted it."

"I cannot believe you just said that."

"What?"

"Pick of the litter. Do you assume all females are dogs or worse, bitches?" Her tone grew angry quickly.

"Hey, I didn't say it to make you mad. It's just a phrase we used to use. I'm sorry."

"No, it's okay. Don't apologize. I'm going to have to get used to being around guys all the time again. I know you guys talk bad about females who act like the waitress, but it doesn't necessarily make it right, though."

"I might need to go to some sensitivity training or sexual harassment training if we're going to be hanging out often."

Once again, she burst out laughing. "You are too funny, Timms. We'll probably both have to complete sexual harassment training to keep our jobs. Most require it nowadays."

"You know already that being in the men's athletic department isn't going to be easy for you, right? How'd you get into kicking anyway?"

We spent the rest of breakfast with her telling me about playing football in high school and college. We laughed at some of our stories that happened over our college days. India was easy to talk to, and I enjoyed learning about how a beautiful woman fit in on an all-male team.

"Y'all need anything else?" The waitress laid the check down on the table, and I grabbed it immediately. No way would India pay for this meal.

"No, I think we're good."

"Great, I'll take the check when you're ready." She turned and walked off doing something with her hips that should have caused displacement. I watched her for a few seconds before turning back to India who was staring at me.

"What?" Busted.

"What? Did you like her show?"

"No, I was wondering how she did that without throwing something out of whack in her back." I smiled hoping she would see the humor in what I said.

"Oh my God, Timms. You're terrible, and she was doing her best to impress you." She pulled her billfold out as we stood.

"If she wanted to impress me, she should have been nicer to you." India stuck out some cash, but I put both my hands up.

"No, ma'am. I'm buying. You're the new kid on the block. It's the least I can do."

"Timms, we have a long year ahead of us. Let me pay my part."

"Next time." I threw some cash on the table and put my hand at her back lightly pushing her toward the door. It felt like an intimate touch when my thumb came in contact with skin above the top of her skirt where her shirt had ridden up. I forced myself not to slide it across the soft skin.

INDIA

After a short tour of the city I would live in for the next year, we drove back to the University parking lot where my car sat patiently waiting. He parked next to it and turned to look at me.

"That didn't take long. The city's smaller than I thought it would be." I picked up my bag preparing to get out.

"Yeah, not too much to it. If you want something good, you go to Austin. It's only about forty-five minutes away. We'll go sometime if you want."

"That's nice of you to volunteer, but I doubt I'll have too much time to waste this semester. I bet you don't either." With class and coaching, there wouldn't be many spare minutes.

"There's always time to take out a pretty lady. I'll make time." He hit me with that smile of his that caused my girly parts to perk up. That was something I didn't need to have going on.

"I'm sure since you just graduated, you still know lots of pretty girls to take out here on campus." He probably had tons of females hovering around waiting for the big Theo Timms to notice them. I bet they were more than willing given his status and looks.

"Not a good idea since I'm employed by the University. Coach didn't say it, but I know the TAs are told to stay away from the students."

"Really? The students are adults. Why would the University care who the TAs took out?"

"Some of them could end up being their instructor, and that might lead to all kinds of problems come grade time."

"Oh, yeah, I guess that's true. Glad I'm not teaching a class, too."

"So you planning to jump into the dating pool here on campus?" He cocked that eyebrow at me like he did before. He must have used that well-practiced look often.

"No, I didn't say that." I took a breath and let it out. "Honestly, I hadn't even thought about dating while I was here. Getting a job is my number one goal for this year ahead of me. Surely, you've thought about working for TAU full-time, right?"

"Sure as hell have." He sat back staring at the building in front of us. "When I got hurt last year on the field, all I could think about was my pro days being over. My football days went up in a puff..." he motioned the gesture, "... of fucking smoke. All the way to the locker room on the stretcher and then to the hospital, I tried to wrap my head around it. Coach Jefferies came to see me the day after my surgery and said he expected me to be on the sidelines even if I had to ride in a damn golf cart to get there."

"You're kidding, right? He expected you to be out there hurt?"

He shook his head slowly from side to side. "It wasn't like that, India. He needed me to be there supporting the team. That's what he said, at least. More importantly, he wanted me to feel like they hadn't abandoned me because of the injury. He and all the coaches busted their asses to help keep my spirits up."

"Oh, well that's different. Good on him to take care of his players no matter what."

"Exactly right. He didn't want me hiding in my apartment while all my closest friends busted their asses to win games every Saturday. I guess he knew how it could mess with my head and cause all kinds of problems."

"That's very true. I saw it happen more than once to good players."

"Coach is not one to play favorites, but he's not going to let his guys flounder around either. He encouraged me to come to practice when I wasn't working out, and then when I started physical therapy, he came to see me again. Told me to get my ass back out on the field to talk to Crew. You know, give him pointers and shit."

I turned toward him. "Did you go?"

"Hell yeah, I did."

"I guess what I wanted to ask is... how did you feel about returning only to be on the sidelines? That would have killed me to watch someone else do my job."

"Oh yeah. It hurt like a son of a bitch to stand aside and see the kid lead my team to the championship, but I was so damn proud of the team and him, too."

"I gotta tell you, Timms, I don't know you all that well yet, but I'm proud of you. If you stood on the side watching and can still talk about it without it messing with you, you're a better man than I am."

He looked at me and smiled. "I sure as hell hope I am."

We both laughed at my comment, but he knew what I meant.

"So I'll see you Monday morning," I called as I stepped out of his low-slung car. He rolled down my window as I shut the door.

"We could go do something tonight if you'd like. I mean, if you don't already have plans."

"That's very kind of you to ask, but I'm sure you already have friends lined up to see. They're all back on campus now so your old teammates will be around, won't they?"

"You're right, and you need to meet the team so we should go throw back a few beers with them."

"No, I don't think that's a great plan. I want them to see me as a coach and not their drinking buddy. You go and have fun with the guys." I started walking away.

"Wait," he called to me. "These guys have girlfriends, too. Most of them are attached at the damn hip. You can meet them since you won't be coaching them. Unless you don't like having friends who are females."

He said it in a taunting manner. I spun around and looked at him. "I can be friends with them, but they might not like me considering I'll be with their boyfriends on a regular basis."

"Nah, they aren't like that. I know two you'll love. Well, one for sure."

"What's wrong with the other one?"

I took a deep breath. "Well, you see, Quinn's mouth is worse than any sailor I've ever known, and some find it offensive."

I laughed out loud. I couldn't help myself. When I finally stopped, I said, "So you think I'm going to find a potty mouth offensive? Wait 'til you meet my sister.

She could teach the Sons of Anarchy Motorcycle Club a few new words."

"Oh, yeah? I suppose Quinn might not be offensive to you then. So how about it? I'll call and tell them we'll stop by this evening? See how it goes from there?"

I studied the toes of my shoes for a few seconds. What would it hurt to meet some new people while I'm here? I needed to have some girl time occasionally. All my friends were back in California. I looked up and saw him watching me through his open car window.

"Okay. I'll go, but you have to promise me that if I'm not comfortable, you'll let me call an Uber and get out of there without an argument from you."

"I'll do better than that. When you're ready to go, just say the word, and we're out."

"Right. Wait! We're not going to a frat house or anything, right?" That would be a big no for me. I didn't do frat boys when I was in college, and I wasn't going to start out of college.

"No, my frat days are over. Damn shame, too. They were some of the best days of my life. Had to turn my gavel over to the new pres before the spring semester ended. Besides, that would be fucking lame, me wanting to hang on to my golden-boy days at this point."

"I just wanted to make sure before I agreed."

His 'golden-boy days,' huh? So, college was the best days of his life. I guess that's great for him.

"I'll pick you up at eight. Where do you live? Nevermind, all the stats about the coaches are in the email from Coach J."

"Oh, okay. So it's Hunter Creek. Are you familiar with it?"

"Oh, yeah. Student housing, huh? You like to live dangerously or at least with no sleep."

"It was on the suggested list, so I went with it."

"Like I said, dangerously sleepy." He laughed and started his car.

I noticed the loud roar it made. Typical guy. I glanced back when I realized he hadn't left. He waited until I got into my car before he backed out revving up the noise.

"That's weird. I wonder what he's waiting for?" I said out loud.

After making my way home, I walked into my apartment as my phone rang. *Chyna, again today?* She must be missing me. I laughed at my own joke.

"Hey, what's going on?"

"Not much, hooker. Just bored. The sorority didn't have any shit going on this afternoon so they could get tonight's big fucking party ready to go for all the pledges. What about you? Tell me your life doesn't suck yet?"

"What makes you think my life is going to suck, Chyna? I'm in grad school, and I have a job doing what

I love. What more could a recent college graduate want?"

"A hot guy with a big dick?"

"Oh please, Chyna. Really?"

"Yes, really. So what did you do today?"

"You must be bored to be interested in my lowly existence."

"I am. I wish my roommates would get their sweet little asses here on campus. So spill, what's new since yesterday?"

"I ended up meeting with the coach and the other intern this morning."

"How'd that go? Same old shit in the world of football?" Her unpleasant attitude told me to make this quick. She'd be asking me for a play by play of my day so far.

"The meeting went great. He's a typical athletic director and head football coach. He's busy and cut straight to the rules and expectations which were nothing new. I'm excited about Monday's practice to get here."

"What about the other intern? Is it a butchy female?"

"Lord, Chyna. You are in a mood."

"I know, sorry. I'm bored out of my fucking mind. It's so lame here that I'm ready for class to start just to have something to do. At this rate, I'll be in trouble before the first damn week's out so I can say I had some action going on. I've yet to see one hot guy."

"I'm sure you're looking in the wrong place then. Get out of your room and walk around. Go sit at the nearest coffee shop and watch the people come and go. Surely some of them will be hot guys."

"Yeah, with their equally cute girlfriends. No, thank you."

"Then quit bitching to me about your lack of fun and games."

"Hey, you never told me about the other intern."

"It's a guy, not a butchy female." I mocked her speech with her words.

"Oh. A guy, huh? In the football coach's office. Is he hot? Would you do him?"

"Chyna, please. Can we have a conversation without you asking stupid questions about my life?"

"Okay, if you wouldn't do him, would I? I mean you know I have standards in that department."

"No, and I don't want to know your standards for a doable guy either."

"India, we are grown women. Despite our mother preaching our entire lives about no sex, we can have a good fucking time if we choose, and I choose. Hey, maybe that's what's wrong with me. I need to get laid. My damn batteries on Fred stopped working yesterday."

I rolled my eyes and took a breath before I spoke, "TMI, Chyna."

"Back to the hottie you *haven't* told me about yet. Give me juicy details so Fred and I can have our way with him in my head later. Do they sell batteries at the bookstore?"

"No. I'm not giving you details... *ever.*"

"Don't be a prude, just tell me. What color is his hair?"

"Black."

"His eyes?"

"Brown."

"Is his dick long and skinny or short and wide or perfect in both directions?"

"I'm done, Chyna. No more questions."

"That's because you don't know the answers. Please tell me you're planning to find out soon?"

Her voice perked up when she said it. This girl did need to get laid. Eww. I don't want to think about my sister having sex, now or ever.

"Okay, last thing, and then I'm hanging up. He's tall, he's hot, he's got tattoos, but I've only seen them peeking out of his sleeve, and he's a coach intern as well. He's going to coach the quarterbacks because that's what he played and apparently was great at the position."

"I bet he's got great moves in other positions, too."

"Bye, Chyna."

"Wait, are you seeing him again, and what's his name?"

"Yes, tonight. His name is Theo Timms. Now bye and stay out of trouble."

"Yeah, yeah. Bye, sister dearest. Don't hit it if you aren't into it," she yelled before I could tap end on my phone.

"God, please take care of that wild child and keep it all away from my mom's ears." I offered up the quiet prayer.

I flopped down on my couch taking my laptop from the coffee table. I needed to spend some quality time restudying the group I'd be starting with on Monday. TAU had the rep and funds to pick the cream of the crop to play for the Rams, so I knew they had stellar high school stats. It would be my job to work with them and decide the best two out of the group of four to recommend for the starting kicker position. I needed to choose wisely, not only for the team but for my job too. Choosing the wrong person could cost us both.

I made a spreadsheet to compare all the necessary numbers for each guy. Too bad a female hadn't tried for one of these spots. I'd love to have the chance to work with a girl. Not as many were as driven as I was.

I started filling in the headers, and my phone chimed with a text from Timms.

> **Timms:** *You might want to slip down to the field and watch your boys.*
> **Me:** *They're there now?*
> **Timms:** *3 out of 4.*
> **Me:** *Be there in 10.*

The eager beavers who truly wanted the starting position must think putting in their own time is a good idea, and they're right. Coach Jefferies might not be there, but I bet one of the coaches is.

You're that coach, dumbass, I told myself and laughed.

INDIA

I slid into my shoes and looked down. "Yeah, can't go like this."

After changing into shorts and a team t-shirt, I headed out. All the way over I thought about approaching them on the field. I finally decided I wouldn't. I walked through the gates and headed up the back ramp to the stands to sit. I looked down at the small tablet I brought with me. I'd never met them so today they would be labeled Blond, Tall, and Muscles. I'd be sure to change that when I put the info down permanently.

They each took turns kicking and retrieving for the next guy so these three could work as a team—points for all of them. Their kicks started at the three-yard line, where college currently kicked extra points from. They did this perfectly which I expected.

It'll be interesting to see who can do it consistently from the twenty or thirty-yard line. I knew with changes in the NFL happening a few years back, it was only a matter of time before the NCAA moved it to college ball.

I watched this action and took plenty of notes for an hour before I took the stand steps down in a run. I saw some good form, some terrible sloppiness, and then some bad habits or poor coaching while I watched. I couldn't stand it any longer.

"Stop. Just stop," I called before Blond could put his foot into the ball another time.

"What's the matter, cupcake? Am I not doing it right? I'll be happy to show you what I can do right." He grabbed his junk and shook.

I came to a dead stop watching this display of stupidity. I knew this behavior so well, but now I was on a different playing field for dealing with it. I wanted to earn their respect, but I wouldn't put up with sexual innuendos from any of these guys.

Taking a few deep breaths, I walked up to him and stood eye to eye and toe to toe. "You think you're going to kick the damn ball with that small, soft appendage better than with your big toe?" I glanced down at his crotch and back to his face.

"Damn straight. It'll get hard on demand, and I can use it on you instead. I bet you have something soft that'll be grateful to house it."

"Is that right?"

"Sure is, sweet cheeks. All nine inches of it, soft."

"Paa-lease," I dragged the word out. "Even a hard nine inches won't kick a ball, dumbass."

"Is that right, and you know this because you've got one and tried it?" He looked around at the other two players who were laughing at his antics.

"No, but if I did, I would know when to man up and use it for the right thing instead of kicking a ball down a field, something you need to learn how to do better."

"Well, now, since you admittedly don't have the right equipment to be out here with the big boys," again fisting his junk, "I suggest you go find a girls' team or squad and practice what you do know how to do. I'm sure the coach would appreciate the ladies steering clear of the players while we practice."

"Is that right? I'm sure a coach is glad to see you trying to do something to improve your kicking, but your particular coach doesn't want to see you continually practicing the same thing wrong every time your foot hits the ball."

He glared down at me. "What makes you think I'm doing it wrong? We spotted you sitting up in the stands watching us wondering what you looked like up close." He looked at the other two. "I'd say, boys, we were off a little. She's more of a six than an eight, but you gotta give her something for having the balls to come out here like she did."

The other two laughed again. "We saw you taking notes on your little tablet, too. What do you do, report back to the coach on what you see? He ought to at least get someone who knows what they're doing before he sends them out to write down how awesome our skills are."

"Oh really." Before I could finish my statement, I caught someone walking up in my peripheral vision.

Calm and quiet words floated over our anger from a voice I recognized. "Well now, if I were a betting man, I'd say someone is in over their head here and doesn't know how to talk themselves out of the situation they've found their shithead self in."

"You're damn straight she has." He looked at Timms and smirked. "Dude, do you know this crazy bitch?"

"Yeah, but that would be crazy bitch, Coach Durham, to you, boy." The slow, southern twang rolled off Timms' tongue. "And I might add, now would be the time to pray to God that she's a forgiving crazy-bitch coach, or you might find yourself packing your shit and going back to whatever rock you crawled out from under that fed your overinflated ego."

Before the words were out of his mouth, the other two kickers were sheepishly backing away from us. They obviously knew the kid was in trouble. At least two of the three had some brains and knew how to use them.

Blond turned his body directly toward Timms as did I. "What the hell are you talking about?"

"Yes, please do go on, Coach Timms. It seems blondie here suffers from a variety of problems, one being that he can't follow directions or he's touched with selective deafness. It's gotta be one of the two so take your pick." I moved to stand beside Timms who glared at the kicker.

"Are you saying, Coach Durham, the recruiters voluntarily brought someone in who isn't capable of filling the requirements of the position? I find that hard to believe since I know TAU only gets the best of the best."

Blondie's face turned redder with each word Timms said. By the time he finished, the kid's eyes were as big as saucers, and I'd swear tears pooled on his lower lids. The big head sitting on top of his body took a major hit, and he had no idea how to use his smartass attitude to get himself out of it.

This was not how I planned to start my coaching career. I wanted the guys to respect me because I was good at what I do. I wanted them to trust my abilities as a kicker and a coach to listen to what I said. I wanted them to try to incorporate my ideas to make them better with their talent.

He finally spoke up. "So, uh. You're the kicking coach? I... I didn't know that the coach was a woman. I had no idea. I'm sorry, ma'am."

"I'd say that's a good start, shit for brains." Timms' easygoing comment lightened the situation some.

"I'd never talk to my coach like that if I'd only known who you were, Coach Durham. My name's Ian Brown, ma'am." He stuck his hand out to me first to shake. I considered this a show of trying to make things right. At least he knew when he'd made a serious error and was willing to step up and attempt to rectify the situation.

I put my hand out and took his with a firm grip. "Thank you, Ian. I accept your apology and think we should put it behind us and start over."

His head nodded in fast-paced acceptance. "Yes, ma'am. I think I'd like that, too."

"I'm Coach Durham, Ian. You want to introduce me to your boys?"

He turned to the two silent faces staring at us. "This is Drew Hastings. It's Andrew but just call him Drew."

I looked up at the tall one. His height didn't match his pubescent face fringed by black, shaggy hair. He vigorously shook my hand smiling down at me. His looks would have him fighting off the women—too cute for his own good.

"Nice to meet you, Coach Durham. I'm happy to be here playing for the Rams."

"Dude, you don't have to suck up first thing. Save it for later when she's yelling at you for your lack of skills," Ian told him.

"Shut up, Ian. I have a lot of skills, or I wouldn't be here on a scholarship like you are, asswipe." Drew stopped and looked at me. "Sorry, ma'am, but he lives to give us shit."

Ian embarrassed Drew if the red creeping up his neck was any indication. While Ian would forever be the jokester, Drew seemed more serious.

"Sounds like you two have some competition going already. I like it. Good, clean competition can make all of you better."

We would still need to adjust Ian's ego as the season progressed, but he had personality, and in the real world, personality got you further in certain situations.

"This is Zac Hernandez, ma'am." Zac stepped up to me and put his hand out stiffly nodding his head. I didn't know if he was nervous or didn't know how to address me.

"Good morning, Zac. What school are you from?"

"Uh, I graduated from West Falls in Houston. Thank you for having me here." He glared over my shoulder as if daring Ian to say anything about his comment.

"No need to thank me, Zac. I'm sure the recruiter who found you is the one to thank. I'll have to see which coach did that."

"It was Coach Jefferies. He watched the videos my coach sent and offered me the spot over the phone."

"That's great, Zac. He must have liked what he saw." This kid had an easygoing personality behind intense eyes. The determination in them told me he'd probably be worth keeping around.

"Yes, ma'am."

I turned and faced all three of them. "This is Coach Timms who'll be working with your quarterback." They all stepped up and shook Timms' hand, too.

I looked around. "Where's the other team member? Have y'all met him?" They all shook their heads.

Ian spoke up. "He hadn't moved into the dorm either. He's supposed to be my roommate. I looked him up online. He's got a lot of followers on *Snapchat*."

"I don't know if that's good or bad, Ian. What do you think?"

"Who knows? I don't use it too much. Ain't got time for that shit." He looked up at me as soon as the words left his lips wondering if he'd stepped over the line.

"Well, okay, Ian. None of us have time for that shit now that we're back to school, right?" I smiled, and it broke the tension with all three of them.

"My job's done here, Coach." Timms smiled at me and turned to go back to the players who waited for him.

"Thanks, Timms." He waved a hand in the air without turning back.

I watched him walk away. The man had a damn fine ass to stare at. How had I not noticed this before? The issued coaching shorts hugged his muscular cheeks in all the right ways. When I finally turned back around, three faces grinned at me.

Busted. "What?"

All three dropped their heads but never lost their smiles. Oh, God. It's middle school all over again. Did guys ever grow up?

"Nothing, Coach. Just waiting on instructions from you but didn't want to interrupt." Ian would be the death of me. I could see it coming.

"Ian, she's our coach. Stop being a dickhead to her." Drew chastised his new friend. Maybe Drew had more of a quick temper than the other two, but at least he didn't direct it toward me. I'd need to keep a watch on that. He had all kinds of potential, and I needed to give all of them an equal chance.

"Let's get back to why we're all standing in the heat, please." I sounded all coachy this time. At least in my mind, I did.

As the sun started down, the guys picked up the footballs they pounded on all evening. Dropping them in bins around the field, they jogged back to where I stood looking at me to give them something.

"Good practice, guys. You're all gifted kickers who've obviously spent time honing your skills. Monday's the first official practice with Coach Jefferies observing. While he devotes his time to the offensive line-up, he also sees what you're doing. Think about that when you want to slack off. You're as much a part of this team as every other member. We can't play successfully without every man giving one hundred percent every time they walk onto this turf. Remember this, please. I'll see y'all Monday after classes."

The three called goodbyes as they sprinted off the field. It had been a good practice. Talent oozed out of these guys. Making a choice was going to be difficult, and I hadn't even seen all of them.

I heard my name called as I made my way out of the stadium. The sun dropped behind the stadium's walls of seating making it hard to see, but I'd recognized Timms' drawl already.

He caught up to me in an easy jog. "How'd it go with the three amigos?"

"You're right about that. Steve Martin and friends didn't hold a candle to these guys." We laughed at one of my favorite movies' reference. "It went well, I think. They're all eager, but it's the first unofficial practice. Monday will be a different story. I tried to pour on the positive today because, with Coach Jefferies here, it'll be tougher. With their jokester ways, I warned them about taking a more serious attitude."

"Probably a good idea. I'm assuming you didn't get any more of the douchebaggery from them?"

"No. Thanks for that." His dark features made it hard to see him at twilight. The thick scruff on his face covered a strong jawline, but those mahogany brown eyes pierced through the darkness. The golden rays that shot through gave a striking appearance.

"None needed. The surprise on their faces was worth it."

"Yeah, your comments broke the tension. I was ready to unload on their smart-ass remarks to me. That was not the way I wanted to start the relationship."

"The sound carried to where I stood with my guys. I knew it was off to a bad start, but you had to know it was going to happen, India."

I turned my head and looked back at the empty field. I'd fought this battle for so long. "Yeah, you're right. I hoped maybe for once it would be different."

His monster hand grabbed the top of my shoulder. "It'll come... in time. You held a big rep in college around the conference and not because you were a female, but because you were a damn fine kicker who your coach could depend on in crunch time."

I saw the tattoos marking his right hand on me, the one he used to take his last team to victory so many times. The warmth seeped through my t-shirt, but I could swear a spark shot through me, too. I looked back up at him. He stood an arm's length from me, but it felt too close.

He dropped his hand. "Come on. I'll buy you a beer. You do drink beer, right?"

Smiling up at him, I said, "Of course I do. What kind of football player would I be if I didn't drink beer with the guys, right?"

He gave me a slight upturn of his lips. "Yeah, with the guys."

Then he winked at me. Winked. How was I going to maintain a professional friendship with him if he kept doing things like that? Ugh. #femalecoachproblems

TIMMS

I opened the door to a packed bar I'd been in a million times before graduation. I should've known better than to bring her here the last Saturday night of summer.

"Timms, my man. Fucking glad to see you. Where you been?" Blue and his girl, Noelle, greeted me as I made my way through the crowd with India in tow. I shook his hand and pulled him in for a tight bro hug. Noelle stood up, and I wrapped her in my arms and lifted her off the floor.

These two had been there for me last season when I blew my knee out. I forced the situation between Blue and Noelle by moving in with them while I recuperated, but it turned out for the best. Now they're stuck together like glue.

I grabbed India's hand pulling her from the crowd to where we stood at the end of their table.

"Let me introduce you to another coach intern. This is India Durham. She's the new special teams' coach."

"Like the India Durham from Cal U?" Blue asked as he shook her hand.

"That would be me." I watched her stare at Blue's face. Him and that damn long, dark blond hair always had the women staring. Good thing he's so in love with Noelle and nothing will come between them.

"I'm Blue Myers, and this is my girl, Noelle Jeffries."

"It's nice to meet you both," she shook Noelle's hand, too. "Hey, Jeffries, are you related to Coach Jefferies?"

"Oh no. People think that all the time. It's spelled differently."

India nodded.

"Y'all sit down. What're you drinking? I need to get Noelle her sangria spritzer." To the side, he added, "You know, sprite with a splash of color added to it."

"That's what I'll have, too," India told him. "Sounds good after spending the day on the field."

"Right. What about you Timms? You want a girlie drink, too?"

"Fuck no. I'll have a beer. I'll go with ya to say hi to some of the others." Looking back at India, "You okay here for a few?" Why did I ask? This is not a date. I don't date. She knows nothing about me, and that's the way I prefer it to be.

"Sure, she'll be fine. I'll take care of her," Noelle piped up.

I nodded at the two before heading to the bar.

"What's up with that, dude?" I knew Blue would say something. I should've never asked her that. He thinks the world should be in love because he is.

"Nothing. She doesn't know anyone. We had an impromptu practice with the new recruits, and it got off to a rocky start for her."

"Shitheads give her hell 'cause she's a female coaching all males?"

"Exactly. Little pricks got in way over their heads too damn fast. One of them stood toe to fucking toe with her by the time I got over there to set 'em straight."

"Well, Monday will be no different. You can damn sure plan on it. She's too beautiful for her own good in that job."

"Yeah, I thought that the moment I met her."

"So you admit she's beautiful." He hit me with a grin I knew was coming.

"Any dumbass can see she's a beauty. Doesn't mean I'm into it, though."

"Right. I saw how you looked at her. Seen it a million times before only she doesn't look the type to hang out at the frat house."

"Nope. Neither of us will be hanging out there. We gotta be 'professional.'" I air quoted the Coach's word. Leaning over the bar, I looked at Blue. "Coach's already talked to me about putting some separation between the team and myself."

"That sucks, dude. How are you going to pull that shit off? You're our friend."

"True, but I can't be your friend on the sideline. I've gotta be the coach. The only good thing is I'll be coaching the QBs only, and Crew's not part of the crew we ran with last year."

"No, but he did hang at the house some. Your legend with all your babes still floats around in conversation."

"Fuck. You're right. I'm glad I got out of there before my last semester."

We picked up the drinks and wound our way through the crowd to the table.

"Here ya go, ladies." I handed India the glass before I sat down next to her in the booth. The seating took on an air of intimacy sitting close, but I couldn't help it. The four of us crowded together so we could hear the conversation which caused my thigh to be stretched along hers.

Her shorts rode up her long leg when she scooted over, and with the briefest of moves, I felt goosebumps form on her skin as it rubbed against my bare skin. Damn, my dick approved of this touch—a zing down to it caused it to jump with interest.

Nope, not happening. Off fucking limits. I talked myself down. I needed to get laid soon and get this need taken care of. Then I could move on to being her colleague on and off the field.

We laughed and talked about some of the antics of last season for several hours. The easy manner that India joined the conversations made it seem like she'd been here at TAU all along.

"I remember you kicked that winning field goal last season with only seconds left. They played that damn clip over and over on TV. It was fucking amazing to watch," Blue told the table.

"Yeah, best night of my life. I was on top that night," India responded.

"Babe, you can be on top every night if that's what it takes to get you into old Timms' bed." The comment came from over my shoulder. What dickhead would say that to a perfect stranger? I turned to see Gerrod and Quinn standing there.

I jumped up and hugged him. "If it isn't fucking Gerrod and Quinn."

Blue and Noelle stood to greet their old friends, too, leaving India sitting behind us. Once I finished, I took her hand and pulled her to standing.

"This is India. She's the new Rams' kicking coach. Good thing you're alumni now, or she'd probably kick your ass for talking about her that way." This brought on a laugh from the whole group. Even with her being tall and built, Gerrod was the size of a small house and could easily take her out.

"Hello, Gerrod. Nice to meet you. You're the new starting tackle for New England, right?"

He took her hand and kissed the back. "My apologies, ma'am. I didn't know we had two loyal subjects to King Jefferies."

"Cut the shit, Gerrod." Quinn quickly took over the situation. "Don't pay him any attention, India. He's so full of himself these days. I'm Quinn, this big douche's girlfriend, and Noelle's former roommate." Everyone laughed. Typical Quinn.

"Nice to meet you both." I could see India taking it all in. She didn't seem like meeting new people caused her any stress which was good with what Monday would bring.

"Join us, we'll make room." I gestured to India to sit and moved in behind her. Quinn joined us causing a tight fit on the one side.

Gerrod got the waitress' attention and ordered another round of drinks for all of us.

"Thanks, dude. I mean with you being the pro player now, I guess you can afford to buy us a few drinks."

"Hell, yeah. I've never had so much money in my fucking account at one time. Hell, I've never had that much during all the time I was in college."

"Good for you, Gerrod. Making that dream come true is outstanding." We all bumped fists.

Gerrod made the draft at the end of his third year of playing ball and was taken in the third round. He graduated in May, and it seemed like he left for the pros the next day. I knew Quinn was happy to have him close even if only for a few days.

The conversation stayed lighthearted as the evening progressed. Remembering all the fun times we had, and some that were not so fun was a great way to spend the evening. Monday, India and I would start a new chapter in our lives, a new season for Blue, a new year for Quinn and Noelle, and an exciting career for Gerrod.

Finally, India leaned into me putting her lips to my ear. "I think I need to head on home." The soft, warm breath touching my ear sent more of the same intense feelings straight down my body. It wasn't enough that her leg rubbed against mine every time she moved keeping my dick on high alert.

"Yeah, we'll go. I've got some last minute things to do tomorrow, too."

"No, you stay with your friends. I'll catch an Uber."

"Oh, hell no. That's not the way I work. I brought you, and I'll take you home." I looked up to see everyone watching our quiet exchange.

"Hey, I'm taking India home and then heading on home myself. Gotta call it a night. We both have tomorrow to prepare for the week of classes so we can be on the field with a bunch of dumbasses every afternoon." I glared at Blue. "You do remember that right, boy?"

"Don't call me boy. I ain't yo boy, old man." Everyone laughed.

"Yeah, Quinn and I need to head out, too. We've got some catching up and planning to do." Gerrod wiggled his eyebrows making us laugh harder.

"And in case you dumbshits didn't understand that he means sex, sex, and more sex. I need to fill my fucking quota since he's leaving for three weeks this time." Quinn's smile didn't reach its usual brightness.

"Right, so let's go now." Gerrod moved like he was exploding off the line after his man.

"Damn, I didn't realize you still could move that fast." Blue laughed some more.

"Given the right motivation, I can move like the wind, and my girl here is a huge motivator." He picked her up. "I'll see y'all before I head out."

"If I let him out of bed that long." She waved over Gerrod's shoulder as he walked across the bar holding her high.

"It was great meeting you all." India gave a little wave to Blue and Noelle. "I hope we get to do this again sometime."

"Believe me, we're here all the time," Noelle said. "I think the two of us need to hang out when you're off the field. I need to do some shopping. And by shopping, I mean walk through one of the shops at the square on the way to my favorite wine bar in the middle."

"Sounds perfect. I might need to buy a few bottles to keep at home," India told her.

"Hell, yeah, we do." The two girls high-fived each other which seemed strange to me. Did females do that?

"We'll see you on the field Monday then, Blue." I tipped my head to him, and he did the same.

India moved when I put my hand on the small of her back, but I quickly jerked it away. This had to stop. She's not a date. Never going to be a date. My mind needed to separate these two ideas when it came to her. I could have any other single girl in this bar with a nod. I needed to do that soon, but right now, I wanted to get her home and away from me.

We stepped out to the car, and India turned to face me from her side of the car once she slid in. "Your friends are really nice, Timms. Thanks for introducing me to them. I had fun."

"I'm glad. You needed some fun. Monday will be a different story."

"What do you mean?"

"You only had a little taste of the shit you're going to see with the entire team on the field. Before we go out of the locker room, Coach usually introduces the new coaches, so that'll be good. They'll know right up front to show some respect. The real respect you have to earn. You know that, right?"

"I know. I've worked with underclassmen when I was in high school. That's been a while, though."

"These guys are going to be braver with the comments than high school boys. A lot of them have a superman complex believing nothing can touch them. Yeah, they earn their positions yearly, but for the most part, they can still be a bunch of dicks with a female. I've seen too many in action."

"And what about you? Are you a dick to females, too?"

I pulled into her apartment complex and parked. Turning to look at her, "Are you shitting me? Have I been one to you?" That statement pissed me off. I'd treated her with nothing but respect the entire time.

"Sorry. I didn't mean to offend you." She squirmed in her seat and then turned to face forward. Guess she didn't like facing me when I called her out.

"I don't treat women like that, India. I have no need to treat women badly."

"Right. I watched them all watching you tonight. Did you have a harem while you were in college?"

"A harem?" I gave a brief laugh when I said it. "Yeah, maybe I did, but I was a prince to them."

She laughed at my comment. "So you were the prince with a harem on campus, huh? Is that how it's going to be now? Women flocking at your every beck and call or is it whistle, and they come running?"

"Do you have a low opinion of all men or just me?"

"It's not a low opinion, it's a realistic opinion."

"Then I have my work cut out for me to change your mind."

"That's good to know you'll be willing to try." She put her hand on the door handle but turned back and leveled those sky-blue beauties on me. "Look, Timms. I'm sorry. I'm not used to guys who want to work for something more than one and done. In the athletic department, the guys I found myself around all the time always seemed to be looking for that."

"I know, and I can't say I haven't been guilty of it. I want to be here for you, though, to fall back on in the battle you're about to engage in." I took her hand. "You have to let me, though. You have to give me a chance to show you I can be more than the low expectations you have of all the athletes."

"I can try, but I'm more nervous about Monday right now. I want to do the best I can. I want my part of the team to be as close to perfect as possible. I can't make them, though, and that worries me. What I saw today was fair, certainly not the best. They're sloppy and have bad habits. It's going to take a lot to break those habits and turn them into what the team needs to succeed in a crunch."

Her nervousness wasn't all about us. I could work with that. "You're right. It will, but Coach Jefferies obviously thinks you've got what it takes, or he wouldn't have stuck his neck out to get you here. He could've chosen any number of coaches for your job. I'm sure there were hundreds of applicants. He chose you. You need to live up to his expectations. You do it right, and they'll do it right."

She let out a long breath. "Yeah, I know."

"Good to hear all that confidence you got going on there." I opened my door and stepped out easing around to her side of the car. "Come on. I'll walk you up." Taking her hand, I pulled her out of the seat. With a little too much force in the tug, her body landed against mine with me wrapping my arms around her to keep us from falling over.

"Oh, sorry." She looked up, only inches away from my face.

Well, hell, not good. Not good at all. The need to kiss her sent a jolt straight through me. She ran the tip of her pink tongue across her plump bottom lip. God help me.

Lowering my head slowly, I brushed my lips across hers to see what kind of response she'd give me. I leaned back, but she reached up putting her hand on the back of my neck, and I knew I was in trouble. She stood on her toes and pulled me down to her level before kissing me back.

Her warm lips connected softly at first, but when she ran her tongue across my lips seeking entrance, that's all I could stand. My hands lowered to her ass cheeks and pulled her into me taking over this assault as I held her firmly.

Our tongues sought each other's in a slow war that quickly turned frantic. She sucked mine back into her mouth, and the movement began mimicking hot, wet sex in every way. My mind drifted to how it would feel if she wrapped her tongue around my dick and sucked it like this instead.

I ground her into my rock-hard cock straining between us, and her low deep growl entered my mouth. Finally, she pulled back releasing my tongue as I let go of my stronghold on her perfect ass cheeks.

She laid her head on my chest, and I could hear her trying to calm her breathing. "Wow. That was... Yeah."

"Yeah is right. I think I better go." My hands never moved.

"Probably a good idea." Her hands never moved.

We waited for a few minutes enjoying the leftover emotions from the scorching kiss.

India backed away as I let her go. "I think it would be better if you didn't walk me to the door." She stared up at me through her dark eyelashes.

"You're probably right about that. You live alone?"

"Yes."

"Best I get back in my car then. I'll see you Monday." She moved up the sidewalk toward her door as I rounded the front.

"Right. Monday it is." She didn't look back at me which was a good plan because, given any indication she'd want me to stay, I'd be hauling her inside that apartment.

I drove home with a hard-on that wouldn't quit. Guess I'd be seeking relief in the shower. At least I had the feel of her warm mouth and tongue, and her sweet, firm ass that felt incredible in my palms.

INDIA

"What the fuck, India!" I said it out loud as soon as I shut the door to my apartment. "That broke all the rules. Why did you let that happen?" No answer materialized.

I went to my fridge and poured myself a few sips of wine to take to my bedroom. I needed to back away from this situation. Could I pretend it never happened?

Opening my phone, I pulled up Chyna's name.

> **Me:** *You awake?*
> **Chyna:** *Hell yeah. I need to be asleep, though. What's up, chica?*

Me: *Had an eventful day that ended bad/good? I don't know.*
Chyna: *How can it be bad and good?*
Me: *It ended with a kiss that was good, great, but it shouldn't have happened, BAD.*
Chyna: *A great kiss is NEVER FUCKING BAD!*
Me: *Yes, it was.*
Chyna: *Was he underage?*
Me: *Really, Chyna, that's what you think?*
Chyna: *That's the only thing I can think that would make a great kiss bad.*
Me: *It was a great kiss from the other coach/intern.*
Chyna: *Is he hot? Is it the same one from earlier?*
Me: *Does that matter? I shouldn't have let it happened. I have to work with him.*
Chyna: *What's the prob? He's not your boss?*
Me: *No. Thank God.*
Chyna: *Then forget about it. Unless you can use it for clit list material.*
Me: *My WHAT?*
Chyna: *You know, your spank bank for females.*
Me: *You're gross, Chyna. I'll solve this on my own. Good night.*
Chyna: *Good night, Priscilla Prude.*

"Lotta good that did me. Now all I can think about is my vibrator," I thought out loud. Good thing the walls of my bedroom don't talk back. I reached over and opened the small nightstand drawer. "Good plan bringing an extra package of batteries. It might be a long semester."

Monday rolled around much faster than I thought it would. I headed to the athletic building after classes anxious to get this first day behind me. I hoped the three younger guys had an open mind about meeting the fourth member and that his attitude lined up with the three I'd already met.

Students streamed in and out of the doors with frantic looks trying to determine which direction they might head to for their next class. I hated my freshman year. If it weren't for kicking at CU, I would have chosen a smaller school.

"Hey, Coach Durham." I saw a friendly face at the doorway looking in my direction.

"Hey yourself, Drew. How's your day going?" He was a cute kid despite his size.

"Great, so far. It's different than high school that's for sure."

"Yes, it is, but you'll figure it out and learn to love it in an entirely new way."

"I already love it." His eyes followed the steps of a cute female walking past us as he spoke. She turned and made eye contact with him giving him a beautiful smile.

"I can see that." I grinned up at him, and he nodded with a smirk on his lips.

"I'm ready to get on the field today. You said yourself we have bad habits that need changing. Let's do it."

"Hopefully, your enthusiasm is contagious. I want you all to perform to the best of your abilities. That's what my job is all about, getting the best out of you."

"No problem getting the most out of me. I'm here to win a spot on the team, not sit the bench. I gotta run, Coach. See you at practice."

"Right. Don't want to be late on the first day." He took off in a run but slowed as he caught up to the blonde female who had slowed her pace after passing by.

"Crazy guys." I walked into the loud building attached to several gyms and workout rooms. Standing inside the edge of the first gym, I watched a few guys playing basketball at one end. The squeak of their tennis shoes and the orange ball dribbling off the floor added to the typical noises.

"Hello, India." Coach Jefferies came up behind me.

"Oh, hey."

"You're done for the day, right?" He looked down at a clipboard in his hand.

"Yes, I am. I won't be meeting too often with classes. Most of my work will involve my laptop and time in the library, which is good because I can schedule it all around my coaching duties."

"Yeah, uh, that's good. Come into my office and let's talk a little."

First day, and I'm called to the office. This didn't sound good.

We walked in, and he shut the door behind me. "Is there a problem?"

"No, no problems. I just want to have a chat about expectations."

"Okay, great. I have high expectations as you already know." We'd discussed this on the phone before I accepted the internship.

"Right, and I'm glad about that. The University prides itself on high standards in all areas." He stopped and looked down at his papers again. "What I want to talk about is you working with these young men. They come to us from all backgrounds. You never know what's going to be a problem for them."

"Yes, I understand. It was the same way when I was playing in college."

"I know I don't have to remind you that treating them with professionalism at all times is imperative, and they should treat you with respect as their coach."

"Yes, sir. I understand."

He threw his pen down and looked up at me. "I'm not going to beat around the bush here, India. What I'm trying to say is don't let yourself get into any situation that might look compromising with these players. Some of them think with their little heads at all times, and you cannot allow that to happen. It's bad for the department and University."

"Let me be the first to assure you it will not happen. I met three of the four yesterday, and we've already established my position as their coach. They know I'm hard-nosed about all things football. To me that includes treating me with the same respect they would treat any of the other coaches on that field."

"Well, I figured it would be that way with you. You came off as strictly business when it came to sports, but I've never had a female coach on the team before. I've had other females working in the department with PT and such. I needed to make sure we were on the same page about this, but I didn't want to mention it with Timms here on Saturday."

"I understand, and I appreciate it being between us. I know I'll have to earn the respect of the rest of the team in time, but for now, having it with my squad is my first priority."

"Your kicking talent got you this job, but your coaching talent is what'll keep it. You understand what I'm saying?"

"Absolutely, Coach. I want to be the best coach for these guys. I know they're some of the best in the nation. I need to make them THE best, though, but if I don't come across as that kind of coach, it'll be impossible."

"Yeah, the bunch of cocky dumbshits on the team will probably test you in the beginning. You need to be prepared for them. Some come here thinking they're above all rules. We make it a point to put their feet back on the ground to walk among us mere mortals. They leave high school strutting like peacocks on hens' day, and we have to show them they're ducklings waiting to be shot down." His smile reached across his face as though he enjoyed plucking their tail feathers.

Another man knocked on the door and opened it. He looked down at me and then back at Coach J. "Uh, that phone call you've been waiting for is on line one."

"I need to take this." He stood as he spoke, so I did too. "Glad you came by, India, but I have one more thing to say to you. If you have any problems with any of these guys around here, you come directly to me. You're my intern, and I look after what's mine. Do you understand? Don't put up with their bullshit for one minute."

"Right, I understand. And thank you, Coach Jefferies. I mean it." I offered him my hand, and he shook it and smiled again.

I walked out thinking, *So, he's human like the rest of us.* I had him up on a pedestal like I'm sure all the players did. I hoped I could live up to his expectations.

Timms came around the corner, and we almost bumped into each other. "Oh hey, Timms."

"We gotta stop running into each other." He leaned forward and softly said, "Can't have another incident like Saturday night."

I could feel the heat slowly prickling my skin up my neck and onto my face. "No, uh. Uh, we can't have that again, ever."

"Ever?"

"Right, never ever."

"Never ever is a long time, In-di-a." The way he dragged out my name with all three syllables in his deep voice caused tingles in all the wrong places for standing in the coaching office area.

"Right. It is, and it will be." Why was I acting like a fifteen-year-old around him? It was only a hot kiss. I've had hot kisses before. It had been a while, but still, I couldn't do this all semester. "So are you done with classes for the day?"

He looked at me for a second realizing I'd changed gears on him. "Yeah. Only one of my classes met to hand out internet instructions. The others meet tomorrow. What about you?"

"I'm done, too. I only have one tomorrow." I looked down at my phone. "I was thinking about grabbing something to eat before we had to be here today."

"Is this an invitation to join you, India?" He gave me a smile that could charm the panties off any female.

"Sure, if you want to come with me."

"Yeah, I was going to join my QB roster, but I'd rather sit across from you anytime."

"No, I don't want to interfere."

He grabbed my arm and started moving me toward the doors. "It's not interference if another coach is joining the team for lunch. Now come on before all the good stuff's gone in the cafeteria. Faculty eats free where we're going."

"Free is good." I smiled up at him.

"Free is perfect."

Moving around the commons was tricky on the first day with so many students taking advantage of the meal tickets. Timms put me before him and placed his hand on the small of my back as we continued through the throng of diners. We picked up our meals and ate in a comfortable silence.

"That wasn't too bad." I looked around as I put my tray down.

"No, and as far as cafeteria food goes, this is the best place on campus. Believe me when I say the football team knows where to get the best damn food."

"I'm sure. The guys on my old team did. We had a lot of morning practices, and some of those guys swore they could tell you which place to eat lunch based on the direction of aromas."

Timms laughed hard at my comment. "I bet that fucking defensive line moved faster after practice to get there than they did trying to get to the quarterback in a game."

I nodded when the noise level rose in across the eating area. We both turned to see what was causing a commotion.

"Speaking of players." He stood and made his way to the noise.

I'd considered taking my lunch and going in the other direction but watched as he greeted a couple of the players. They spoke with ease, and then three followed him back to our table. I found myself surrounded by guys bigger and taller than any I'd seen the day before on the field.

Timms spoke up. "Let me introduce you to some of the upperclassmen on the team, India. Uh... I mean Coach Durham."

The looks I received from this group made me want to laugh out loud.

"We'd heard Coach hired a woman to coach the kicking team," one of the players said.

Would I ever live down being the woman on the coaching staff? I prayed they would come to see me as just another coach to work with, but earning that was going to take time.

INDIA

"This is Jenko, Tucker, Crew, and you've met Blue already." They all nodded their heads as Timms introduced them.

"Hey, Coach Durham. Good to see you again." Blue seemed more formal to me today than when we were drinking beer together. It relieved me to know he took this approach and could separate the relationships.

I looked over this group of huge guys standing here staring down at me. I needed to stand up to get more on their level, but with Timms leaning on his hands grasping the back of my chair, it wasn't possible.

Finally, I spoke up. "It's great to meet you. Tell me what position you play." I looked at Blue first. We hadn't discussed it before.

"I play tight end mostly but can play safety, too." Blue's smile showed the pride he had in the ability to play both offense and defense. Most colleges didn't allow it.

"I'm sure you prefer scoring over tackling, right?" I asked him.

"Hell, yeah, I do, but I like intercepting passes, too."

The others made noises about trying to be the star on the team and the one who does it all. Blue's teammates obviously looked up to him and his outstanding ability.

The new quarterback, Crew, leaned over and put his hand out to shake it. "It's very nice to meet the person who's going to make sure the kickers add points to the scoring I do."

So this must be the cocky little shit Timms talked about. "Nice to meet you, Crew. I see your ego proceeds you." Timms had his work cut out with this one.

He stood tall, and I thought he might strut around in a circle. "Well, I plan to live up to my potential or ego, whichever you call it, ma'am."

I laughed at this comment. Turning to Timms, I jokingly said, "You have so much work to do. Might want to go ahead and buy some waders to wear to practice. He's so full of shit you'll be standing in it daily."

Timms looked at Crew. "Boy, you know talking like that's only going to cause you more trouble than you're worth." He glanced back at me, "Oh yeah. I forgot he's worth a lot more than he looks, though. His dad's a rock star."

"Oh really?" I looked up at Crew, who turned a nice shade of red.

So he did have some humility mixed in with the cockiness.

Tucker spoke up. "This dumbshit, Crew's dad is Ryan Powell, lead guitarist for Assured Distraction."

"Oh God, is that true?" I looked at Crew waiting for a reply. He finally mumbled something and raised his head. "Yes, ma'am, it's true."

His reaction surprised me. "You don't like people knowing this?"

"It's not that I mind people knowing, but I don't want to be known because of who my dad is."

"I can understand that." To help Crew out, I turned my attention to Tucker. "I'm sure you're a great player as well, Tucker, or you wouldn't have made the team. What position do you play?" I wanted them both to feel comfortable around me.

"Running back, and I can line up as wide receiver, too." His lips turned into a beautiful smile when he said this. He did like playing football but didn't seem to have the cocky attitude of his friend, Crew. Guess time would tell on that. I couldn't imagine these two not being mirror images since they knew each other so well.

"That's great. I'm sure you and Blue here are double threats to the opposing teams when they have you both on the field."

"Yes, ma'am, we are." He turned to Blue who stuck a fist out for a bump.

"See, dude. Coach Durham's cool. She already knows who to depend on when we're playing," Blue added.

It made me happy to see the two bolstering each other and not feel in competition. A team should be this way. These guys thinking I was already cool didn't hurt either.

I felt my phone vibrate in my pocket. Pulling it out, I looked at Timms and shrugged my shoulders.

"Hello, Coach Jefferies, this is Coach Durham," I spoke loud enough for all of them to hear me. Last thing any of these guys needed was to say something to make the coach mad. He kept the conversation short, and all my answers were yes and no.

"What'd he want?" Timms asked as soon as I hit end.

"He said some last-minute changes were made to the kicking squad, and we have a new, more experienced player coming in today to join the team."

"That is kinda last minute, isn't it?" Blue asked, looking between Timms and me.

"That's for damn sure. I thought we had the roster set last semester during spring training," Timms told the group.

"He wants me to come back to his office after lunch."

"Then I guess we better get finished." I didn't ask him to go with me, but I was happy he included himself.

The others said bye and drifted to the food lines while we finished up.

Stepping back outside into the heat, I looked at Timms. "He said it's a kicker with more experience. I'm surprised he'd be able to find anyone worth a damn this late."

"Yeah, seems strange to me, too. Coach J wouldn't take someone who wasn't going to be an asset to the team."

"Well, I'm sure the three freshmen I worked with yesterday aren't going to be all that thrilled to have an upperclassman stroll in and take over."

"Seriously, I'd be pissed."

"Hope he's not a dick to my guys." I already thought of the three from yesterday as mine.

"Yeah, we got enough dicks to go around."

I rolled my eyes at his wordplay but had to smile. "Please." He grinned back at me.

I walked into Coach J's office for the second time. I could see someone slumped down in the chair, but when I opened the door, an average size, lanky-built guy stood.

"Oh good, good. You got here fast." Coach looked behind me and saw I wasn't alone. "Oh, Timms. I didn't know y'all were together."

"Just enjoying the fine cuisine the cafeterias offer, sir." A slow smile ghosted his lips. He looked at his boss as though they shared some secret knowledge of food.

"Yeah, I bet that's right."

"So, this is your coach I was telling you about. Coach Durham meet Conner..."

Before the older man could finish the new kid's name, I did it for him. "Graham."

"You two know each other?" Coach J looked at me.

Conner spoke up. "You could say that. We played against each other in the playoffs last year. Her kick is what ended up beating us out of our rightful place in the next round where they got beat, I might add." He had the audacity to glare at me the entire time.

"Well, I'm sure y'all will work that out since she's your new coach," Coach J added.

The smartass smirked at me making a harrumphing noise that was laced with sarcasm. Coach J heard it and looked at both of us. "This isn't going to be a problem is it, Coach Durham?"

"Not at all, Coach J. I can work with anyone willing to be coached." I stared at Conner.

Conner looked down crossing his arms in front of his body. "Yeah, I can learn to work with her if she'll give me what I need." He looked back at me and smiled.

I didn't like what he implied with the comment given the way he delivered it with another smirk. The suggestiveness of it followed by a lecherous smile caused the hair on the back of my neck to rise.

Timms, who had leaned against the wall when we came in, stood up. I couldn't see him without turning around, but I heard a hike in his breathing.

"I'm sure with my help we can make you the best kicker you've ever been." I wanted him to know I was in charge.

"I am the best kicker on this campus already, so it shouldn't be too difficult for you." This guy was going to be trouble. His sorry attitude bordered on belligerent, and we hadn't even made it on the field.

"Well, we'll see, won't we, Coach Durham?" Coach looked at me when he said it and then turned to Conner. "You, young man, need to remember she *is* the coach with the *final* say of who goes on the field. Do you understand what I'm saying, son?"

"Yes, sir. I get it. Can I go now? I still have to unload my car."

"Sure. Be back here by four. We start the first official training day today."

"Right. Thank you, sir." He glared down at me as he walked toward the door never bothering to acknowledge my presence.

"See you this afternoon, Conner," I called after him, but he never looked back.

When the door closed, Timms spoke first. "I don't like him."

"Doesn't matter what you like, Timms. You worry about your QBs and let Durham here worry about the kickers. You understand me?"

"Yeah, I understand, but does he?" He nodded his head toward the door the kid disappeared through.

"Why don't you go on out and let me talk with India."

Timms moved off the wall again and opened the door. "See ya later."

I nodded at him. I needed to get this problem worked out already, and I didn't want Timms fighting my first battle for me. I got here on my own and would prove my worth on my own.

"So what do you think about him? Is he going to be too much to handle? The three freshmen all come with great high school kicking stats, but this guy has proven himself in college ball already. It'll give the newbies time to grow up for the coming years. He's a ready-made kicker that shouldn't require too much of your time. It'll free you up to work with the others.

"I guess my first question is, can he take instructions? His attitude could be a problem. He thinks he's above me already. That's what's going to be a problem. If he can't listen when I try to coach him, then he doesn't have a place on special teams."

"That's all true. He does have to listen to you. I want you to work with him just like he's the same as the others. No special favors, but you need to remember that he's good at what he does."

"If he's good at what he does, then why did you get to take him away from another big school?"

"It's a fair question. I got a call from a friend at another school saying he was looking to change schools for his senior year. Word has it, he might have worn his welcome out."

"Great. You and I both know what that means." He wasted an opportunity at the other university for one thing, but I wondered what else the phrase encompassed.

"I understand it looks bad, but before you walked through the door, he was a perfect player. Answered all the questions correctly. Said all the right things. Always wanted to come here to TAU. Had lots of friends who thought this was the best school and they convinced him to come. Those were his reasons for wanting to change schools. I had to make some calls to find out the other information."

I stood. Talking about it wasn't going to get me anywhere. I needed to prove to him that I could be the coach he needed under all circumstances. He wouldn't be the last player with a cocky attitude and overblown ego. I'd deal with him for one season.

"Okay, so I have a project for the fall. It'll make life interesting."

Coach stood and rounded the desk. He put his hand on my shoulder and then quickly withdrew it. "Sorry."

"For what? Touching me is okay, Coach, just like you would any of your other interns."

"Right. They drill that sexual harassment thing into all of us."

"We're a team, Coach." I patted him on the back and smiled.

"Good to know, India. Anyway, I'm glad you're taking a positive attitude about this. It'll be a challenge for you."

"A challenge is right."

After our goodbyes were said, I walked out of coach's office to the front doors of the building thinking about my new challenge—a pain in my ass was more like it. He would fight me on every level.

"Hey." Timms leaned against the brick with his foot propped up behind him. Damn, the hot look piercing through the fringe of black lashes and his tanned skin dark against the simple white t-shirt stretched across his arms, made his ink stand out creating a look most females would swoon over. I stared at him for a minute before I spoke knowing creating coherent speech would take effort.

"Oh, hey. Sorry. I had my mind on my new challenge as Coach J called him." I made myself break eye contact with him. "Come on. Walk me to my car. I'm going home for a little bit." He pushed off the wall coming to my side as we moved down the wide sidewalk together.

"He's gonna be trouble for you and probably for the rest of the fucking team. I don't like him or the badass attitude he tried to shove down your throat, and in the damn coach's office, no less."

"I know, but like it or not, he's on my squad. It's going to be one hell of a pleasure working with him that's for sure."

"He's going to give you nothing but shit, and you know it. Little fucker. I wanted to slap that bullshit grin off his face."

"Timms, calm down. It'll be okay. I've dealt with egotistical males my whole career. I'll have more control this time around."

"You won't control him, India. I know too many douchebags like him. Been around them the entire time I've been here."

"Well, he's not your problem, so don't worry about him." We turned the corner, and he reached out and pulled me around to the side of the building leading to the parking lot. When I was pressed up against his body with his arm tight around my waist, he looked down at me.

"If he's your problem, he's my problem, India. I'm not going to let that dickhead treat you like he probably treats all women." Sliding his hand up my back to my neck, he pulled me into his chest kissing the top of my head. Heat followed his hand up my back as a slight shiver involuntarily took over. He brought forth feelings I hadn't felt in a long time or maybe ever. I knew his possessiveness had potential to cause problems.

"Timms, this isn't a good idea. Students know you and will see us." Saying I didn't like being held against his warm hard body would be a huge lie. Even with my height, he still towered over me, and hard muscles held me close. Looking at him and allowing the embrace made me feel good all over, as though he tried to provide me with some of his strength.

"Let me come home with you then?" Softly spoken, slow words and warm breath drifted over my ear with his mouth hovering close.

"Do you think that's wise after yesterday?" I looked up at him.

"Yeah, especially after yesterday because given a chance to do that again, I'll take it every time. You're right, though. This location is a bad choice to continue what we started."

I stepped back out of the intimate embrace staring at him. I wanted to consider the consequences but looking up at him solved the battle. I couldn't have said no if I'd tried. He looked completely edible standing there with those tattoos sticking out of his shirt forming a sleeve of interesting designs. I knew there had to be more. Maybe I'd see them all... soon. "Come on."

TIMMS

I thought of all the things my body longed to do with her, starting with leaving kisses along her long toned legs as I worked my way up her luscious body. This real woman could match me in every way, unlike the females I'd dealt with the last four years. Smart, athletic, and beautiful were only a few of her best qualities.

I planned to work through the list I mentally formed last night for us to experience together. Standing in my shower when I got home last night, I dreamed of having her luscious body in so many ways. If not today, then soon. She didn't back down when we kissed, but that didn't mean she was prepared to take this to another level so quickly.

My mind said slide to the finish, but I knew she'd want more than what I'd spent my college days doing. As frat president, snapping my fingers brought me the pick of women whenever I wanted them, but with India, this needed to be a slow waltz to a perfect finish. For the first time, I believed I could do this dance... with her. The moves would be different—more steps involved with more time taken to learn them.

Planning the execution involved some work on my part. I'd never wanted this before. The question I kept tumbling over was why? What was it about India that made me realize there had to be more footwork for us to make it all gel, to become an us?

I pulled in the parking lot behind her, my engine rumbling announcing my arrival. As she gathered her things, I opened her car door. When she finally stood and looked at me, I caught a glimpse of hesitancy.

"Are you okay? I mean, are you good with this?"

Her only answer was a stiff nod of her head sending alarms going off in mine.

"Nothing has to happen, India. We can talk if that's what you want."

"What do you want, Timms?" She looked hard at me and then started for her door where she unlocked it, and I followed her in.

"I want you, plain and simple." I watched her face to see her reaction. She managed to offer no reaction.

Maybe she didn't feel the same, but I didn't believe it, not after the way she returned my kiss yesterday.

"That's getting right to the point." Dropping her bag on the table, India came back to me where I stood in front of her couch. She stopped directly in front of me before she pushed me back until I sat looking up at her. When my hands gripped her hips, she moved forward straddling my lap.

"Talk about getting right to the point." I grinned at her.

"Isn't this what you expected me to do?"

"What?" She confused me. Getting a read on her seemed impossible.

"Isn't this the way you're used to women treating you?"

"What women?"

"Come on, Timms, I'm not naïve. Is this what you're used to after the last four years? Accessible women on demand?"

I looked at her trying to decide where she was headed with her comment. "What's that got to do with anything between us?"

"Timms, I went to enough parties in college to know jumping right into bed for a hit it and quit it was the kind of relationships you guys always wanted—nothing lasting, nothing long term. So, let's skip all the romance, all the clichéd lines, and get to it. I'm good with it. I want you. You want me. Let's fuck."

"Wait a second. Wait a second." I pushed her to the side, so she sprawled across the couch. Her wide-eyed look told me she thought I'd lost my mind.

"What's the matter? Did I do something wrong?" she asked with a puzzled look.

"No, but that's not how I saw this going."

"Really? It's how I saw it happening. I mean yesterday when you kissed me, we were both into it. I saw how you looked like you wanted to devour me, and I'm good with it. I don't expect anything else from you."

"Wait a damn minute. You might not expect anything, but I sure as hell do."

"I know you're trying to change my mind, but right now, sex sounds like an instant stress reliever so can we get on with it?" She started toward me again.

"No, we can't. This is what I was talking about before. I don't have expectations of jumping into the bed with you, India."

"I don't have any expectations, Timms... except sex."

"Wrong."

"Ever?"

"I didn't say ever, but if I'm going to convince you I'm the kind of guy you can trust and fall back on when you need me, then we need to take this slow."

She turned and put her feet on the floor. "This has to be a first for both of us."

"Yeah, I'll admit it is. But for the first time, I want to be more than just a good fuck. I want to be the kind of guy you can depend on when you need me."

"And what if all I need is a good fuck?" She took me by surprise.

"I can be that, too."

"Just not right now."

My hand moved to the back of my neck as I rubbed it trying to relieve the tension that suddenly hit me. "No, probably not happening tonight."

"That's why I thought you came home with me." She gave me a hard stare.

"I know you did, but you're wrong." It might have been until she informed me how she looked at me and my past. "What were you coming home for anyway?"

"I'm tired. I didn't get much sleep worrying about today. I thought I might watch some mindless TV and sleep through it with my alarm on. The last thing I need to do is be late for today's practice."

"Me either." I slid my shoes off and put my foot behind her pulling her up my body. "Where's the remote?" She grabbed it off the coffee table. "Tell me you have *Netflix*. I have some shows to catch up on."

"And no *Netflix* and chill, huh?" She smiled a beautiful smile at me.

"No, *Netflix* and sleep. It's a brilliant new concept. Set the damn alarm first."

"Right." She snagged her phone and punched it a few times before she laid her head on my chest. I wrapped my leg around the back of her knee. She glanced down at our entangled legs and then back at my face with a raised eyebrow.

"Gotta keep you on the couch while you sleep."

"Yeah, okay." She laid her head back down, and I turned on season three of *The Ranch*.

"Oh, right. I said mindless TV."

"I hadn't caught the next season yet."

It didn't take long before I felt her firm body relax against me in sleep. Picking up a piece of her dark blonde hair, I slid it through my fingers. The honey vanilla fragrance I smelled happened to be one of my favorites and coming from her made it even better. I dropped it and ran a finger down the soft skin of her arm.

My dick cried when it figured out there would be no real sex again today. If she fell asleep believing I didn't want her, she was mistaken, but I spoke the truth. I wanted to be that man she needed, the one she could turn to for anything. If that meant not fucking for a few more days or even a week, I was on board with it.

It made me happy to know she voiced what she needed, but leaving her hanging was a first for me. No female could ever accuse me of not coming through for them in bed—until now. This was different, though. I had something to prove and was determined to follow through to the end, whatever that might be.

We rolled into the parking lot with time to spare. Neither of us wanted to be late on day one. I felt secure in my position with the University, but I still had to prove to the coaching staff I deserved to be kept on as quarterback coach.

She jumped out of her car ready to take on the world. If a short nap did this for her, maybe I should try one tomorrow. I smiled watching her bouncing on her toes waiting for me to step out.

"Come on, Coach." I found myself feeding off her energy. Her exuberance might've been contagious.

"A little excited to be here, babe?" She put her hands on her hips and tilted her head giving me a look.

"Please don't call me that in front of the team. And hell yeah, I'm excited. What clued you in on it?" She continued smiling.

"Talking at warp speed maybe, but it's the bouncing you're doing." As I walked toward her, I glanced down at her tits that kept in time with her feet. "I suggest you not make that little move on the field. You'll have every player staring at you."

She looked down at herself finally realizing what I was referring to. "Oh, yeah, probably not a good idea."

"It is if you want to cause busted plays during practice. Hey, maybe in a crunch you could pull that trick out to keep the other team from scoring." I laughed.

"That's not funny, Timms, so stop."

I put my arm around her but quickly removed it realizing where we were.

"None of that either. We'll have trouble right off the bat if you touch me or show favoritism toward me."

"Oh, right, but your sports idioms are mixed up."

"Eww, look at you being all Englishy." Her playful mood continued with the grin that followed.

"Englishy? That's not even a fucking word, India. What'd they hire when they got you? Doesn't know her sports and makes up her own shit. Don't they teach anything in California universities?"

When we reached the doorway, I opened to let her through.

"Well, it's my interns deciding to show up a couple of minutes ahead of schedule." I knew Coach's kidding voice when I heard it, but the change in India happened so fast I wanted to laugh again.

"Oh, Coach, I'm so sorry. I didn't realize you wanted me here early. I'll be here whenever you want me," she quickly addressed his comment.

"And what about you, asshat?" Coach asked me. "You going to be keeping her busy in your down time?"

"Come on, Coach. You know me. I'm innocent in all this. It's her fault."

India glared at me for throwing her under the bus—not laughing out loud was so difficult.

"Uh, Coach. It's my fault. I needed a quick nap. I didn't sleep well last night worrying about today." The sheepish look she gave him was priceless, and it was all I could stand. I busted out laughing, and the coach smiled.

"India, we're just busting your chops here. I didn't need you earlier than anyone else. Your new friend here knew that, but I take it he didn't tell you I like on time but not early. I'm usually busy and don't like people bothering me until I walk out my office door."

I stopped laughing immediately. He'd outed me on the spot. "Sorry. Yeah, he hates to be bothered before practices."

"You are so in trouble." Each word spoken plainly, she held the steam in because the coach watched her. "Paybacks are hell. You know that, right?"

"Yeah, I know. Sorry. I should've mentioned it. He also loves playing jokes on people so be ready anytime."

We followed the coach out the doors to the field. "You are so dead, Timms. I'll get you, and you'll never see it coming."

"Bring it on, newbie. You have no idea what you're dealing with. I've had years of practice with the shitheads I've lived with. You'll never survive."

After introductions, we broke into our specific assignments to begin where we'd left off in spring training. Crew and I reviewed what he practiced all summer. The kid acted like he was born to be a quarterback. His skills continued to improve every time he picked up the football. He delivered his leadership with quiet enthusiasm, using a lot of one-on-one with his teammates. They followed his cues knowing he would lead them to a sure victory if they did their jobs.

"Dude, did you spend the entire summer with a football in your hand?" I should have known better to phrase it as I did.

"Hell, no. I took some time to put my hands on more important things than a football." He wiggled his eyebrows at me. "You know, Coach, all work and no play is bad for you, but I'm sure you know this. What about you? All your time spent thinking of new ways to torture me out here or were they in their usual location around a hot female body?"

I took my cap off and looked at him. This comment would have been funny last year, but today, not so much. We needed to put his comments on my personal life to rest. Coach Jefferies had people listening all over the field.

"Okay, Crew. Let's talk."

"This sounds serious."

"It's serious for a lot of reasons." With my hand on his shoulder, I led him off to the side. He liked the individual approach, and today I'd use it in my favor. "My opportunity to coach here is the best damn thing that could've happened to me considering where I was last November with my injuries. I don't want to let anything happen to fuck it up. You understand that, right?"

"Sure thing, but Coach J knew what he was doing after the finish to the season you helped me have."

"True, but now I'm your permanent coach, at least for the season. I've gotta prove my worth at making you the best. One thing he's observing is whether I can make the transition from being a teammate to coach. There's going to be times when I'm going to ask you to do shit you don't feel is the right thing."

"Well, yeah, probably."

"As teammates, you'd see the calls as suggestions. As your coach, you've gotta see those calls as instructions that you damn sure better execute. It won't be an option. Are we still on the same page here, Tuck?"

"So you're saying we can't be friends anymore? We've gotta be coach/player all the time?"

"Pretty much or at least during the football season." I turned and looked directly at him to gauge his understanding and feelings on what I said. "I mean, I'm still here for you to talk to or help you when you need it. That won't change."

He looked down like he needed a second to take it all in. "So no more hanging out with us at the frat house?"

"No. I was out of XOX the day I walked across the stage. I'll show up to special events y'all throw for charities or on occasions for the team and shit like that, but otherwise, I'll never be at the house. There's things that go on I don't need to know about anymore." He knew what I referred to.

"Yeah, you're right about that, Coach. I understand what you're saying."

"It's all about earning your respect, Crew I plan to earn it every damn day with you and the rest of this team. Part of that is going to be calling you out on your shit from time to time. The way you respond to me will determine whether or not I've earned that respect. If the QB doesn't respect my position, none of the team will." Crew and I stared at each other for a few seconds. I needed him to grasp this concept and relay it to the team through his actions. It didn't take long until a subtle change came over his face.

"I get it, Coach Timms, and I'll make sure the others see it, too." He looked at me and smiled a genuine Crew smile. He'd do his best to show others how it had to be now.

"Thanks, Tuck. I appreciate you." I stuck my hand out to shake his. Crew might barely be twenty, but I knew he'd been an adult for a long time with his background as a musician's kid.

Taking my hand, he shook it firmly. "Okay, *Coach Timms*. Let's do this," he said loud enough for the others in our squad to hear.

"Yeah, let's do this." I turned to look at all of them. "Huddle up guys. We've got a few things to cover and then start drills."

INDIA

I ran over to meet with the squad at the five-yard line. The short jog warmed me up. My excitement hadn't waned from earlier, so I was ready to take on the world. Ian, Drew, and Zac all jogged over to meet me calling hellos.

"Where's Conner?" I looked behind them.

Ian finally spoke up. "Haven't seen him, Coach. We thought maybe he was with you."

"No, I haven't seen him this morning." They all stared at me. "Have you all met him?"

Again, Ian spoke. I could see him emerging as the leader of this little band. "Not exactly."

"What does that mean, Ian?"

"Well, we kinda, uh... all went out to a frat house last night for a bit, and he was there."

"Oh really? I thought he was new to this University. He's already pledged?"

"No, Coach. He transferred from the other university, so he's in."

None of the three would look at me.

"Guys, look at me. If you're going to party, at least own it. I know this whole college thing is new to you, but we've gotta be on the same page. Did something happen I need to know about?"

They finally raised their heads. Sometimes I felt like eighteen-year-olds didn't belong off at college. "So?"

Ian looked at the other two. "Well, we don't think he's coming today."

"What? He's not coming?"

"No, ma'am. He said... and these are his words, not mine... 'I don't need to show up with you bunch of pussies to listen to some muff muncher tell me how to do my job.'"

I felt my eyebrows shoot up before I could get a word out. *Who the fuck did he think he was?* I knew my face was red. I could feel it. The three standing before me knew I was pissed. My inner bitch said to have a fit, but the coach in me knew better than crucify the messengers for one dumbass' mistakes. The University would not put up with a homophobe using derogatory comments.

I took a few deep breaths before speaking. I needed to think before I said the wrong thing to these guys.

"Oh... he did, huh? Well, as far as we're concerned, we don't need him here either. This squad will do the practice the way I've lined it out, then we'll join the team if Coach J asks us to, and finally, we will meet with the team for anything he wants to say to all of us before heading to the showers. Everyone good with that?"

They collectively said yes.

"You all need to warm up and stretch." I paused and then said, "Wait. I have one more question. Who heard him say this?"

"Uh... I think only us. We were outside when he said it," Ian offered.

"Yeah, no one was around, Coach Durham," Drew added and Zac nodded.

"Okay. Let's get to it." I pushed down my seething anger for a later time.

The rest of the practice surpassed my expectations. The group worked hard to execute all the drills I had them do, and the different scenarios I had them work through. I wondered if these three tried harder than usual trying to make up for the missing player and his comments. Once we finished, we joined the team midfield where Coach J addressed the entire team.

I walked around the outside of the circle looking at the other players. These kids were some of the best players the nation offered. Recruitment in college was all about money, and TAU had plenty designated for football.

Pushing Conner's insolence out of my mind was necessary for a productive day. Practice would have gone to hell in two seconds if I didn't. As I looked over the team and the other coaches, I took in a deep breath and let it out slowly. Would an easy first day be too damn much to ask for?

Timms looked at me when I glanced in his direction. He turned his lips up in a brief smile, and I nodded but immediately looked away.

I knew I would have to deal with shit before I took the job but not on this level. Who the hell did that little prick think he was? Calling me such a derogatory name made my blood boil so badly I wanted to kick him off the squad without even questioning him. I needed to be careful not to betray the others by telling Conner I knew what he said since they were the only witnesses.

I needed to talk to Coach J about the policy for missing practices. He wasn't going to get away with that. The name calling would have to be dealt with differently, and I needed to think on that for a while.

As soon as practice ended, I jogged off the field and straight to Coach J's office. The longer I waited, the more the anger built up in me. Knocking on his office door, he raised and hand and motioned me inside.

"Quick question, Coach."

"What's that, India?"

"What happens to the players who miss practice?"
This got his attention. "Who?"

"The new recruit, Conner."

"Little prick already starting problems for him and the team, I see."

"I haven't talked to him yet. There might be a good excuse. I wanted to check in with you about the consequences in case his reasons are lame."

"Right. Good call. If they miss for no reason, they don't play in the next game. That goes for everyone, even starters."

I nodded my head.

"If they miss because of an appointment or some bullshit excuse, we'll issue a punishment."

"Seems fair. They can schedule around practice." I agreed with the rules so far.

"If players miss with a legitimate excuse, death in the family, something along those lines, it'll certainly be excused."

"Absolutely. Family should come first." We both nodded our heads.

"Let me get him in here tomorrow morning. We'll set the kid straight." The older coach stood and stretched his back.

"No, I'd rather deal with it myself. Conner needs to understand I'm his immediate coach. He needs to answer to me when he screws up."

"True, India, but I can stop this in one meeting. I talked to him about playing for a woman before I agreed to take him on the team. He assured me no problems would arise with whoever coached him."

"But if you take over, he'll see me as incapable of being a coach with authority over the squad. It's necessary for me to show him." Backing down wasn't in my nature, especially when it came from doing my job. In college, my job was to kick, and I did it even with the team on the other side of the line of scrimmage taunting me. Now my job is to get my squad ready to kick under any circumstances.

"So you want to try to solve this battle. I can already see it's going to be one, India." Coach never took his eyes off my face, judging my determination.

"My squad, my problem. If I can't handle it, then I don't deserve to be coaching at this level. You took a chance on me, and I'll prove to you it was the right choice." Faltering at the first problem would never work for me. My game face was on, and it wouldn't fail me. I'd used it more times than not navigating this all-male sport.

"All right. I let you have your way this time, but don't think I won't be watching. His insolence won't go unnoticed from here on out. Do you understand?"

"Yes, Coach. I get it. I'll never allow it to fester to a problem that affects the outcome of the team's game." I wanted to smile and high-five Coach J, but I kept the celebrating hidden away until later. "Guess I'll head out then, Coach."

"See you tomorrow. Oh, and good job out there today. Even when I'm not standing there, I'm still keeping up with progress everywhere on the field."

"Thanks, Coach J." I closed the door behind me.

Go me! I whispered to myself as I walked out of the building. The name calling still had me fired up, and I should have mentioned it to Coach J, but I wanted to handle this situation myself.

Making my way to the car, I slid in and started off. My phone rang, and I saw Chyna's name pop up. I pushed the talk button on the steering wheel as I drove out of the athletics parking lot.

"Hey girl, what's up?"

"Ugh. My classes are going to be such a bitch."

"Yeah, those freshmen classes are designed to weed out the slackers."

"I'm not a damn slacker, and you know it, but they're going to fucking kill me with all the reading."

"Been there, sweetie. You'll get used to it."

"Never. I'd rather do a thousand fucking physics problems over reading some of the shit from a five-thousand-page anthology for English."

"So you called to complain or was there something you wanted?" I was in no mood to listen to it right then. My mind was on dealing with Conner.

"Yeah, I wanted to ask what kind of shitastic day you had? You know with your first hot-as-hell practice and all."

"It was that and more. I'm not sure I was cut out for Texas if it stays this hot."

"Then let's talk a different hot. Did you meet all the hot guys? Any trips to the locker room to get a peek behind a towel?"

"Stop, Chyna. I'm not talking about my team like that."

"Well, hell. You're no damn fun at all. I needed a good dick story to cheer me up. Guess I'll have to go find my own to have my way with."

"No. Go home and read, remember?"

"That's about right, my prude, princess sister. I'm talking dicks, and you're talking *Jane Eyre*. You can't give me anything?"

"Well, I did get referred to as a muff muncher today."

"A muff muncher, huh? Was he hot? The guy who said it?"

"Really, Chyna? I get designated as a lesbian because I'm coaching football, and you want to know if he's worth your time?" I let out a huge breath. "No, he's an asshole in the worst kind of way."

"Oh. It must be pretty damn bad for you to call him a name like that." She chuckled. I didn't.

"He's a douchebag, sewer-sucking slimeball with a god complex."

The car next to me could hear Chyna laughing over my speaker. "Oh my God, India. That's the worst combination of 'not bad words' I've ever heard you say."

"This isn't funny."

"Yeah, it is." Once she caught her breath, she asked. "What'd he call you a muff muncher for anyway?"

"He told the other freshmen on the kicking team that he wasn't listening to me tell him how to do his job. Like he already had the damn spot as head kicker, which he doesn't because I get to say who is the starting kicker, and he will only be that over my dead body—"

"Stop, stop. *Stop!*" She ended my tirade. "Wow, you must be mad to get that worked up."

"Glad you finally caught on." I pulled into my spot turning off the motor. "Look, I'm home now and not going anywhere tonight, so I'm gonna let you go. I'm hot and tired."

"And pissed. Don't forget that."

"And super pissed. Right. I'm gonna go take a shower and cool off."

"Okay. Well, make sure your vibrator is waterproof if you don't already know. A good orgasm would take the stress away, but I'd hate to read about a coach dying from being BOB shocked."

"Funny. Bye." I pushed end to stop any other smart-ass comments she had for me.

After walking inside, showing and eating something, finally crawling into bed felt so good. My fluffed pillow felt perfect, and my head sunk down in it ready to turn off for the night, but someone had other ideas. My phone vibrated on the nightstand.

"Ugh. This better be good."

Timms' name flashed on the screen. I expected to hear from him after practice, but it never happened.

"Hey." My voice held an angry tone to it, but I didn't care.

"Hey, yourself. Did I wake you up?" His deep, even voice sounded so sexy over the phone. I pictured him relaxing against his headboard without a shirt. Damn, I needed to stop thinking of him this way.

"No, I just got in bed. It's been a long day, and I'm glad it's over." I didn't want to be angry with him, but I couldn't help myself.

"Practice looked like it went well every time I looked over there. Am I wrong?"

"No, you're right. It went great, except..." I dragged out the last word. Did I want to tell him what I learned? It wasn't his problem to deal with, but he did tell me I could talk to him about anything.

"I don't like the way that sounded. Want me to come over for a few minutes."

When I didn't answer right away, he added, "To talk."

No, I wanted him to come over and do dirty things to me. He needed to make me think about anything other than dealing with the shit I knew needed to happen tomorrow.

"I don't know. I'm already in bed."

"I find talking in bed one of the best places to get the truth out." His light tone told me he must have been smiling when he said it.

"Well, yeah. If you can't tell the truth in bed, where will you tell it?" I chuckled a little. Two minutes of talking to him, and I already felt better.

"So, you want to open the door for me?" A brief knock surprised me.

"You're here already? I'm not dressed."

"I'm sure whatever you're wearing is fine with me."

With only my tank and some lacy boy shorts on, he would more than appreciate my state of dress. I pulled some sleep shorts out and hopped down the hallway stepping into them.

Swinging the door open, he looked like sin standing in my doorway. Maybe I needed a little sin right now. Wearing loose-fitting basketball shorts and a tight-fitting white tee, I didn't even try to stop myself. I grabbed his shirt front and pulled him inside. My neighbors didn't need a show on the sidewalk.

The door slammed behind him, but not before I had my lips on his. The kiss started out hard and heart-stopping. I slid my hands across the tattoos on both sides of his neck to clasp together behind the thick, hard muscles. I desperately needed his mouth on mine. I craved this connection with him with everything inside me.

In seconds, he realized my demands needed to be met from the hot, frantic kiss I poured my soul into.

Reaching under my thighs, he lifted me as we spun around pushing me back against the door responding to the urgency I sought. Anyone spying on us would think it was closer to mauling than a kiss. My tongue dueled with his in a dance to say what I wanted from him. Our coming together turned frantic, messy even, but it's what I wanted.

His hands slid under my tank and ripped it over my head, the hard peaks of my nipples strained against his t-shirt before I could get the soft cotton off him.

"Put me down, Timms, please." He let go of my legs, and I slid down his body feeling the tightness of his abs rub against my skin. I kissed across his chest looking at the darkness of the tattoos as I went, his skin hot to my tongue as I licked my way down. I swiped the tip of my tongue across his taut nipple, and he sucked in a breath pulling on my hair that he'd wrapped his fingers in. The prickles of pain he caused sent shocks to my core making my desire for him heighten even faster as I felt the liquid of my desire pool.

He pulled me back up to attack my mouth, but this time he led the way. His warm hands drifted from my tangled hair to my neck where he used a tighter grasp than needed. If this hold was meant to show force, he proved his point, and I felt myself melting against him.

My hands inched around his narrow waist stroking the taught, straining muscles until I tugged him closer to me. He let go of my neck and moved down to my breasts to tug my stiffly-pebbled nipples between his thumb and index finger. Each squeeze and twist caused my breath to hitch from the exquisite form of torture. His mouth started a torturous descent across my jaw and down my neck where he nipped at my skin before running his flattened tongue over the places to soothe the sting. He left each spot with a wet kiss causing the skin on my arms to tingle as the hair stood on end.

The zing of lust shot through me when he finally took one nipple between his teeth and lightly bit the hardened flesh. Letting go, he lavished the swollen nub with his tongue and then finally sucked the nipple into his warm mouth with force behind it. My body was so close to orgasming that I cried out when he abandoned the tight pink button.

"God, India. Your tits are pure perfection." He'd replaced his mouth with fingers to continue the smoldering torment. Grabbing both breasts, he pulled them together tightly as he kissed and sucked from one peak to the other.

I needed more. I looped my fingers under the elastic of his shorts and pushed them down as far as I could freeing his hard cock for me to wrap my hand around him. The smooth flesh's length felt perfect, but the girth caused me to suck in a breath. I doubted my ability to take him inside me.

I'd only had sex with a few different men, but they were nothing like this. As I slid from the base to the head, my doubts grew more. I squeezed tightly on my way back down taking the drops of precum with me to offer a smoother glide.

"Stop, babe. It feels too fucking good. Don't want to ruin this before we even get started. It's been a while, since I've been waiting for the right time with you."

"Now is the right time, Timms. I need you to fuck me now."

"Then I want it to be perfect. Bedroom?" He nodded down the hall.

"Yeah."

I reached behind me and locked the door when he picked me up again. As I wrapped my legs around him and held on, I had a feeling the ride of my life waited beyond that bedroom door.

TIMMS

The street light coming through the blinds offered enough light when I entered her room. As I laid her on top of the comforter, my eyes drifted down her fine body. "I need to see you, India." The lamp flipped on before I worked my way to the foot of the bed. This needed to slow down. I planned to savor every minute of our first time together. Rushing this had the potential to ruin everything between us. Her desire for me was apparent, but I wanted this to be more than just a fuck to satisfy our lust.

With my knee on the foot of the bed, I reached up and grabbed the tiny sleep shorts she bothered wearing. "You put these on just for me?"

She looked down at my hands on both sides of her body before I started sliding them down her tanned legs. "Yeah, I didn't want to answer the door in my panties."

"No, bad idea. Well, unless it's me, then I'm good with it." My lips turned up into a slow smile. "Hell, you could've been naked and saved us some time."

"That'll never happen."

A soft grin held my attention. "You should smile more often, India. Your entire face lights up when you do making you even more beautiful."

"Come on, Timms. You've got me in bed mostly naked. All the flattery isn't necessary." Her hands rested on top of mine trying to help me get her completely undressed.

"Is that right? Are we back to you wanting to use me for sex?" I looked up at her.

She laughed this time. "Well, I don't know if I'd say use you for sex. More like I'd like to enjoy you having sex."

"You're a strange woman, India. Most females enjoy the compliments, the cajoling. You're ready to jump in and hang on for the ride."

"Come on, Timms. We both know that's all it is. I've been told this before. I'm sure if I had the time, I'd discover plenty of girls on campus who had all the gossip about you being the hot quarterback with a different girl every night."

"That was before." My hands traced down her legs to her ankles and back up to her knees. The silky feel of her skin made me want to pick up the pace. Damn, I wanted this woman, and the idea of having her all night sounded perfect until now. "I told you I planned to change my ways, and I have. I want you, India, in a different way than the others."

She glanced down at my dick standing at attention waiting patiently. "Yeah, I can see that." She wiggled her eyebrows.

What was there about her? The only time she expressed any interest in me was when she was horny or frustrated and needed a quick lay. I began to believe that's the only thing she saw sex for, and I could supply her with a means to an end. She puzzled me at every turn.

I rolled over and sat down. She jumped up and sat beside me. "What's going on? One minute you're completely on board with fucking, and now you're having second thoughts. There's something wrong with this dynamic, Timms."

"You're telling me." I turned sideways so I could watch her while I spoke. "Look, India, there's so much about you I like. You're talented, smart, and God knows you're a knockout in the looks department." I reached out and took her hand rubbing it between both of mine. The look on her face expressed her confusion with my words.

"I'm dying to get you in bed and do things to your smokin' hot body that you probably don't even know can be done."

"But..." The blue eyes that captured attention from everyone who saw them stared at me waiting for what I needed to say. "But not this way. I need it to be more than a quick fuck with you. I want us to have sex because it means more than just a way to release the tension of the day. I mean, I get needing that kind of sex. God knows I've needed it, a lot, but I never had it with someone I cared about. Do you understand what I'm trying to say?"

"Even though I want to have sex, you don't want to because you care too much about me? That's just weird, Timms."

I took in a deep breath and let it out slowly. I needed to choose my words carefully, so I didn't ruin this moment. "Yeah, you're right. It's weird, but I want us to have a chance, India. I want us both to enjoy sex because of the connection it'll create."

She fell back on the bed and stared up at the ceiling fan that formed a breeze across our skin. "And what if I don't want a connection? What if I only want to hook up when I feel the need?"

I didn't look back. How could I answer this? If we weren't together, would she go out and find someone else? She'd have no problem locating a participant more than willing to fulfill her request. Hell, most of the team would stand in line for a shot to fuck her.

"So, all you want is a quick fuck and move on to the next guy?"

"No, I didn't say that. I mean, I hadn't thought about hooking up with random guys. I've never done something like that."

"Good to know."

"I'm not a whore, Timms."

"Never said that." I felt my anger rising. I rarely got mad about anything. I let things roll off my back, but this might be something I couldn't let go of so quickly.

"No, but it sounded like that's what you thought."

I stood and turned toward her. She lay there mostly naked looking like a goddess enjoying the freedom of clothes. It did nothing for my anger, though. My gaze traveled up her body past her legs, the curves, her perfect tits up to her gorgeous face.

"Fuck it." My shorts hit the floor, and I finished yanking her panties off her body before I gave another thought to what I was doing. As I pushed my thigh between her legs parting them, I stroked my dick. Her hand snaked out and pulled open the nightstand drawer producing a condom. I had one in my billfold, but in my anger, I had forgotten about it. Stupid mistake on my part that I'd never made before. She had my mind so fucked.

She watched my hand clasped around myself as I rolled it down the length before she bent her knees giving me better access to the ultimate destination. If she wanted down and dirty fucking, we'd have it. I spit in my hand to add to the slickness in case she wasn't wet enough.

"You ready for this." I looked up at her, and she nodded. It tore me up inside. I slid the head up and down her crease and found her more than ready for me. I pushed forward just inside her, and she sucked in a breath.

"It'll feel better in a second." Again, she nodded, so I plunged forward until I was buried inside her. It was the tightest pussy I'd felt in forever.

"This is what you wanted, right?" The nod came fast, and she wrapped her legs around my waist holding me tight against her. When she finally relaxed some, I slid out and pushed back in easier this time. If we were going to do this, she would damn well enjoy it.

After a few easy strokes to get her used to my size, I rolled us over, and she straddled me. India wanted it, so I decided to let her lead the way. With her hands braced on my shoulders, her movement and the friction it created was what was needed to race to the finish.

Reaching down, I ran my thumb over her clit knowing it would speed this along. She would cum before I did if it killed me. Satisfying her lust was more important to me at this point.

I circled the engorged nub moving down to our joining to grab some liquid to spread around her. It didn't take long before I felt her walls constricting on me, evidence that the end was getting close. I raised up and took one of her pebbles in my mouth. She'd driven me crazy watching them bounce with each thrust. One easy bite of the distended tip and she contracted over and over.

"Oh God, Timms. Oh God. Yes. Timms. Yes." Her screams and trembles on my dick created what I needed to follow her over that edge. I grabbed her hips and pulled her down in several hard thrusts to empty all I had into her willing body.

She accomplished her goal with the fast and furious fucking she controlled. My goal went out the window before we started.

When I could breathe again, I rolled us back over and climbed off the bed to dispose of the condom in her bathroom. I walked out, and she still lay exactly as I'd left her. Her dark hair fanned across the light pillowcase, and again, the idea of a goddess lying before me came to mind. Only now I knew she'd never be my goddess to worship which pissed me off, too.

I snatched my shorts off the floor and stepped into them with her watching me. "See you on the field tomorrow." I turned and headed for the door.

"Where are you going?" she called, but I didn't answer. I twisted the door lock before I shut it. I heard her unlocking it before I got five steps down the sidewalk. She jerked it open peeking around it. "Timms, where are you going?"

"Home," I called before climbing in and squealing my tires as I pushed the gas pedal down harder than necessary. My foot mashed it to the floor, knowing she watched me. I didn't care. I had to get out of there.

Angry at her and myself for letting it go that far, I slammed my fist down on the steering wheel over and over at the first stop sign. Why the fuck did I go through with that? It's so far from what I wanted, what I'd planned.

I heard my phone go off with a text seeing her name on the screen.

"No way, babe. Not now. Maybe not ever at this point."

If I drove straight home, I'd brood about this on my patio for hours. At the frat house, I spent many nights sitting on the front porch thinking about shit. I watched people come and go from that spot. My apartment didn't offer that distraction.

I turned at the end of the street and headed out to another place where I knew I could think. I picked up my phone, and Siri found the number I needed.

"You home?"

"Sure. What's up?" Blue replied.

"Noelle there?"

"Nope, she went to her parents this evening to get some things we need."

"You got beer?"

"Don't I always?"

"Be there in a few."

"Come on."

I ended the call. I didn't want to talk to Blue. I only needed a place to go where other people would be, so I made my way there.

The door to Blue and Noelle's new apartment faced the pool and play area. The complex catered to college students, so people always had something going on in the common area. I saw a few people I recognized before walking through their door.

"Hey, dude. What's up?" Blue-eyed me with suspicion.

"Not much. Just felt the need to stop in for a beer. There's no one at my fucking place except old people or married couples who never step a damn foot outside."

"Okay. No problem." He handed me an opened cold bottle. "Let's sit outside. It's a great night."

"Yeah, it is." We sat without speaking until I drained the bottle. I stood to get another. "You good?" I glanced at his beer.

"Yeah, I am, but don't let me stop you." One thing I liked about Blue was he wouldn't question me. He knew me well enough to know that I'd talk if I wanted to say something. Right now, I didn't know what I wanted to say. I'd probably fucked up with India, but why did I feel bad about it? It's what she wanted from me.

When I sat back down a few of the other teammates sat on Blue's porch.

"Hey, Timms." Some acknowledged me. Knowing I shouldn't party with this group, I considered leaving. I looked at Blue about to say my goodbyes.

He spoke first. "Guys. Timms and I were doing some strategizing about the first game. We need some time to finish this shit." They all stood and jumped back in the pool.

"Thanks. Coach J would fire my ass on the spot if he found out I spent my fucking evening drinking with the team."

"It's cool. I understand." He looked at me with a smirk. "But you know I'm part of the team, too."

"Yeah, I know, but you're my friend first."

"True." He waited a beat before continuing. "Speaking of that. You want to talk about why you're here drinking beer on my fucking porch watching freshmen make douchebag moves on women?"

"I'm thinking about it."

"Is that what you call it? Sucking back beer, making huffing noises, shuffling your feet like you're about to take off in a sprint?"

"Maybe."

"So, are we talking women here?"

"What do you mean?"

"Dude, I've known you a long fucking time now. Shit never gets to you. It's gotta be a female."

I watched the dumb asshats trying their fuckery at getting the girls to go home with them. "God, were we ever that stupid around women?"

"Hell yeah, I was. Just last year, remember?"

I had to laugh because that comment held such truth. If it weren't for falling in love with Noelle, he might still be.

"What's got you all tied up?" He watched me for a second before he continued.

"It's kinda funny, Timms. I've seen you about to play in the biggest damn game of your life, and you never hardly broke a fucking sweat worrying about it. This must be serious."

"I thought it was serious, but hell, she must've been on a different playing field."

"Is that right?"

"For once, I wanted to take it slow and easy. See if I could do the relationship thing with someone I thought was worth it."

"You? In a relationship? No shit?" Blue smiled but didn't laugh.

"It is no shit because it ain't happening. She showed me real fast that all she was in it for was a quick fuck when she was desperate."

"You mean like we lived for the past three years?"

"Hell yeah, we did." We bumped fists on it.

"So what the fuck's wrong? She wanted to get laid, and you're turning her down? Did an alien abduction happen while we weren't looking?" He chuckled.

I sat back, looked down at my crossed sandaled feet and guzzled some of my beer. I'd barely remembered to get my beer cap Reefs before I walked out of her apartment seething through my anger.

"When I got hurt last season, I had a lot of time to think. Living with you and Noelle showed me a different kind of life. Unlike me, you've got a woman who cares for you when you need her. She knows when that need is strong. She knows when you only need to be close and when it's okay to pull back and give you time. You get each other that way. I watched it, and I gotta say, it looks great on both of you."

"Yeah, we do have that. It was a hard road to get there, though. Hell, I don't even know how we got there. What I sure as shit do know is, I'm fucking glad we did."

"Right. You see, that right there... you don't hesitate to say it either. You two figured each other out, got your act together, and made it work."

"So, what are you saying, Timms? You want what we've got?"

"Exactly, and I thought I'd found the right one, but she's not on board with the damn plan."

"Then get her on board."

"Not that easy. Hell, maybe she's not ready, or maybe I got it all wrong, and she's not it."

"Dude, you gotta get her ready."

"What the fuck does that mean? Either she's in, or she's not."

"Not always. Could be you gotta show her what she's missing by not being with you."

"Oh, she wants to be with me but apparently only for the sex."

He laughed at me and was so loud that the asswipes from the pool turned to look at us. "Timms, you've got half the damn battle won then. Usually, sex breaks the deal for women. She wants you already. Now you gotta show her for the other reasons, too."

He had my attention. "I'll have to give this some thought."

"This oughta be a fucking cakewalk for you, dude."

"Shit, something tells me nothing's going to be cake with this girl. It's going to be all piss and vinegar."

"Turn on that Theo Timms' charm and knock her over."

"My charm might not be what gets me there when all she wants is my dick."

"Then maybe you'll need to fuck her into loving you instead of charming her into it." Blue laughed out loud at his comment.

"That's what I don't want to do. Like I said, I gotta give this approach some thought since it's a first."

"You do that, man, and get back to me. This season's going to be interesting watching you trying not to get into a girl's pants for a change."

INDIA

"Well, damn. So much for basking in the afterglow of sex. Great job, India. Guess my hopes of a fuck buddy fell through." With the door closed and locked, the bed called my name. The one that still smelled like him. Damn, his scent buried in my bedding made me want him even more. The abrupt departure stung and left me wondering what I'd done wrong.

The way he took control before we made it to the bedroom, I assumed he would continue showing the same intense passion, but he turned the tables on me. How did that happen?

His rock-hard cock proved he was into it, but something changed when he rolled us over for me to ride him. He gave me total control like he couldn't be bothered. The position gave me everything I needed taking him deeper inside. I loved the sensation, but he seemed like he only participated in letting me have my way and nothing more.

My phone rang, and Chyna's name flashed on the screen. "Great. You're timing's too perfect, little sister."

I pressed the speaker button. "Hey, sis, waz up in Texas?" Her speech told me all I needed to know about her intoxicated ass.

"Not much." I huffed after my words.

"Doesn't sound like it. You pizzed?" She formed real words only with a new sound. "Was it those little freshmen fuckers? They can be cocky bastards like all the rest of the jerk-off jocks."

Her wording caused me to laugh. Chyna always had a way of cheering me up. "No, it wasn't a player. It's a coach, a friend."

"The hell you say, seester. Tell me that cocksucker's name. I'll come to Texas and whoop his ass for you. Oh, wait." She spoke to others in the loud room. "Can someone give me a ride to Texas? I got some ass to kick." The laughing echoing in the background told me I needed to keep this conversation brief. She might tell the world my problems in her state of drunkenness.

"Look, I'll find that fucktard and take care of him for you. It's him, right babe?"

"Oh my God, Chyna. You need to ask someone who's not been drinking to take you home before you make some serious mistakes."

I jerked the phone away from my ear since her loud laughter echoed through the phone.

"Joking, India. Joking. Lighten up biatch. We're only having some fun."

"I'm not joking, Chyna. Please don't drive home. Order an Uber."

"And what even gave you a fucking idea I was going home tonight?" She emphasized the *even* loud and clear.

"Could be you have classes in the morning?" I knew she'd never make them at this point.

"Oh yeah. I forgot I've got that fine-ass professor in the morning. I met him at orientation. He's got a hot body that won't quit, just like I like them."

"Chyna, stay away from your professors."

"Yeah, yeah." She held the phone out again. "Hey, all you dirty hos? Isn't Professor Duke the hottest fucking thing on campus?" I heard resounding whoops and catcalls. This conversation was going nowhere.

"Okay, Chyna. I'm gonna run. Please get a safe ride if you do leave, and for God's sake, remember to use a condom."

"Yes, ma'am, mommy dearest." The cackle coming through the phone didn't offer any surety on taking my advice. "Bye, bitch." She ended our call.

I looked at my phone and wondered if there might be a person to call to make sure she got home but knew better. She'd find her way both from the party and through life.

Rolling over, I looked at my phone. Maybe I should call him, but he might think I was desperate. The evening didn't go anywhere that I wanted it to except for the good sex.

What was his deal anyway? Isn't that the way it's supposed to work with these guys? Timms' reputation with the women around campus made me believe it would be easy to have him for a fuck buddy. It looked like I needed to gather more intel on this situation from the women I'd met so far. I wondered if they would be forthcoming with what I needed to know.

After checking in with my classes the next morning, I knew going to school would be the easy part of my day. Grad school for interns all happened on the web which was fine with me. Getting the initial info and going over term assignments didn't take long, and I found my way to the coaching offices long before practice started.

Coach J needed to know some things about the fourth team member, so I hoped now would be a good time. After playing against him last season, trouble between us might be in the works. He had an attitude from hell and a real problem with authority. Part of me suspected that's why he changed schools at the last minute.

As I rounded the corner down to Coach J's office, loud talking between two men slowed me down. I didn't want to get into something that was none of my business. All the doors to the other offices stood closed except the one I needed to be in, so I stopped and leaned against the wall waiting for my turn.

Coach J yelled at someone about not coming to practice.

Hmm. Maybe he was yelling at Conner. Maybe I needed to be in there after all.

"You will not skip practices and expect to play on this team, young man. I don't care how good you are at kicking."

I heard a chair scrape slightly across the floor. "Well, Coach J, I never had to go to practice at my old school because they knew I would do my job when the time was right." The smart-ass tone Conner used confirmed what I already knew about this guy—I didn't want him on my team.

"Does this look like your old school, boy? Hell no, it doesn't. You got cut from your old school probably for pulling this same shit with them."

"I didn't get cut. They didn't need me anymore, so I chose to leave."

"You chose to leave after they announced you would no longer be part of their team."

A similar scraping noise from the chair came again, but this time the chair hit the wall. "Those dumb sons of bitches didn't know what they were saying when they told me I was off. The team knew I was a necessary part of any good football team. They needed me."

"If that's so, then why didn't any of them come forward to speak on your behalf? I don't recall being contacted by a single person in your defense." Coach J's voice got louder. "That's because they were glad to see you go. I only wish I'd had a chance to talk to more people before I signed on that dotted line getting you here. We needed a player we could count on, and not one who would cause trouble from the first day."

"Well, you don't have to worry about that now, do you? That bitch, India Durham, will know how to use me. I promise you I can show her a thing or two about kicking."

Coach J's voice strained to maintain control. "First of all, you will *never*... and I repeat... *never*, refer to her with another derogatory term again. Coach Durham graduated as one of the top kickers in the nation. She's not 'a bitch' or 'your bitch.' Do you understand what I'm saying?"

"Yeah, yeah. I feel ya, but I don't understand why you felt like I needed to have some sweet meat to help me on the field. Her soccer background isn't exactly my style."

Coach's chair rolled from behind his desk and hit the credenza. "I'm not sure we have a place for you on this team either, son. Your comments are going to cause more trouble than you're worth."

"Now don't be like that, Coach J. You know I need this year to finish, and I'm a damn fine kicker. Let's forget I let that slip. I promise to watch my language around her."

"I don't know," Coach J responded. "You came in here walking a fine line, and if your comments are the reason, I completely understand why they pulled your scholarship. I only agreed to let you come on-board because their coach is a friend who said you could pull your weight in the kicking department, and I have a group of green-horn freshmen."

I couldn't believe he was letting this fucktard off so easily. There was no way in hell I would put up with his mouth. Who the hell did he think he was talking about in there? I'd had enough listening, my turn to voice my opinion.

I walked in the doorway of Coach J's office.

"Oh, India, uh... Coach Durham, I was discussing the need to attend all practices with Conner here."

Conner stood and smiled a huge smile at me. Damn, he was tall. His smile wouldn't phase me, though. He was a douchebag right off the line.

"Is there a problem in here, Coach J? I thought I'd heard some yelling."

"No, not at all, Coach Durham. Conner here was simply telling some stories about his former college days."

"If you mean about how he treats women, then yes, his reputation proceeds him."

This shut both men down completely. Coach J's eyes bulged to the point I started thinking they might pop out of his head. The little smartass dropped his face to the floor refusing to meet my stare. Today was not the day I wanted to fight after last night with Timms, but I guess it's better to get it all out in the open.

"I exchanged texts with a few friends who knew of Conner from his last university when he failed to show up to practice. Former students there said they had an opportunity to watch his raw talent be put to good use until he let his mouth overload his ass."

"Now, Coach Durham, we don't like to base our players' reputations on hearsay and innuendos."

"Remember, too, Coach J, I played against him last season during a playoff game. He didn't impress me with his kicking or his attitude."

Conner stood. "I'm telling you both I've never been in trouble. I know how to conduct myself professionally when I'm on the field. I'm a gifted kicker which you will see as soon as I post one through those uprights from fifty yards out. That's what my reputation says."

I stared at him, and this time he held my gaze. "And while that's an impressive stat, it won't do you or this team any good if you're sitting your ass on the bench because you can't keep your mouth shut. Do you understand what I'm telling you, Conner?"

"Yeah, I understand you loud and clear. It's a good thing Coach J here knows how valuable I am to this team, him being the head coach and all." He had the nerve at this point to smirk at me. What an asshat.

I took a deep breath and let it out slowly before I spoke. "Yes, Conner, you are right on one thing you said. Coach J is the head football coach here at TAU. As far as having the last call on who goes on the field to kick the ball, though, well... you see... that's my call. Isn't that right, Coach J?"

I turned to the older man and looked him square in the eye. If he didn't back me up on this, I could kiss this internship goodbye.

Coach J nodded his head. "She's telling the truth. When we took her on as the kicking coach, we knew she would have the best knowledge as to who needed to be kicking. I can't be everywhere, so my assistant coaches are considered my eyes and ears. Coach Durham will be making the call every time this season, Conner. You better get used to it because, at this point, I believe you'll not be the first person listed on the kicking roster."

I turned and stared Conner down. His face told me all I needed to know. At that moment, I doubted he would ever kick this season. Instinct said to tell him to turn in his uniform, but I knew that would be overstepping my bounds as the assistant.

Conner stood and addressed Coach J. "Well, I guess I'll just have to prove to you I'm the man for the job, Coach J." The insolent dumbass purposely ignored me deferring to Coach J. When he finished, he spun around and walked out of the office.

We both watched him around the corner before I turned back to look at Coach J.

"That didn't go too well."

"No, it didn't. I'd been told he was a handful and would test us at every opportunity, but I never realized we were taking on someone with no sense of respect for authority. I'm sorry you're strapped with a player of his caliber. The only good thing I can say is, he is an outstanding kicker."

"And that's great, but I seriously doubt you'll ever see him kick for TAU. A bad attitude, a smart-ass mouth, and disrespect for women will get him nowhere with me. I'll work with one of the others night and day, if necessary, to make sure they surpass anything he can do on the field. They're worth far more than Conner in my book."

I spent the afternoon watching all the videos I could find of Conner kicking at his previous university. He was good, I had to give him that, but his mouth and attitude were far from it.

I pulled up videos of the other three on the team. They needed work, but it didn't mean they couldn't pull it off during the season. It would require a lot of practice on our part to get them there, but it could be done.

Voices came from another part of the building. Almost time for practice. These next few hours should be interesting considering I had to face Timms and put up with Conner. I wasn't looking forward to either.

I stood and walked into the women's restroom that was designated as my locker area. I knew they had accommodated me with my own so it wouldn't cause a problem. I'd dealt with this all before.

When I walked out, Conner came down the hallway alone. I didn't even acknowledge his presence. Dealing with him on a one-on-one basis needed to be avoided.

"Well, hello, Coach Hottie." His comment caught me off guard. I knew he was audacious, but to be glaringly so in the middle of the locker area was too much.

I crawled up into his personal space as I put my nose even with his. For once in my life, I was ecstatic with my height.

"Listen here, Conner. You may have wormed your way onto this team, and I may be stuck with you for a short period, but don't think I can't chew you up and spit you to the sideline."

"What was that, Coach Durham?" he said loudly. "I don't think you telling me you're willing to eat my dick to keep me on the team is appropriate. Sounds like sexual harassment, Coach. I would never want to have to file charges against you. You know that kind of problem happens when you least expect it."

Timms walked through the locker room doors. He hadn't heard the conversation, but he knew something was wrong. Of all people to happen along right then, he wasn't the one I wanted to see.

"Is there a problem here, Coach Durham?" He stepped up to form a triangle of bodies.

I looked at the slight smile on Conner's face and wanted to scream. "No, Coach Timms. It's all good. We're about to go out on the field and warm up for practice."

Conner stepped back and slid his helmet on halfway. "I'll see you shortly, Coach." He made the pretense of team enthusiasm with jogging out the door to the field.

Timms and I watched him as the doors closed. "What's going on, India?"

I blew out a breath, "Nothing, yet. He's going to be trouble the entire damn season."

"Yeah, I can see it." He looked at me with a questioning look as though he wanted to ask more but didn't.

"Watch yourself around him. Guys like that have a way of working their agenda so they come out looking good but can take you down."

"Right. I can see it happening."

The locker doors opened, and the remainder of the Rams' team jogged out in their clean practice uniforms. It was going to be a long season if I didn't get this straightened out.

TIMMS

My hands were full with the new quarterback recruits and working with Crew. He caught on to the new plays quickly which helped me have more time to work on his backups. No one ever wanted to think about injuries being a possibility, but my situation always hung around like a ghost waiting its turn to come forward and scare the hell out of me.

At the front of my mind was India since I'd had several days to think about our time together. Something was going on with her other than our situation. I'd played the scene between our time in bed over and over. What could I do to change her mind about it? Did I misunderstand her intentions? Was she through with me so quickly? Other than a few nods and brief necessary conversations, we hadn't spoken all week. I wondered if this lack of communication had bothered her as it did me.

Every time I glanced down to her end of the field, she seemed to be in a confrontation with Conner. She said he was trouble, and while I believed her, I didn't know what had gone on. I needed her to trust me enough to share the problems. I couldn't help fix something I wasn't aware of. But then, India seemed to want to handle everything on her own.

"Coach?" The name brought me out of my own head.

"Yeah?" Crew was talking to me. "What's going on?"

He put his hand on my shoulder. "You okay? We were talking to you, and you spaced out on us."

"Sorry. Just thinking about something we need to work on." This lie would never fly with these guys. Why did I even bother?

"Yeah, right, Coach. We see you watching her. We're not total dumbasses, you know. You keep an eye on her all the time and you should."

The others made some positive noises to add to Crew's.

"What are y'all talking about?" I glanced down to the thirty-yard line where her squad practiced different techniques—at least three of them were.

"Coach Timms, Conner is nothing but trouble. You should hear the things he says about her when we're out or hanging around the house." Crew removed his helmet and took a knee. The Texas sun drained the players in a hurry, so they never overlooked an opportunity to rest.

I yelled over to the sidelines to get the team trainers to bring us sports drinks. If we were taking a break, it needed to look legit.

"What are y'all saying, guys? Is there something going on to report?"

"Report? Don't know about that but getting him straight, yes. That needs to happen."

"Tell me, guys. What do I need to know?"

Mixon, one of the freshmen, stopped spraying liquid in his mouth. "Conner thinks he's too good to be coached by her. He's so full of himself that he can't see how she could make him even better."

"He's sneaky, though. It's going to be hard to catch him doing anything wrong," Crew added.

"How, Crew?"

"He's made some comments about getting her alone and making trouble for her. Thinks the University will fire her and maybe make her dreams of being a full-time coach never happen."

"Oh, yeah?" Anger rose with each comment.

Who did this little shit think he was?

"Yeah, Coach," Mixon added. "But when we ask him about it, he plays it off as trash talk. Says he doesn't mean anything by it, or he denies he said anything at all."

"Maybe I need to have a talk of my own with him." I stared at the troublemaker standing around on the sidelines.

"You do that, Coach, and let us know when, so we can watch. He's a big talker, and we'd love to see someone take him down a few notches," Crew added.

"He thinks he's a badass because he's a senior, and he's constantly trying to lord it over the rest of the guys in the house. We're sick of the bullshit he consistently spews," Mixon said, but the entire group nodded in agreement.

"Sounds like we've got an arrogant prick among us."

The group laughed, and while I laughed with them, I wondered how this problem could be fixed without getting myself in trouble with the University. I also didn't want anything coming back to India from it.

"Okay, slackers, let's get back to work." The moans started, but this QB squad knew hard work paid off.

After practice, the fifty-yard line meeting ended quickly, and we headed for the locker rooms, while I watched for India. We needed to get back on some solid ground. I'd let her stew for the week on what happened between us before, and hoped she would see things in a different light.

Soft footsteps approached from behind me, and I knew they had to be hers, so I slowed down.

"Hey, Timms." She appeared beside me.

"Hey yourself, India. How's practice going?" Her lustrous blue eyes meeting mine made me want to stop and stare.

"Oh, you know. It's practice." I hated that she played it off instead of telling me the truth.

"That's good." We moved forward a few more steps without speaking. "Some of my guys told me differently." I knew I had to tread softly around this conversation.

"Oh, really. What'd they say?" I figured she'd give me nothing.

"Something along the lines of you having a prima donna causing you all kinds of shit." I wrapped my hand around the smooth skin of her upper arm and turned her, so she had to look me in the eyes. "What's going on?"

The blue irises widened with a hard look. "What makes you think something's going on?"

"Don't pretend like it's all fun and games out there on the field, India. I've heard already."

"What have you heard and from who?" Her stare turned into a glare.

Pulling her to the side so others wouldn't watch or hear our exchange gave me a second to think. "Look, I'm not trying to make this a thing. I only want to help. The guys on my squad told me Conner's been saying shit, so tell me the damn truth this time."

She stood still. I could see she was trying to decide what to say or if she was going to say anything at all. Her chest rose as she took in a deep breath.

"I don't even know where to start, Timms. He's the worst. He says things when others aren't around to hear. At practice, he starts crap every chance he gets. The others refuse to go against him. I think he's threatened them at some point, but I can't get them to admit to it."

"Wait, back up. Let's start at the top. What kind of things is Conner saying?"

India looked around before saying another word. "I don't want to talk about this here."

"That's fine. Let's go somewhere else then."

"No, I can't. I have to meet with my advisor. I've put it off twice already."

"Then come over when you're done. I'm heading straight home." I wanted to pull her into my arms and hold her. The look on her face said she was scared which surprised me. I would have thought that scaring her took some doing.

She crossed her arms over each other and gave herself the hug I wanted to supply. It took her a minute to finally answer me.

"Okay. I'll stop by."

"I'll get dinner, and we can talk about what the hell's going on. You know... spend some time together talking, just the two of us." This gorgeous woman needed to know I still had her on my mind, and what we shared wouldn't go away anytime soon.

When she lifted her head, turmoil surfaced on her face.

"India, please."

"Okay, sure. Dinner. I can do that."

The way she said it struck me as strange. Where did that strong woman go that I first met? The one who intrigued me? The one willing to go toe to toe with anyone inside that coaching office? Had something already happened with Conner?

"I'll be waiting. Are you going inside?" I wanted to go with her to the locker room. If he had her spooked, we had to put a stop to this now. I wouldn't allow her to continue holding this in any longer.

"No, I've got my stuff. I'm leaving now."

I turned around. "Let me walk you to your car."

"That's okay. I'm getting in and leaving. I've got to get to my appointment."

"I'm still walking you." I led her to the parking lot with my hand on her elbow. All the way to her car all I could think of was pulling her to me and surrounding her in my arms. I wanted to offer her my strength, but I was afraid of her reaction, so I stopped myself.

"Thanks for this." She looked up at me before she stepped forward and wrapped her arms around my waist. Thank God. I encircled her body pulling her close. I loved the feeling of holding her sweet body against me.

When India pulled back, she glanced up, and our foreheads met with me still looking in her eyes that drew me in.

"Hey, Coach." The address separated us. It crossed my mind to hit whoever it was. I turned to see Crew and Tucker standing at the hood of her car.

"Oh, hi. What's up?" I reached down and opened her car door as I spoke. She immediately jumped in as though escaping.

"We were going for a... soda. You want to join us? Thought we might relax before going home." Crew grinned as he said it, then he glanced through the windshield at India. He never took his eyes off her, but added, "There're some things we need to talk over."

She finally looked up at me, concern written all over her face. "Maybe it's a good idea. I'll text you when I leave my advisor's office."

"Yeah, sure. I'll follow y'all but not to the XOX house, right?"

"No, we'll meet at Chewz," Crew added.

India started her car as I tapped the roof a couple of times. "See you shortly." She nodded.

Sitting in a booth where we sat so many times as teammates, the waitress delivered three cold beers. Her dark eyes never left me while she stood there, and last year I would have been all over that. The attention felt awkward now. I shook my head as she finally walked away, and the two players across from me followed every swaying step she made back to the bar.

When Crew's eyes met mine, he had a shit-eating grin plastered on his face. "Hey, Coach, I think you had all her attention. Think I'll ever get that kind of notice?"

"No, asswipe, you're too fucking ugly for a girl to want to stare at," Tucker said before I replied, and we both laughed at his joke.

"Tucker's right. Besides, been there, done that. I'll pass, and you should, too." Both guys looked at me and shook their heads.

"Dude, I'm not into your sloppy-ass seconds." Crew picked up his beer and guzzled a long drink from the frosted bottle.

"Good to know." I glanced around at the other women in the bar. "Guess you better find another place to pick up chicks then."

Tucker almost spit his beer at me. "What the fuck, Timms? All of them?"

"It was a long, damn four years, remember?" My lips moved into an involuntary smirk. "Just giving you advanced warning. There're a lot more fucking bars in this town."

"Yeah, but we like to hang out here with all our friends." Crew sighed. "You've ruined this shit now."

"Awe, poor Crew. Can't get laid, and he's the starting quarterback. Must be a personal problem." Tucker laughed out loud. "Hey, try talking to Half sac. He'll know all you need to learn about finding beautiful women."

"Shut the fuck up, Tucker. I don't need Blue's advice on finding a woman, and dude, you better watch out calling him Half sac. He's gonna beat your ass if he didn't say you could."

"Really, dude, because from where I'm sitting and sleeping, I don't see or hear too much action going on in that department for you. And as far as calling him his nickname, I think we're cool." Tucker almost falls out of the booth with his laughter this time.

"You only know this because no female in their right mind would be sleeping in that hellhole you call a bedroom. The rank smell alone through the damn open door is enough to make rats run the other way. Who the fuck knows what you got growing in there."

"You lying bastard. You know my room smells like roses compared to the nasty-ass odor that reeks in your room."

"Enough, children." I'd had all the antics I could stand for now. I knew they were both twenty, but they acted like thirteen sometimes. "Hire a damn maid to come clean that shit up if that's what keeping the women afraid to sleep with you. Hell, get your dads to hire one. They've got the money."

"You know it's not like that. My dad could care less about my sex life," Crew said before finishing off his drink. "Shit, if it were left up to him, I'd be a virgin until I was married. He thinks I'm too stupid to count or something. My mom had me before they even tied the knot."

"Oh yeah? Why don't you ask him about that sometime?" Tucker added.

"Hell no. I value my ass more than that. He'd probably tear me a new one if I asked something that even remotely disrespected my mom."

"As it should be. Have you thought maybe that's the reason you can't find a woman?" I gave them both a pointed look.

"What's that?" They both said in unison.

"No respect for females. If you want a decent woman, you gotta treat them with more respect than being an easy lay when the urge strikes."

"Right, right." Tucker smiled at me. "This coming from the exhibitionist at the frat house. Hey, Crew, remember that story Blue likes to tell about our coach and that psycho chick having sex under the beach towel in a lounge chair during a party?"

I leaned forward and spoke low and with purpose at these two. "That was before, you little prick. If I ever hear you refer to that again in a public place, I'll make sure you don't get a piece of ass for the rest of your college days. You get what I'm saying?"

"Yes, sir." Tucker's attitude did a one-eighty.

Now it was my turn to laugh hard. "Nah, we're good, but honestly, we can't be talking about my fuck-ups anymore. I made mistakes back then, and you two need to learn from them. Shit like that could've caused me problems the rest of my life with videos being made you know nothing about. Hell, I probably have my own channel of public sex on *YouTube*. I thanked God every day back then that women were down with whatever fun I wanted to get into, but that doesn't make it right. And I like my new position with the team. Trash talk of my former escapades could cause it all to go down the drain quickly."

"Right. We get it." Crew and Tucker nodded in agreement.

"So, now that we've established that you two'll never have girlfriends or even fuck buddies, what was it you wanted to talk about?"

"Oh yeah. I'd forgotten already," Crew commented. "We've been hearing some noise about what went on with that new guy, Conner. You know he's in XOX as a transfer, right?"

"Yeah, I saw that. What's going on?" I hoped I was ready for what they were going to tell me.

Tucker continued speaking in a low tone for only us to hear. "He got wasted at the house last week and told some of the other guys he had to leave his last school before they kicked his ass out."

"Did he say why?" This couldn't be good.

Tucker spoke up, "I was there and heard it all." He leaned forward before he spoke. "He said he had trouble with some of the girls on campus. They apparently reported him to the dean of student welfare."

"For what?" I knew where this was going before Tucker even continued.

"Said there'd been some misunderstandings with a few of them over what was consensual sex and what wasn't."

Crew picked up the story. "I heard from some of the guys he supposedly had extra rough sex with a few girls in the frat house, and they were going to turn in the fraternity and him."

"Shit. I knew this was bad. The guy has no respect for women. He didn't change his stripes when he came here, he simply moved the problem to our campus." We all knew the stories about this kind of thing happening in fraternities and colleges, but we'd never had it on our doorstep. This could affect XOX and the Rams if something of that nature went down here.

"Yeah. We've seen and heard some shit's already happening with Coach Durham, too. Is it true?" Tucker asked.

"Nothing's happened so far, and it won't if I have anything to do with it." India became my number one priority right then.

"We knew you'd want to know this kind of information, Coach. What we don't know is what to do with it. If we go to Coach J, it could turn into a huge problem." Tucker leaned back and took another drink.

"Since nothing's happened yet, there's nothing we can do but have a little chat with the fuckwit." I needed to handle this by myself. "Y'all do know he and India have some history already, right?"

"What kind of history?" Tucker asked, then drained his beer.

"Her kick last season eliminated his team from the playoffs, and even worse, he missed one in the same game."

"Damn, he's going to have it out for Coach Durham for sure."

"Yeah, that's what I'm afraid of."

"Well, we're in, Timms. Coach Durham doesn't deserve that, and the house doesn't need him starting a fucking investigation. They'll put a stop to everything," Crew chimed in.

"No, you both need to back off and keep your ears open for information we might use if necessary."

"That fucker could cause problems for all of us if he starts his shit in the house." Tucker's tone told me he was pissed.

"Yeah, but if you jump in and start asking questions, he's going to know we're watching his every move. Y'all gotta keep his ass in line for a while.

Don't let that happen at the house. Assign someone to keep an eye on his room all the time."

"Dammit, that's not right. What if the fucker hurts a girl somewhere else? We won't be there to stop it. None of us are going to put up with roughing our girls up." Crew's voice got a little louder. This conversation needed to end. Of course, he was right, but we had to figure out what was happening first.

"I need to go. I gotta talk to India."

"Oh, okay, right. Go 'talk,' but when you're done talking, will you make sure she knows what's up?" Crew added.

"It's not like that, yet. Get your head out of your ass and quit thinking about sex all the damn time." I gave them a brief smile. "Oh yeah, you're both still horny fourteen-year-olds."

"The hell you say. Dude, I had more women at fourteen than I do now. Something's not right about this." Crew's bragging on his younger self, sounded like something Tucker would have come up with. Crew always seemed a little more mature than his sidekick.

"As I said earlier, you're too ugly now," Tucker said again to piss Crew off.

"Right, children. Be good, please." I stood throwing cash on the table to cover all the drinks.

"Yes sir, big daddy." I didn't know which one said it before they both started laughing so loud I could hear them at the doorway.

INDIA

I walked out of my meeting feeling better. At least the educational part of my life flowed smoothly. A plan existed, and I knew where I was going and where it would end. Having some peace of mind on one front kept my life on track.

As I climbed in my car, a white paper stuck under the windshield wiper caught my attention. All the time, people were advertising parties this way, and passing them out helped some broke college kids earn a buck. When I tugged it out from under the rubber of the wiper, I saw the plain handwritten print. Weird. Who did this anymore with text messaging?

"I'm always watching..." That's all there was to it. I slid into the driver's seat and read it again. "Watching

what?" I commented aloud to myself. Maybe they got the wrong car. I crushed the note up and threw it in the passenger seat. I didn't have time for this shit. I started the motor and took off for Timms' apartment.

Blasting music to keep my mind occupied, I needed to unwind from all that assaulted me today. How could I convince him to allow a mutually beneficial relationship? My life would be so much easier if he would agree.

The front door opened before I took a step in the direction of his apartment. Timms walked out looking so damn hot. His dark features and the tattoos only added to the constantly tanned skin and made my heartbeat speed up simply thinking about touching him.

"Hey." He handed me a glass with something frozen waiting to assault my senses. "I figured you'd appreciate something cold after being out in the heat all afternoon."

The tart coldness melted slightly on my tongue as I swallowed down the frozen margarita. "Mmm, you're right. I think I could drink a pitcher of them... brain freeze and all."

"How about a blender full instead?" He wrapped an arm around my back and pulled me into him leading me to the doorway. "I kinda like you coming home this way."

"I like it, too. Hot guy, frozen beverage, and air conditioning. You trying to make a girl swoon or something?" I grinned over the top of my glass before sucking more of the icy goodness down.

"Swoon, huh? I don't know about that, but it sounds good."

We both sat down on his couch and propped our feet up on the coffee table. "It's been a long, hot day, Timms."

"That it has. Relax a little. I know you need it."

"Yeah, but I want to talk before I drink too much of this. Something tells me these could sneak up on me. They taste too good, and I could down several before I knew what was happening."

"Maybe that's part of the swooning I planned." He gave me one of his smiles that takes a girl's breath away. Damn, this guy is so dangerous to my senses.

I looked at his lips as I sipped another healthy amount. "Well, in that case, maybe I should wait to finish this one." I leaned forward and put it on the table.

"They aren't that strong."

"Actually, not as strong as I am. I need a shower after being on the field for four full hours."

"Feel free to use mine. I'll put your drink in the freezer with the rest."

"I think I'll take you up on that." Standing, I made my way down the hallway to his bathroom. I knew getting the sweat off me and cooling down my body temperature would help this go better anyway.

Dropping my clothes, I climbed into his personal space he showered in, enjoying the smell of his manly body soap—so perfect for him. I guess we'll smell the same.

"Eek!" I squeaked as an arm came in around the curtain with a bottle of something in his hand.

"Sorry, didn't mean to scare you, but I thought you might like something that smelled a little more girly."

"Oh, so you keep vanilla and lace shower gel for guests?" I said it with a laugh. Good for him to take care of his women.

"No, it was some of Noelle's that got mixed in with mine when we all moved. I saved it just in case she needed it sometime."

"Good job, Mr. Thoughtful." I peeked around the edge of the plastic curtain. "I'm sure I'll smell better than the woods your... stuff... smells..." He stood there staring at me, and I couldn't finish the sentence.

A dark-haired Adonis stood naked in front of me. No way could I stop my eyes from drifting across the tattoos displayed on his pecs to the well-defined abs that begged my tongue to trace. Drifting down passed the words marking his tanned skin, the sight of his hard cock begging for permission stole the breath I barely maintained. My eyes tore away from the thing of beauty to continue down his muscular thighs and calves. His body was a thing of beauty even with the slight scar left from the career-stealing surgery. I swallowed and drifted back to the eyes waiting for me to look my fill.

His lips gave a slight upturn, and he cocked an eyebrow. I knew what he was asking. I didn't come over for sex, but right at that minute, it sounded like a perfect way to get rid of the tension I harbored. I gave a curt nod in his direction and stepped back behind the curtain.

What are you doing, India? He wants more than you're willing to give. He stepped in before I could start to contemplate that thought. I felt his warmth as it invaded the narrow confines created behind the curtain.

"Shit, that's cold." He adjusted the temperature and then turned to me. His gaze moved down my body causing everything in me to tighten—my nipples hardened, my core clinched, my muscles contracted. With one simple look, my entire body responded to him with a strong, powerful desire.

I reached forward placing my hand on his chest. His tattooed pecs felt hot to my touch. His chest expanded as he sucked in a breath. My eyes moved up from his chest, past his throat, over his perfect lips, across his flared nose, and finally settled so I could stare into the dark melting chocolate his eyes had turned.

He reached for me slowly pulling my body closer to him. "I want you, India."

"Then have me, Timms." He spun me around and pushed me to the end of the tub. As he took my hands in his, he raised them to the bar embedded in the tile. "Hold on tight."

"Tight." I gripped it.

I heard the bottle open behind me and felt the liquid drizzle across my shoulders. His hands smoothed the stream across my shoulders mingling with the mist of water. The warm hands came around under my arms moving the silky soap to my swollen breasts that waited for his attention.

A ragged breath filled my lungs when he tweaked the nipples that begged to be touched. Then his hands encased the swollen fullness and squeezed forward pulling until the strong fingers reached the pebbled flesh again where he tugged and twisted causing a moan to slip past my lips.

My back arched into him from need, and I felt his hard cock sticking straight out as if it pointed to where it wanted to be. His hands traveled over my ribs leaving a trail of soap suds until he reached my hips. Both hands wrapped around them pulling me back into his warmth. I felt his length settle into my valley between my cheeks.

"God, India." That's all he said before he quickly reached both hands around me, one holding me to him and the other finding the nub that begged for his touch. The assault he launched on my clit caused a gush of liquid to coat me so when he ventured further down, he felt more of the urgency of my desire for him. Using a finger to take it back up, he circled the tense nerve endings and worked me into a complete frenzy ready to fall over the edge at any second. Finally, he moved his hand under my leg and pulled it up propping it on the side of the tub.

"Yes, Timms, now. I need you now." It sounded like a cry instead of a request.

"Yes, beautiful. The trembling of your body told me all I needed to know, but, babe, I don't have a condom in here."

"It's okay. We were both tested for the job. I've not been with anyone but you, and I'm on the ring. What about you?"

"Since I met you, no one else has crossed my mind. You're all I want." His admission hit me hard and made me want him even more.

I laid my head back against his shoulder. "Then have me, Timms. Now." He took me at my word and lined the thick head against my entrance after sliding it back and forth hitting my clit each time. I tried to push down on a few passes and end my anticipation, but he wasn't having it. He held my hips in place with strong arms around me. When I said it, he pushed the thick head of his cock inside me stopping only long enough to maneuver us, so it was a smooth entrance.

He plunged in balls deep, and I felt them graze my ass as he began the rhythm made to give us both the pleasure we sought. With my hands clutching the bar,

I pushed as he plundered causing him to hit the very spot meant to send me spiraling to an orgasm so strong I cried out. My inner walls convulsed over and over on him as he continued to pump into me making the orgasm seem like it went on forever.

When my body finally went limp, held only by his strong arms, he pulled my fingers loose from the bar and used my arms to trap me to him. "Get down on your knees, India. I can't have you falling."

I went down on all fours, and the cooling water sprayed across my back. "You okay?" he asked as he ran his hand up my spine.

"Yeah, better than okay." I smiled to myself. This was the best sex I'd had in ages. Maybe ever.

"Good, because I'm not finished with you yet. Hell, at this rate, I may never be finished with you." His hands grasped my hip bones, and he kneeled behind me, as he slowly buried himself inside me again. "God, India, this feels so fucking good. Your pussy is so damn tight, and when you came all over me, I had to battle to keep from cumming right then."

"Don't stop." I wanted him to pound into me. I craved the need for a hard fucking. I wanted to feel the desire he had for me.

"Not a chance." He leaned down covering me and put his fingers back on my clit adding another exquisite punishment to the perfect assault on my swollen, bundled nerves.

"Oh fuck, Timms. Keep going. You're hitting the best spot each time." I began pushing back to his thrusting causing the coupling to be deep and more intense until that familiar sensation started at my toes. Each digit curled under, and the feeling shot up my legs causing me to cry out.

"Fuck me," was more of a drawn-out oath than a request. The shockwave of the intense orgasm took over, and I couldn't move fast enough against him. My walls around him began to milk his hard cock. I wanted him to experience this pleasure with me, so I continued contracting the muscles that begged him to stay.

He rose, his back ramrod straight, and ravaged me with the pumping as I felt him release rope after rope with each plunge. He made unintelligible sounds as it happened. If anyone heard, they would think he was being tortured, but I knew better. This kind of torture was pure pleasure.

After a few minutes, he pulled out of me, stood, and stepped out of the tub. I collapsed on the bottom, but he rolled me over.

"Hey, beautiful, are you okay?"

Opening one eye, I give him a slight smile. I was too tired to do anything else.

"That's okay. You lay there, and I'll bathe you." He heated up the cool water, rolled a towel and put it under my head, and softly washed my body with the vanilla-scented soap. I'd hadn't had someone bathe me since I'd been old enough to do it myself. The way he tended to me spoke of luxury paying close attention to the spots he knew would be sore.

He stood and leaned down picking me up so he could set me on a towel before wrapping me in it. "Let's rest a while."

"Sounds perfect." I tried to stand, but he scooped me up holding me close to his naked body heat. Laying me down on the bed, he climbed in beside me pulling the blanket from the foot to cover us. I snuggled in close to him and drifted off into the sleep of the dead.

TIMMS

I woke a few hours later to the most gorgeous sight in my bed. Dark blonde hair fanned across the silver pillowcase caught my attention before I ever lifted my head. Her pink lips, still swollen from the intense kisses we shared earlier, called to me. I wanted nothing to disturb this scene I needed to commit to memory.

Her shallow breathing told me she slept deeply. The sheet barely covered her beautiful, perky tits. If I slowly moved it down, I might stand a chance to see them peek out and greet me. Damn, why hadn't I done this before? Waking up to something this hot lying next to me could get addictive. How would she feel about that? Probably too soon to find out, but the idea would be filed away for later consideration.

It was getting late. I could see the setting sun barely peeking through my curtains, so I knew we needed to face reality and get up. She came here to talk. I think I got the best of this encounter, though.

I reached out and ran my finger down her collarbone, across the divide, and over the other one before retracing my steps. Her skin felt like silk. Reluctantly, I moved my hand off her and put it down by my side. Just watching her sleep and the gentle touch of her skin caused my dick to perk up. It was ready for round two, or was this three? Either way, he was ready, but I knew we needed to hold off. If nothing else, she had to be sore from the aggressiveness we attacked each other with.

I heard her phone go off in the other room. Damn, reality bites. I watched to see if she heard it in her sleep, but she didn't flinch. It chimed again, so I knew whoever wanted her would probably continue to message until they got a response.

"India," I barely whispered her name.

Nothing.

"Hey, beautiful," I said a little louder.

This got some eye movement.

"India, darlin', you gotta wake up."

A sound came out that mimicked "No."

"Yeah, I'm afraid your phone's going off. Someone wants to talk to you."

"Tell them to go away," she barely whispered it. I knew right then she probably didn't like being awakened by loud noises. Another tidbit to file under beautiful India.

"Well, I would, but then I'd have to get up. You look so sexy lying next to me all warm and naked and smelling like a vanilla confection. I just can't bring myself to do it."

"When you put it like that, I guess it's asking too much." She smiled but never opened her eyes.

I leaned over and nuzzled her jawline and dropped a soft kiss on those lips. Some things couldn't be helped, and tasting her lips was one of them. When I pulled back, she smiled a bigger smile and opened her eyes this time.

"Good evening, beautiful."

"God, do you have to look so good first thing?"

"What's that supposed to mean?"

"You look like a *GQ* model waiting to do a bedroom photo shoot. How am I going to get out of this bed and go in the other room knowing I'm leaving that in the bed?" She ran her hand down the side of my face. "You're too hot for your own good."

"Now that's a first. I don't think I've ever been told I was too hot. Maybe too hot to handle." I wiggled my eyebrows at her.

She reached down and wrapped her small hand around my dick. "Nope, not too hot. As a matter of fact, I think it could use a little warming up." I didn't know what she had in mind, but I was all for anything that involved her hand staying right where it was. Before I knew what was happening, she disappeared under the covers and replaced her hand with her mouth.

"Shiiittt, babe. You know you don't have to do that." Breathing was difficult.

She popped the head out of her mouth. "Does this mean you want me to stop?"

"Oh, hell no. Have your way with me. It's all good." I rolled onto my back taking her with me before sliding the covers down so I could watch. If I were getting a blow job, I needed to watch it for the full effect.

She sat back on her calves between my legs and looked up at me as she ran her tongue around the rim before taking the length in her mouth. Dark blonde locks of hair fell forward to curtain off everything else but her sucking me. I needed to see her face as my dick hit the back of her throat. Her sky-blue eyes never left mine. Watching my cock disappear behind those pink lips as she swallowed me down over and over started the familiar tingling in my spine.

"Sweets, that feels so fucking good."

She hummed *uh, huh* sending more excitement through me.

"Keep that up, and I'm not going to last long." The erotic feeling traveled down my spine, and I knew it was coming hard and fast. "Babe. I'm gonna blow. You better decide how you want it right now." I cried out as the feeling overtook my body. "Fuck, Indy. Now, Indy. Don't stop, Indy."

When my pelvis lurched forward, she swallowed down all I offered her before sitting up between my legs. Now I'm the one who felt like Jell-O.

"Can we go back to sleep, please?" I whisper-growled.

Indy climbed over beside me, and I pulled her into my side. She walked her fingers across my tattoos. "You can, but I can't. I heard my phone again. Someone wants me."

"No, please. Stay here. It's too great having you here beside me right now."

"I wish. Sorry." She kissed my right nipple, rolled over, and stuck her foot out trying to get up, but I grabbed her arm and pulled her back over to me and then up my body. I held her and kissed her hard.

"This has been the best evening I've ever had in my life, India. I mean it, ever."

"Hmm. I'll have to give that some thought. Ever is a long time." She grinned at me and stood up, so I popped her perfect ass cheek before she got away.

"Oww."

"Yeah, that's for being a smartass." She laughed as she disappeared into the bathroom and shut the door. After all that, she's still modest enough to close the door to take a leak. Women.

I dug out some clothes for both of us. "Hey, beautiful. I left you some clean clothes at the end of the bed."

"K. Thanks." I heard the water running in the sink as I stepped into boxer briefs and workout shorts with an old Rams t-shirt. Old was always better in my book. Well-washed clothes always felt soft and easy to wear.

Her phone lay on the coffee table where she dropped it when she walked in. I was tempted to look at it but decided that was none of my business unless she asked for it to be. I dug around in the drawer and found some food delivery menus for her to choose from. After the evening we had, venturing out for dinner didn't sound appealing to me. We still needed to talk.

God, I hope this didn't ruin what we started.

"It's a good thing these have a drawstring in them." She walked in tying the cutoff workout shorts from the athletic department. The t-shirt hung almost to the bottom of them, but damn, she looked good in my clothes.

"I like these. They smell like you." She pulled the hem of the shirt up burying her nose in it.

"I like them on you, too. Of course, you could have forgone the shorts all together with the shirt being so long. And no panties is fine with me."

"What makes you think I'm wearing any?" She stared daring me to ask her.

"Oh, you're just a little too conservative to go commando, babe." I only said it hoping it would goad her into showing me.

"Nope, not falling for that. You'll have to wait to find out."

Was this a test? If so, I failed.

I sprinted around the end of the bar and dropped to my knees in front of her taking the shorts down with me. Her completely bare pink pussy was directly in my face.

I looked up at her. "I guess I lost this bet. Now what?"

She grinned. "Now pull my shorts back up because if you keep looking at me like that, we'll get no supper, and I won't get to talk to whoever is bothering me." The phone sounded again.

"Well, shit." I pulled the shorts back up and tightened the stretched strings of the waistband. "Can't blame me for trying."

"Later, tiger. Much later."

"Tiger, huh? I like it. King of the jungle."

"Uh, that would be lion, not tiger."

"Not if there's pepper involved."

"I think you're mixing up your movie quotes." She giggled a little.

"Tigers love pepper, but they hate cinnamon," I informed her.

"And tell me what that has to do with lions and kings of the jungle? Didn't you ever watch *The Lion King*?"

"Oh yeah, you're right. Anyway, here are some menus for delivery. I'm not feeling going out. Is that okay with you?"

"Sure, I'm good with whatever. You decide." She picked up her phone to see who was blowing it up. "Dammit."

I looked at the end of the bar. "What's wrong?"

"It's Ian. Campus police have him."

"Great. Let's go. No telling what the little shit did."

She didn't budge. "Do you think it's a good idea for you and me to show up together?"

"Why? What we do in our own time is none of their business, India." I didn't like the idea of her trying to handle these guys on her own.

"You're right, but we don't need to add to campus gossip either. I think I should go alone."

"I don't. You have no idea what he did or who he was with. Besides, I know all the campus police. Getting them out of trouble might be easier with me there."

She thought about this a second and decided I knew what I was talking about. "Okay, come on."

We dressed and left quickly arriving in front of the athletic dorm with blue lights flashing everywhere. India bolted from the car before I could put it in park.

"Wait," I called to her, but she never stopped. After parking, I walked up to the scene trying to gather all I could from what the cop said to her.

"So let me get this straight," she repeated his words. "An anonymous tip called in saying they spotted Ian carrying drugs into his room, and you located them after turning his room out?"

"That's correct, Coach Durham. Just like the caller said. She told us where he hid them."

"Do you know what drugs you found?" India's face had a red glow to it. Her anger was apparent.

"He had some weed and the paraphernalia to go with it." The cop held up an evidence bag.

"Like what?" She clipped her words as she spoke.

"Bong, papers. The usual stuff."

Ian sat on the curb with his hands tie-wrapped behind his back. I rolled my eyes at that sight. Did they think he was a hardened criminal?

"Can I speak to him?" India turned some charm on at this point. I'd yet to see her use that sweet side for anyone but me. I didn't like her pulling it on a stranger.

"Uh, sure. I guess." The cop stumbled over the words.

Yeah, those light blues turned to snake charmers when needed.

She stepped to Ian with me on her heels, but she chose to sit next to him. The scared look on his face said it all as far as I was concerned—no way Ian lit up in the dorm. I seriously doubted he smoked at all, but he was smart enough to know what it would cost him and how easy getting caught in the dorm would be.

India spoke softly to him, so I squatted down to listen.

"Ian, what's going on here?"

Without raising his head, he spoke, "I don't know, Coach. I was in bed reading, and someone pounded on the door. I didn't answer it thinking it was somebody from the team, and I needed to get the work done for class."

He shook his head back and forth visibly upset with the retelling. "They knocked again and said they were the police. I didn't answer it. These shitheads will do anything to stop me. Saying it was the police wasn't anything unusual if they wanted in.

"Then I heard keys in the lock. That was going too far, so I jerked open the door before they got it unlocked. Before I asked anything, one cop had me on the floor, and one was tearing through my closet. When they pulled out the bong and baggie, it shocked me. I told them it wasn't mine, but all they said was, 'Yeah, right. They all say that.'

"Coach, I swear to God it's not mine. I'd never do something that stupid. I'll lose my scholarship if I can't fix this. I can't lose it, Coach. I've gotta finish college." Ian's eyes and nose turned red as he fought to keep the tears back.

Even I knew this didn't look good. We had to get someone here who knew what to do to help him. He'd need a lawyer if they charged him. The amount in that baggie wasn't going to end up being jail time, but it would get him suspended from the team.

"They can test me, Coach. Will you talk to Coach J for me? I'll take a test for any drug. I swear I'm clean." Desperation seeped in his speech.

"I'm sure that's an option, Ian," India told him.

"I think we better call Coach Jefferies," I told them both. India looked up at me and nodded. He needed to know.

Students stood around, and I spotted Drew and Zac but no Conner. With him living in the frat house, I wasn't surprised. Those guys never ventured over to these dorms unless made to. I motioned for them to come over and moved away from Ian and India.

"What's going on, Coach Timms?" Zac asked first.

"Guys," I jerked my head motioning them to walk further away. "Y'all know if Ian lights up sometimes?"

"No way. He's too afraid. From what he's told us, his dad would kill him if he lost the scholarship."

"Is that right?" I looked at Drew.

"Yes, sir. Ian's only here because of the scholarship. He may talk a big talk, but he's living his dream of getting an education, sir," he said without taking his eyes off India and Ian.

"How do y'all think a bong might have been in his closet then? Who's his roommate?" I should know this about my squad, but I didn't. After tonight, I'd know where every one of my guys lived and with whom.

Zac answered. "He doesn't have one. He's supposed to live with Conner, but since he's in the frat, he only came by and looked in the room. He laughed and told us what he thought about living in a dorm and left."

Interesting information. "So, does that mean he had a key to the room?"

They both looked at me, the information I requested told them where I was going with the comment.

"Well, yeah. I guess. I never thought about it. Ian probably knows, though." Zac provided this, and I decided he was right.

Turning back to the two sitting on the curb, I squatted back down. "Ian, do you know if Conner has a key to the room?"

"I don't know. Probably. He came by and opened the door when I was there. I thought he turned it back in when he said he wouldn't live there."

"Does anyone else have access to your room?" All the bases needed covering.

Zac spoke up. "Yeah, Drew and I do. We share a bathroom between our rooms, and we never lock the doors on each end."

"Y'all leave them open for anyone in the other room to walk in?" I knew the answer before he spoke.

"Yes, sir. They're our friends and teammates," Drew confessed.

I understood. They trusted the other guys to be the same as they were—honest and dependable. They should feel that way about the guys on the team. Trust among players should be a given, but in this case, maybe not.

India looked up at me. She knew what I thought. Ian was the best of the three kickers. If Conner could get them off the team, he'd have to be the kicker. I motioned for her to join me over with the others.

"Do you think he would stoop so low as to start getting rid of the competition so I'd let him kick?" She looked to all three of us. The other two wouldn't look at her. What the fuck was that about?

She realized it, too. "Guys, if you know something that will help Ian, you better start talking. They are about to call the city cops, and he's going to be spending the night in jail."

Finally, those words got their attention. Their heads jerked up and met her eyes. Drew spoke quickly. "Conner's been threatening to cause problems for us if we outkick him at practice. Ian told him to fuck off. Oops, sorry. No disrespect, Coach."

"It's okay. Go on, Drew." She glanced at me wanting to smile, but this was too serious.

"He's caught all three of us when we weren't together and told us the same thing. If we do anything to make him look bad on the field in front of you or Coach J, he said he had friends who would hurt us. Ian didn't believe him, but I did, Coach Durham. I think he did it to get one more of us out of the way of him being the starter."

When Drew took a breath, Zac started, "We all thought he meant like break our leg or something. We never considered he would do something to get us kicked off the team like this." He pointed to Ian being loaded into the campus police car.

Ian looked devastated. "You keep talking to these two, India. I want to talk to campus police. Before I made it over there, Coach J drove up and sprinted from his car to the police car.

"Are you charging him with something?" Coach J asked first thing.

"Not yet. The city police will do that."

"You know for a fact that it was *his* dope?" His term was drastic, but I guess in these guys' eyes, it was all the same.

"We found it in his closet, right where the caller said it would be," the cop told the coach. "Look, Coach, we don't want to have to arrest the kid, but this stuff happens all the time. They think they're off at college and can do whatever they want for a change."

"Officer," Coach spoke. "While that might be true of many students on this campus, my players are hand-picked to be here. They've never caused a problem. This kid has never been in trouble with drugs or the law."

"Right, Coach J, we know. We ran his I.D., and it comes up clean, but still, he had the drugs, and we can't overlook that. Sorry, Coach."

"I understand. You're simply doing your job, but you have to admit this all looks a little suspicious. For no reason, someone calls to report drugs in a dorm room and knows where they are? I know you can't tell me the name, but can you say if it was male or female?"

"It was a female, and that's all I can say. He'll be here on campus until morning. We'll make him call his parents when we get him to the station."

"Thanks, Officer." Coach Jefferies turned to me. "You know something about this that I need to hear, Timms?"

"Yeah, probably so. You want to talk to the other two on the kicking team as well?"

"I do. Bring them over to my office." He turned and walked back to his car.

The four of us walked into Coach J's office together. The kickers hadn't spoken a word since we left the sidewalk.

"Come in and shut the door. You never know who's lurking around here," Coach J told us. He sat down in his big chair. "Now boys, I want to hear everything you have to say. Who wants to start?"

Drew spoke up. "Coach, there is no way Ian had that marijuana. None of us use drugs. I wouldn't even know where to get them around here. Ian's thrilled to be here and part of the team."

Zac added, "Right. He would never risk his scholarship. He can't go to school without it."

"Yeah, I knew that already. Now tell me what else I need to hear. Timms seems to think there's other things going on. Coach Durham, do you know anything about other problems with your squad?"

"Conner is the other trouble with our squad, Coach J. Apparently, he's threatened the other three if they do anything to keep him from being the starting kicker. Isn't that right, guys?" I wanted them to spill it all. Coach J needed to know what type of guy we were dealing with.

They only nodded. "Speak up, you two. This all needs to be out in the open, so we can deal with the situation. Tell Coach J everything you've told Timms and me."

Once Drew and Zac started, the problem had a lot more to it than we knew, and these two seemed to be a wealth of knowledge.

After the two finished spilling their guts on all that had gone on with compelling information, Coach J dismissed the two players for us to talk.

Coach J shook his head. "I don't understand this at all. I've only had to deal with this kind of shit a few times in all my years of coaching. I recruit better than this. Ian's better than this. Why would someone want him off the team?"

He gave me the green light to speak my mind. "Don't you think it's probably someone who stands to gain from him being off the team?"

He leaned forward and looked at me. "You think another player did this to him? Why?"

Timms rested his head on the wall behind him. "Think about it, Coach. There's only one spot open for this position. You've got four people vying for it."

"That's bullshit. Y'all both know I recruited those others to build for future teams. I'll probably red-shirt one."

I spoke up. "That still leaves three, though. If this person eliminates one and you red-shirt one, then the fifty-fifty odds look better."

Coach stood and paced across the floor a few times. "Say that's the case, who do you think the one doing it is then? We can shut this down right now."

Timms' opened his eyes. "You know already. Why are you asking us?"

"That damn Conner. I knew better than to take him on when James called me. He caught me at a weak moment. I knew those freshmen needed more time, and this looked like a good way around it. I should have started preparing for Howell's graduating last season, but we needed detrimental positions filled first."

"That's in the past. Fixing the problem fast is the current issue. We're going to have to prove it, though," I told them both.

I wanted to tell them about the note situation, but we had more important things to worry about. Conner's bold attitude required him to show himself at every opportunity, not hide behind anonymous notes.

INDIA

We walked into my apartment drained. "This day has lasted forever." I plopped down on my couch. I wanted to come home and vegetate, but that was impossible. After Ian talked to his dad, his parents decided they wouldn't come down until more information could be decided in the morning. They lived twelve hours away so deciding to come down would depend on what happened tomorrow.

Timms landed beside me and propped his feet on the coffee table. "True that. We never got to eat either."

"I'm too tired to eat." I laid my head over on his shoulder as I tucked my legs up under me.

"You need to have something. You burned a lot of calories out on that field today. The last thing your squad or the team needs is for you to get sick."

"Missing one meal isn't going to make me sick." I smiled. Timms trying to take care of me was cute.

He pulled out his phone and pulled up a number. Speaking to whoever answered, he ordered a meat lover's pizza to be delivered ASAP.

"You have Pizza Heaven on speed dial?" I never moved my head off his shoulder.

"You don't?" Smiling at his comment, I squirmed into his side more. His warmth felt amazing since Coach's office had icicles hanging off the registers.

"Can you believe Conner's been doing his own form of hazing or bullying or whatever you want to call it, and the three amigos never said a word about it?"

"Yeah, I can. Happens all the time especially since he's in the fraternity, and they're not. Our chapter isn't big on it since most are athletes, and we tend to look after our own. The last thing XOX needs to have is problems with coaches causing problems with their players. Maybe the chapter he belonged to operates differently."

"That's something you need to tell Blue to address since he took your place as president."

"Right, first thing tomorrow. Right now, all I want to do is eat and sleep. Between practice, bed gymnastics, and your gorgeous lips wrapped around my cock, I'm spent." He laid his head back on the couch.

"What?" I sat up looking at him. "I think it's the other way around."

"No way. That blow job was all on you, sweetcakes."

"Well, yeah, maybe you're right about that, but you just looked so good, I couldn't resist." I rubbed a hand around on his abs. "I didn't think you'd object."

"You keep doing that, and pizza will have to wait."

"I thought you were hungry." I grinned at him. Guys were so easy.

"I'm starving, and I know something I'd be happy to have as an appetizer." He wiggled his eyebrows and pushed me back on the couch.

The doorbell rang.

"Dammit. Just when it was getting good." I laughed as I said it.

"Not to worry, sweets. Dessert is always worth waiting for."

After we finished pizza, I patted my tummy as I stretched out on the couch. "Damn, I'm stuffed. That's pretty good pizza for delivery."

"Best in town, and after four years I should know." He picked up the remote. "Let's jump on *Netflix* I'm trying to finish up on *Sons of Anarchy*."

"Are you just now watching it?" I found this information hard to believe.

"Yeah, for the third time. I love that show. Next, I'm watching *The Outsiders* since Opey's in it. He's got to make a good hillbilly."

"Three times? Really?" How could anyone watch the same show that many times?

He turned the show on and climbed in behind me. "We can do *Netflix,* but there will be no chilling. I'm too tired."

"Whatever you say, sweets. Just lay here and watch it with me."

"Mmm hmm."

I woke up to my alarm going off on my phone on the coffee table but no Timms. I wrapped my arm across my eyes to block out the sun. Taking a deep breath, my mind went back over last night's events. Surely, there was a way to get Ian out of this problem. Conner needed to come forward and do the right thing, but somehow I didn't see him volunteering.

My shower called to me so I could wake up. I needed to get down to the campus police department and see what was happening. This wasn't my problem, but I still felt responsible for helping Ian however possible.

The hot water rushed over my skin. I hurt some but in all the best places letting me know I'd been thoroughly fucked. Damn, it was good. I perked up just thinking about all the things we did to each other's bodies.

Maybe I wasn't looking for a relationship, but I could see me spending time with Timms. What was not to like about the guy? He was hotter than hell in the looks department. He had a body to die for. His eyes drew me in every time he leveled them on me. Thinking about the sex and the way he played my body made me wet in anticipation of more of the same.

Get out of here before you have to finish this off on your own, India.

I shut off the warmth of the water and wrapped a towel around me.

I heard someone talking in my living room. "Hey, I'm here."

It scared me at first until I recognized that warm voice. It made me tingle all over again. *I should have finished this in the shower.*

"Honey, I'm home," the loud voice thundered.

With my robe wrapped firmly around me, I hurried down the hallway. The closer I got, the more I smelled coffee.

"What are you doing here, Timms?" I beelined to the to-go coffee cup on the table. The aroma of warm, sugary donuts caught my attention when I picked up the coffee. "Nevermind. I don't care why you're here. Anyone who comes bearing yummy hot donuts and freshly brewed coffee with vanilla creamer and lots of sugar is perfect in my books no matter what time it is.

He wrapped an arm around me and kissed me above my ear. "Good morning to you, too. I figured you'd be happy to take a few of these off my hands. Personally, I prefer protein for breakfast, so I got tacos, but you can have one if you want."

"You found a place that sells tacos and donuts?"

"Stick with me. I know all the best places." He winked at me, and we both laughed.

A nice, easy, simple morning. I liked it. I could handle it. Probably a bad idea, but for now, I'd enjoy the donuts. "Guess you'll think I'm easy if you can have me for coffee and donuts at this hour."

"Indy, you are anything but easy." He sat down on the couch.

"I am too easy. What are you talking about?" My feathers ruffled.

"You want me to list them? Number one, you're one damn hard-headed woman. You depend on no one. Didn't anyone ever tell you it's okay to rely on your friends?"

Sitting down next to him, I popped the last bite of sweet confection in my mouth. Licking my fingers and following it up with a sip of coffee with my eyes closed, I finally spoke. "Mmm. That was good."

Once the sugar rush safely hit my stomach, I looked at him. "No, I am not hard-headed. I do what I have to do to get by. I'm used to depending on myself. Being on a team with all guys is a lonely position. It's not like the cheerleaders want to cheer for me except when I'm out there winning a game in the last five seconds. Then I'm the most popular person on the team. Outside of that, the majority of my time is spent alone."

He picked up my hand and put each of my sugary fingers in his mouth sucking off any leftover goodness. Well damn, that felt almost as good as eating the donut tasted. "Sorry, sweetness, I never thought about that. You're right, though. The kicker's spot is a personal position, and so I guess I'll give you that. And being a female on an all-male team would make you feel like the odd man out."

"Odd woman out, you mean." I leaned in and kissed him. This man could worm his way into my heart. I'd have to be careful. As much as I enjoyed spending time with him, I'm not sure we needed to have anything that felt like a relationship. My days here at TAU were numbered, I felt sure of it. If I'm moving on at the end of the semester or the end of the year, the last thing I needed was having to do anything to break our hearts. Long-distance relationships didn't work.

"That brain of yours is working overtime," he commented when our conversation died.

"Oh, sorry. I'm still trying to get fully awake here." I downed more of the coffee. "Thanks so much for bringing me this. I needed it."

"You're welcome."

"When I woke up, and you weren't beside me on the couch, I thought you'd gone home." I watched his reaction to my comment over the brim of the cup.

"I'm usually an early riser. You didn't have anything to eat or drink, so going out for Taco/Donuts made sense to me. You look so beautiful lying there making that little snoring sound, I didn't have the heart to wake you."

"I know you're exaggerating since I don't snore, but thank you for the compliment."

"Exaggerating? Girl, you kept me awake through the whole rest of the series. I started to move on to the other series, but I needed some sleep, too. I turned you a little so you'd stop, and you went to sleep. I did put that piece of the blanket you keep here on the couch over us and tucked it under your face."

"What? Why under my face?" I looked at him not understanding what he referred to.

"When your drool started down my arm, it felt weird, so I put the blanket under you to catch it."

I grabbed the throw and searched it. "I did not drool. There's no wet spots on it."

He laughed out loud at me. "Well, no. You got it all out on my arm. You know having spit roll down your bicep feels weird. It's kinda thick like—"

I grabbed the pillow and hit him with it. He pulled me back in his lap and tickled me.

"Stop, wait."

He held me down but quit moving.

"What?"

"How would you know what that feels like?"

"Like what feels like?" Surely, he knew what he alluded to in his comment.

"You know. Like your..."

"Oh, you mean like jizz rolling down my arm?"

"Eww." My nose scrunched up. "That's just nasty talking about it like that."

"India, it's a real thing. Jizz, cum, manjuice—"

"Shut up." I put my fingers on his mouth to stop the gross terms he spewed. He laughed behind my fingers.

"You might play with the big boys on the team, but you're all girl."

"I hope so after what we've done in the last twelve hours to each other."

He wiggled his eyebrows. "We could start on another round." He rolled me over on his lap, and I straddled him, my robe parting revealing my lack of lingerie underneath.

"We could." I rocked my pelvis against his thin basketball shorts. "Feels like you're halfway there, but I've got some things to do before practice today. Sorry." I jumped up, but he grabbed the dragging end of my belt before I could get away.

"Uh, huh. You started this talking about my cum, then teasing me with no panties, and rubbing that sweet bare pussy against me." With each phrase, he tugged me closer until I stood in front of him again. "It's not nice to wake up and be teased, India."

When he said my name in that slow, deep voice, he had me. I knew I'd be taking another shower.

"Let's start right here." He parted the robe. It slid off my shoulders and fell to the floor. His eyes turned a darker brown as he looked directly at my bare skin causing a hot zing to shoot through me.

Big hands covered my hips tugging me forward. He met my body halfway, and his tongue started just below my navel and traced a wet line down to the crevice below. I couldn't keep from burying my hands in his soft black strands, scraping my nails along his scalp as he slipped his tongue through the crease and lapped around the swollen nub.

His palms moved down so his fingers could reach the bare skin that pulsed at my center. He parted the skin and assaulted the throbbing in the best possible way.

His tongue circled the nub before he sucked it into his mouth causing a moan to start deep inside me and work its way out. He lifted my right leg until my foot rested on the couch beside him, opening me for easy access.

The warmth of his tongue moved down further to my wet opening that begged for his attention. His tongue ran around and around the opening lapping at the flood of juices that edged out. Moving his tongue back to circle my clit, he replaced it with his fingers. At first push, one slid in, but two found their way on the second plunge. Before I could react, the third push

Thia Finn

came with a third finger filling me more. When the three fingers bent forward and rubbed across the roughened patch of secret nerve endings at the same time he sucked my clit harder than before, I cried out as my entire body shook with exquisite pleasure spasming over and over.

"God, Theo. Oh God. Yes, right there." I couldn't help myself from screaming out. I bent forward resting my head on his. I had to hold on.

He finally pulled out when the spasms allowed him to remove his fingers my muscles held hostage for the duration of the pleasure. He moved them to his mouth and lapped up the juice I covered him in. Watching him taste me sent an erotic jolt through me. This man could hold me here for the sex alone, but looking at his face, I knew it might be more than that.

An hour later, we walked out the door, and I turned and locked it behind me. Our cars sat parked on each end, mine a little further away. I glanced down the sidewalk toward mine and spotted something white on my windshield.

"Again?" As soon as the words left my mouth, I wished I'd kept them to myself. Timms didn't need to deal with this shit, too. I remembered I hadn't told him about the first note, and that would make him angry with me. It could have been something stuck on the wrong car. Two meant the person knew where I lived, and that I was at the University. This was trouble.

"Hey, I was thinking about going to the library later. Maybe I should take my car." I hated lying, but I didn't want to cause more worry.

"Let's just take mine, and I'll drop you back here later." He assumed I'd go along with him, so he got in and started his loud car.

I opened his passenger door. "I think I'll just take mine since all my things for practice are in it." I wanted to get over to my car without him to read the new message.

"We'll be back before practice. Get in, please. We need to get down to the police station."

Dammit, there was no good reason not to do it his way.

"Okay, but let me run down and get some things from my car that I need." Before he had time to respond, I shut the door and took off.

Whoever left the note wanted to make sure I didn't miss it. Bold block print of my name stood out when I approached my car.

I quickly pulled the note out so I could read it and open my car for something I might have to have. Leaning into my car, I opened the note. *"Too hot for your own good leads to bad."*

"What the fuck?" Whoever wrote it has my apartment bugged or was at my window long enough to hear what we were saying. My hands trembled, and I dropped the note as I heard a car stop behind mine. I looked back and saw Timms through his opened window.

"Hurry, Indy. We need to get down there."

"I'm coming." I grabbed my phone charger wire and shut the door.

As I stepped in his, he looked at me. "What's wrong?" He took off before I clicked my seatbelt.

A sentence right then was impossible. I didn't know if forming a coherent thought was even possible at the moment. "Nothing," a whisper squeaked out.

"You look like you've seen a ghost. Are you feeling okay?" He kept looking at me, and I knew I had to give him something.

"Yeah, I'm fine. Just thinking about what poor Ian went through last night. It had to be his first night in jail." I managed to cover my fear up, but it wasn't easy.

"No way that kid's been to jail. Coach J would've known that and never offered him a scholarship."

I knew this to be true. Coach J wouldn't award the money unless he checked out the players. Surely, he checked out Conner, too? I needed to ask him. With the new kicker coming in so late and taking him on a recommendation from another coach, maybe he didn't bother. What a mistake that was if he didn't.

INDIA

What looked like a disturbed ant bed greeted us at the police station. Police must be heading out for the day as they made their way from the building's entrance to their cars. Timms easily slid the car into an open slot not capturing any attention.

He looked at me again. "You ready? No telling what we're going to find when we get in there."

"I know. Let's pray for the best possible outcome." He met me at the hood and took my hand. Looking down where we were joined, I realized the warmth he generated. He didn't understand how badly I needed that connection. Timms would assume it was for Ian, but I knew differently.

Coach J sat waiting in the entrance. "Took y'all long enough to get here." He looked down at our hands. I couldn't deal with that right now, but I wasn't about to let Timms go.

"Sorry, Coach. It was a long night, remember?" Timms offered.

"It's my fault, Coach J. I forgot to change my alarm and overslept." I took the blame for the tardiness.

Timms looked at me and then turned back to Coach J. "Have you seen anyone yet?" I shook my head.

The police officer walked around the corner with Ian in tow. We stood, and he introduced himself, shaking our hands.

"Nice to meet you, Officer Guerrero. These two are assistant coaches." We nodded our heads to him.

I wanted to hug Ian. He looked like he hadn't slept at all. I wondered if they'd put him in a cell by himself. Orange wasn't his color, that's for sure.

"Hey, Ian," I finally said to him. The officer hadn't included him in the conversation.

"Hey, Coach." His mumble could barely be heard in the noisy station.

"Let's go down the hall so we can talk." The officer led Ian with him as we followed behind.

The room was small and crowded with all of us inside sitting around a conference table. Officer Guerrero opened a folder and read over the information.

"It looks like a pretty simple case of being caught with the goods from what I'm reading here."

I couldn't help myself. "I believe it's far from simple. Someone wanted him caught and set him up."

The officer looked at me. "Uh, huh. What makes you think that?"

"First, Ian's a good kid."

"Stop right there, missy." If he thought he gained points with that horrid pet name, he had the wrong woman. Fire brewed inside me and built toward my ears.

"Lots of good kids come to college to try new things. I can show you an entire file drawer full of them. You're going to have to give me more than that."

"Okay. I can give you ten people that will vouch for him never doing drugs."

"Can't rely on friends. They'll say anything to get him out of this," he countered.

"He has no history of drug usage, and we can verify that with the drug screenings he's had to take."

"Now we're getting somewhere. Factual evidence, but I'm willing to bet that was while he was at home with momma. He's off at college now, and we're back to my original statement."

Timms joined the cause. "What about the fact that an anonymous caller told the police exactly where the drugs and bong were located in his room?"

Guerrero looked down to read some more from the file. "Yeah, I see that. Other than knowing it's a female, we have no way of verifying the caller."

"So you're going to take an anonymous girl's word over the victim?" I spoke louder than I should have, and Coach J put his hand on my shoulder before he offered his words on the situation.

"Looks to me like it's a 'he said, she said' thing at this point, Officer." He turned to Ian. "Ian, son, whatever you say they can use against you in here, so I'm not going to ask you to talk, but you can volunteer if you know anything we need to know."

Ian glanced up for the first time since we entered the room. "Coach J, Coach Durham, I don't do drugs. Never have, never will. I would never do anything to risk losing my scholarship either. I need it to get an education. My parents can't afford to send me to college. They're doing all they can to keep me here since my scholarship only pays so much."

Officer Guerrero jumped in. "Okay, that's all good, but we need to know how those drugs got in your closet, kid."

"I honestly don't know. The only guys I hang out with are on the team. They're the only ones I've had time to meet since I got here. I live by myself, so no one else goes into my room unless I'm there."

"Could someone get it there if you went down the hall to another room? You leave your door unlocked?"

The officer honestly seemed like he wanted Ian to be innocent in all of this.

"No, sir. Our doors lock automatically like a hotel door. You never leave without your key."

Timms spoke up. "You're the only guy who lives alone. How come?" Timms already knew this answer, but the officer didn't.

Ian's eyes perked up for the first time. "I live alone because Conner was assigned as my roommate. He never moved in because of the frat house."

"And he has a key to your room?" Guerrero asked.

"Yes, sir. He does." I looked just in time to see a brief grin ghost Ian's lips. It disappeared quickly. He knew what the information meant for him, but he kept hope to himself.

Guerrero took a breath and let it out slowly. "Thought this was going to be a done deal when I opened this folder. It looks like we have some things to clear up before any charges are filed. I'll talk to my supervisor and see about letting Ian go if you'll vouch for his whereabouts for the next forty-eight hours or so. Where can I find this absentee roommate?"

"I'll give you his address," Timms told the officer. He knew the address by heart.

Coach J stood. "We sure can. He'll go live with Timms until the time's up, and we'll make sure he's accounted for the entire time he's on campus."

The officer stood. "Works for me. You know we like to see a good ending to problems, Coach, especially involving team members, but we aren't going to give him more than he deserves."

"Right, and I respect that, Officer Guerrero." Coach J stuck his hand out to shake hands with him, as did Timms and I.

"He'll be out in about thirty minutes." He led my player out the door, and we returned to our bench out front.

"So will he get to practice with the team today?" I needed to decide how to play this.

"He was arrested but not charged, so he can practice. Now, whether he'll get to suit up this week for the game is another story. For now, we'll assume he can't so we won't be caught off guard if it comes to that." It sounded like Coach J had his mind made up already.

"What about Conner?" I felt stabby, all of a sudden, as in I wanted to stab him for doing this to Ian and bringing bad publicity to the team.

Coach stood and took a few steps toward the door. "Guess we'll see what's what when the officer talks to him. He'll be in the same shape as this kid, though, until an arrest is made."

"Am I expected to come down here and support him, too, since he's a member of my squad?" I wasn't feeling this generosity in any way.

"Yeah, I guess you better. Can't be playing favorites. Give them your number to call when they get him here so you can show up, too." He turned and walked through the glass doors.

Turning back to Timms, I said, "I suppose I'll be doing this alone since you're on babysitting duty."

"Nope. Not leaving you to fend for yourself with that numbnuts. Let me think about this for a second. I need to call someone who's not involved with the team." He scrolled through his phone and then hit dial on a number.

"Gerrod? Dude, you in town? Yeah, I need a favor." He stepped outside to talk about the time Ian came around the corner.

"Thanks, Coach Durham. You don't know how much I didn't want to call my dad. He's going to be so disappointed if we can't straighten this out and clear my name."

I put an arm around his big shoulders and gave him a little side hug. "We'll get it cleared. Don't worry, but you shouldn't lie to your dad. I'm sure he only wants what's best."

"Yeah, he does, but I don't want to tell him until we know. My dad wants me to have a college education so badly, and this would shatter his dream."

"That's good your dad pushes you, but is this what you want, too?"

"Yes, ma'am. For sure." He smiled a big smile as we walked out the door where Timms stood waiting on us.

"It's all set. My friend, Gerrod, is coming to practice today and then to the police station with you. You met him the first time we went out, remember?"

"Okay?" I drew the word out. "You must trust him to send him in your place?"

"He'll do the right thing, and he'll make sure you're okay. That's all I'm worried about."

I caught the grin on Ian's face and assumed it was over Timms' comment about me as I climbed in the backseat so the two long-legged guys could fit in the car. Great, I suppose Timms and me seeing each other off-campus couldn't be kept quiet.

TIMMS

After running through *In-N-Out* for some lunch to take back to campus, I sent Ian inside with his food. Having a constant companion for a few days was going to put a halt to me spending all my extra time with India. This thing between us blossomed faster than I'd imagined it would even with her resistance to it.

"Want to sit outside in the shade to eat?" I pointed at the tables under the portico at the end of the building.

"Sure, why not. You know you didn't take me by to get my car on the way back." She gave me an evil eye.

"Yeah, do you think you're going to have time to be on the field since you know you're going back to the police station at some point?"

We sat down across from each other. Doing normal things with India seemed so easy, and having the opportunity to watch her made life a lot sweeter. I never realized until now what I might have been missing all along with having someone all my own. I'd never wanted to have someone before now.

India's perfection measured in more ways than simply her beauty. Her determination to be a good coach shined through this morning at the police station. The fact she went to bat for her player said it all. She genuinely cared for Ian's well-being, too. Now here she sat facing the prospect of going back to the same station to make sure a player—who had caused nothing but trouble—would get a fair shake. Some coaches would've written him off the first day.

Thinking back to last night and this morning, I realized I'd gotten a more private side of this woman. Her free spirit in the bedroom allowed her to take what she needed and give what I wanted without question. The confidence she exuded let her express her desires, so there was no guessing how to please her and no fumbling through the awkward stages hoping I made the right moves with her.

Those thoughts needed to be set aside since I felt my dick twinge remembering her kneeling before me with plump red lips and her sky-blue eyes looking up at me. All I had to do was close my eyes...

"What are you thinking about over there?" She interrupted my wet daydream of her.

"You. You caught me replaying our time together last night and this morning." To throw her off, I laid my best panty-dropping smile on her.

"Stop, right now. Don't even look at me like that." She laughed as she bit into her burger.

"Who me? What are you talking about? I'm just admiring the way you rip into a damn hamburger. Most girls can't stand the idea of pigging out on something good and greasy. Not my girl. She bites into it like it's the best thing that's ever been in her mouth." I looked up at her with the same smile. "Well, maybe not the best thing."

India paused for a second. I knew she heard me say 'my girl' and wondered if she would comment on it, then she threw a French fry at me. "Shut up and eat." She then added, "Your cheeseburger." This time she gave me a smoldering look. "I remember this morning, too, you know."

I laughed out loud. I couldn't help it. "Yeah, that was a pretty eventful morning we had."

"A little too much for me. I'm not used to being in a police station." She grinned.

"Yeah, that, too."

Gerrod showed before practice started and while we sat around listening to Coach J talk about plays and strategies for the season opener on Saturday, he kept a slight smile glued to his lips. What was that about?

Loud voices came from the locker area, and we knew the team trickled in from their classes to get started on learning and honing their skills. Most of these kids played football for as long as they could remember, just like Gerrod and I did. Coach J wrapped up the meeting and India, Gerrod, and I stood and headed out the door.

India spoke up. "I haven't gotten a call from Officer Guerrero, yet. I thought he'd have picked up Conner by now."

Coach J called us over talk to him.

"Looks like they're having trouble finding Conner. I heard from my friend at the station, and he said they are calling him a person of interest and want to question him, but he's not shown at any of his usual haunts today."

Loud voices coming from the locker area halted the coach. The sound escalated quickly, and I knew fighting when I heard it. Teammates fighting against each other was never a good thing.

Running in, we saw Conner pinning Zac down surprising me at his strength since Zac had size on his side. When the rest of the team stepped back instead of breaking up the fight, problems existed. Usually, the team broke up petty arguments but not this time. Before we could get to them, Zac rolled the fighting over and started punching Conner in the face. The others cheered for the quiet kid to do his worst.

Two coaches were needed to pull the athletes apart. I realized then that India stood in the middle of half or mostly naked males. "I looked at her and jerked my head for her to leave." She only looked hard at me and then was up in Zac's face.

"What the hell do you two think you're doing in this locker room? Fighting among teammates is not, and will never be, acceptable." She turned and got up in Conner's personal space. "Both of you, put your clothes on and go to Coach J's office." When neither attempted to move, she screamed a loud and deep, "Now," breaking their adrenaline rush enough to hear her words. They backed away from each other.

She spun around looking at the rest of the team. "Do any of the rest of you dumbshits feel the need to go at each other? If not, I suggest you get your asses in gear and get on the field. Your coaches won't wait forever." The group turned away and went back to putting on their practice gear.

Yes, India stood in the middle of players in all states of undress.

Yes, she got up in the faces of two members of her squad and got their attention.

Yes, she told the entire team what to do, and they listened.

Yes, this woman had me by the balls.

I might as well hand over my man card. I was in love.

Passing Coach J's office, I wanted to go in so badly I could taste it, but I knew I had players warming up and waiting for me. Gerrod met me at the exit doors to the field.

"What the fuck, dude? Has it been like this since the beginning?"

"Hell no. Not until that prick Conner joined the team. I don't know what Coach J was thinking allowing him to be part of the Rams' program. He's been a damn detriment since day one when he didn't bother to show up for practice. He claimed he didn't need to practice with someone who didn't know how to kick his style. The douchebag has done nothing but cause problems for India."

"Why's he still here then?"

"Hell if I know. His conniving ass needs to be kicked off the team and out of the school. He'll never kick one damn extra point if India has her way."

"From the sounds coming from Coach J's office, I doubt he will."

"Especially if he's in jail which I'm beginning to believe is where he belongs."

I barely got the words out of my mouth when a police car drove up with Officer Guerrero and another cop getting out.

Gerrod looked at me, and I knew he was puzzled. "You a damn psychic now or you have something you need to tell me?"

"About that. You're going to need to go with India to the fucking police station. She's gotta make sure the dipshit's okay like she did her other player this morning."

"That's what you were doing at the police station when you called?"

"Yeah, we were all down there together."

"Hell, I don't remember having this much fun when we all played together during our four years."

"This ain't fun." I gave him a hard look.

"No, I guess it's not."

The police strongly suggested Conner go down to the station, so India and Gerrod took him. I carried on with practice, but my mind wasn't in it.

"Coach Timms, you might as well call the practice and head down to the police station where she's at. You're not doing us any good," Crew informed me. "We can run these plays without you standing around."

"Just do your job, Crew. Same as I'll do mine." The pointed stare I gave him let him know he was dangerously close to crossing the fine line of our relationship.

He looked at me and gave me one nod. "Sure thing, Coach." The kid knew when to listen which made him invaluable as a player and a friend."

I stalked the backfield watching the plays being executed yelling when something didn't go right until Coach J came over to me and stood between them and me.

"Timms."

"Yes?"

"Go to the police station, and call me so I'll know what's going on. Your head's so far up your ass, you can't see the light of day. You got no business being on this field right now. Never seen you tied up in a knot before even on a big game day." He didn't wait for me to speak, but turned around and walked away yelling something at the team.

As I walked past him, he glanced in my direction. "I expect a phone call in less than thirty minutes. You understand what I'm saying?"

"Yes, sir. I do." I jogged to my car and took off.

Pulling my car up and getting out, I walked inside. "What's happening in there?" I asked as soon as I spot India and Gerrod.

"Don't know. They haven't been out yet." Her tone of voice read frustration. She had every reason to be frustrated, too. Causing trouble for one member of her squad was one thing, but now it appeared two could get booted from the team.

"Who's in there?"

"Just the officer and Conner. I asked if he wanted me in there, and he laughed in my face." She huffed. "I should have gotten in my car and driven back to practice. What good am I sitting here?"

I put my arm around the back of her chair. "At least here we'll find something out. I doubt Conner would be forthcoming with information."

Gerrod spoke up. "If the kid were smart, he'd come clean now. He's only making it worse for himself."

"Yeah, but I think Timms is speaking the truth. Doesn't make sitting here any easier." She turned and looked at me. "How is this going to affect the team if both are kicked off? I mean, I know we only need one person, but things happen. Muscles get pulled. Zac and Drew are not the best kickers in the world. I mean, given enough time, they could be good, but we might not have time. They both want a position, though. They work hard during practice."

"Whoa, whoa. Take a breath, Coach. You're getting way ahead of yourself. We don't know what's happening yet. Thinking about it, though, of your three players, which one is next in line in ability behind Conner?"

She dropped her chin and looked at me through her long, feathery eyelashes. "Ian, naturally."

Thia Finn

"Then who?" All the evidence pointed to Conner, but we needed to be sure in our accusations.

"Zac and then Drew," she explained.

"Right, and look who the person who did this took out. His closest competition. You and I both know it was Conner." She verified my comment with a nod.

The door opened, and both the officer and Conner walked out. Conner took a minute to drop his eyes to where India sat and gave her a hard look before lowering his black sunglasses. They covered his eyes with the blackest of glass. Everything he did prevented India from trying to help or even like this asshat.

"See ya at practice, Coach," he called to her sauntering through the door like he owned the world.

I turned to her. "That piece of shit needs to be gone today."

She nodded and looked at Officer Guerrero. "So what do you think? Is Ian going to be charged with anything?"

He didn't respond to begin with choosing to look at some paperwork in the folder he held. "Let's go back in there and talk a minute."

"Hey, Gerrod. There's no reason for you to hang around here. I know you're here for Quinn, and I'll be with India the rest of the day." I stuck my hand out, shook his hand, and patted him on the back. Our friendship went deep. We'd always be there to help each other out.

P a g e | **214**

"Thanks for everything, Gerrod." India hugged him. "You don't even know me but stepped in when I needed you. You must be a good friend to this guy." She nodded in my direction.

"Absolutely. I'm glad I was here for him to call on. You know where to find me if you need me again." He gave us a little salute and headed out the door.

I grabbed India's hand, and we filed through the door to an empty room. Guerrero shut it firmly behind us.

India immediately dove in. "Did you learn anything we didn't already know? I mean, are either of them going to be charged? They are both part of the same squad on the team. Charges will change everything."

I put my hand on hers. "India, let him talk."

She stopped with the questions. I turned my attention to him. "She's a little anxious, Officer Guerrero."

"Yeah, I think you're right." He took a deep breath. "Okay, so here's the deal. Your boy, Conner, says that he lost the key a week or so ago. Thought it was somewhere in his new room but couldn't swear to it. Said he'd given a half-assed effort to find it but wasn't all that concerned since he could pay for it at the end of the semester."

"Great. So, he's off the hook for his dumbassery," India stated exasperated with the news.

"Not completely. When I asked about the drugs, he stumbled over the answer which took me by surprise.

He's seemed so sure of himself when he talked about the key and never living in the dorm."

That's the first damn piece of news that sounded even close to positive. I prayed he had some more.

"Well, where does that leave Ian?" The tone of India's voice told me she'd lost some of her determination. It was less than forceful like it was when we walked in.

"Here's the thing. Ian has no priors. Hell, the kid's only had two speeding tickets since he turned sixteen. He exhibited a respectful attitude when we spoke to him which goes a long way with me." He stopped and closed the folder. "This one..." he nodded toward the door, "... gives off a lot of bad vibes in my opinion. He needs to be watched. In other words, I don't trust him as far as I can throw him. Given his size, that wouldn't be far."

"Yes, I feel the same way," India piped up. "To be honest, he makes my skin crawl."

I had to know. "What about priors on him."

"He has some minor offenses and some information tied up in juvenile court we can't access without a court order. I'm not sure this problem is pertinent enough to go that route."

"Minor, as in?" Guerrero seemed reluctant to tell us something that was a matter of public knowledge.

"He's had a few run-ins with the law in his hometown involving drugs, but nothing he ended up being charged with, just like now." Guerrero looked up at India. "For now, we aren't going to be charging either one, so it looks like your kickers gain back their eligibility as of today, and no more babysitting for Ian."

A deep breath caused her chest to rise before she spoke. "So good news and bad news, and I get them both."

"Looks that way to me, Miss Durham. Getting down to the season opener, too. Better make the best decision."

My eyes met his when he said that. I found the comment strange. Was he trying to tell her something without spelling it out plainly? Did he think Conner was a threat to her if she made the wrong choice? I hated bringing it up with her. Guess we should run it by Coach J when we get back to campus.

Standing, we shook hands again and left the officer at the doorway.

INDIA

The ride back to campus happened too quickly. Having some time to think about what to do or say would have been great. When Timms parked the car, he grabbed my arm before I opened the door.

"Wait. I want to talk to you before we go in there."

I stared at the building. "You know, this was supposed to be an awesome fall for me. Getting to coach the kickers, going to a new university, proving myself capable of being a coach on a football team. Those goals I set for myself seem like forever ago. With all this other shit going on, I may never get a chance to do any of it. Coach J might decide I'm not worthy of this position."

"Don't be so hard on yourself about this. None of it reflects on you or your coaching. You had no control over any of it. Hell, you didn't do the recruiting."

"I know, but it still looks bad that I can't exhibit some control over my squad."

"India," he threaded my fingers through his and pulled them into his lap, "Coach J is a fair man. He looks at all sides of situations. He knows the shit that went down had nothing to do with you because he's been dealing with college guys for a long-ass time. They are not the first to fight or the first caught with drugs in their rooms. He'll make the right decisions when the time comes, you'll see."

He picked our hands up and kissed the back of mine. The contact made me feel better. Timms' constant thinking of how to be there for me had gone above and beyond what I expected. I leaned over and pressed a light brush of my lips against his. When we separated, he pulled me back in and turned it into a hard, heated kiss. Finally, he let me go.

I smiled. "Thank you. I think I needed that."

"Yeah, me, too. I wanted to do it earlier, but the time and place weren't right."

"No, the police station with my players would be a no go on PDA."

"I know where it can be a 'yes' go. Come to my apartment tonight. I know a place we can go to relax in a hot tub. I think we both could use it."

"Not at your complex, right? I've seen who lives around you and risking disease isn't my form of relaxing."

"Yeah, that's the damn truth. No way would I climb in that thing. Been there, done that." His comment and the face he made caused us both to laugh. We needed something to laugh about.

"Come on, Coach D, let's go see what we missed in the world of TAU football today. That Crew better have shined for the coaches. I might have to do some ass-kicking if he didn't."

Later, as I drove over to Timms', I thought about everything Coach J said. Conner didn't show back up on the field, but Ian did which impressed the head coach even more. Ian met his team head on knowing he'd done nothing wrong. Apparently, the team welcomed him back. Would they have done the same for Conner?

I knocked on the door hearing some Twenty One Pilots' music playing. It sounded like some music I needed for the night. He answered the door in his swimsuit but no shirt. The tattoos decorating his body started a slow burn inside me. He looked so damn hot standing there with designs playing across his skin. My first instinct was to start at his pecs and trace downward with my tongue. The hills and valleys his abs created were made for admiring up close.

"You through with the eye-fucking, sweets?" he teased.

My eyes immediately looked up. "Oh, sorry. You just look so, so, so..." I had a hard time finding the right word. "Freaking hot."

"I'll take freaking hot." Grabbing my hand, he pulled me inside and had me up against his door. My bag slid to the floor as he assaulted my senses with a kiss that added to the simmering burn inside me.

He broke the kiss and rested our foreheads together. "Damn, I needed that." His words came in a warm breath across my face as we both regained needed oxygen.

"Me, too."

"Glad we're on the same page. Let's save it for the cool water."

"Where are we going?"

"You'll see." He picked up my bag and one of his own and headed to his car as I followed behind him.

"Hop in, and I'll put this in the trunk with the rest of our stuff."

"What kind of stuff are you bringing?" I started to the back of the car.

"Stop. It's a surprise. Wait till we get there."

The fifteen-minute drive quickly passed as we made our way to the edge of town where huge homes sprawled across beautifully landscaped lawns.

"This must be where the other half lives. Sure as hell doesn't look like this on the campus side of town."

"Actually, we're in another city altogether. This is Callan Crossing. It's where the real people live, unlike Cauldon, where the University is. When one city ends, the other begins. Guess the University's founding fathers didn't want to risk living that close to a bunch of fucking heathens sent to college on daddy's money."

"Probably not. The homes are ginormous, though. Whose house are we going to?" I watched as the meticulous green spaces drifted past the window.

"It's two of the players' dads' house. They bought it together when the boys came to TAU so they'd have a private place to stay."

"So like a vacation home?"

"Something like that." I couldn't understand why he was so secretive about the owners.

"How did you get access to it? It seems like they'd want to keep it private all the time."

"Oh, it's private. Not a problem at all. The caretakers only come in to check on it a couple of times a week and when the owners are coming to stay."

"These people must be rolling in the dough."

"Yeah, they are."

He turned and stopped at a gate to put in the code. As the huge scrolling fence opened, and we drove through, the sight took my breath away. The majestic home stood against a backdrop of large oak trees. I'd never seen anything like it before.

"Are you sure about this, Timms? We're not going to get arrested, are we? I've had enough police action for the day."

"No, baby, we have permission." He grinned at me in a wicked way that caused my fear to amp up quickly.

"Stop the car," I yelled, and he complied by slamming on the brakes.

"What? Was there a deer or something? They're all out in here."

"Hell no, there wasn't a deer. Tell me who owns this damn house and how we're allowed to be here. This feels wrong to me."

He put his hand on the back of my neck. "Indy, I would never do a damn thing to put you in danger or get you in trouble with the law. You need to have more trust in me."

"Answer the fucking question, Timms." I knew I acted paranoid, but after the day I had, I deserved it.

"It belongs to Tucker and Crew's parents. Remember us telling you they have a band?"

"What kind of band is it? Hell, is it like Foo Fighters or something?" He slowly turned his face to me. His countenance completely deadpan.

"What the fuck, Timms? Who are their dads?"

"Assured Distraction, at least Tucker's is. He's Ryan Powell, the lead guitar player. Crew's dad writes all their music, Hayden Devillier."

I picked my chin up off the floorboard. "You've gotta be shittin' me?"

"No, sweets. I'm not. Both come from great families. I love them, and thankfully, they love me, especially after I got hurt and Crew moved into my position." He started moving the car forward and turned to follow another driveway going around back to a portico where it rumbled to a loud stop.

"Timms, it's unbelievable. Why don't Tucker and Crew live here?"

"Uh, that'd be a big hell no. Their moms would never allow it. Together those two dumbasses can do some fucking damage. Besides, it's too far from campus. They're all fine with them living in their rooms in the XOX house. Unfortunately, I doubt the damn house survives the terrible two."

"Is that what they call them? That's cool they're the same age."

"It's got some history, but I've never been brave enough to ask about it."

"Oh, best-kept band secrets, huh?"

"I don't even know if it's secret info. I decided if they wanted me to know more, they'd tell me. The little shits both know the story, so it's not a thing to them." He stepped from the car and opened my door for me. I liked that he had good manners and wanted to treat me special when time allowed.

"If you'll take our bags, I'll get the rest of it." He handed them to me and then brought out a huge ice chest.

"What all did you pack away there for only the two of us? It's going just to be us, right?"

"Sure is. I checked with dumb and dumber before practice was over to see. I know they come out sometimes and use the pool, but they don't bring groups of people out here. Their parents made it a rule right up front. The band values their privacy, and it's hard to have it when you're as well-known as they are. The more people who know it's here, the more likely they are to be stalked."

"True. I bet they hate it."

"Hell, Tuck and Crew had problems from the beginning when they first came to campus, but the paparazzi got tired of trying to keep up with them. Now and then one will show up at the house, but it's strictly off limits. We let the fuckers know we weren't putting up with their shit."

He lifted the heavy chest, and we walked around to a gate. Timms used a key on his ring, opened the lock and locked it behind us. "Can't be too damn careful."

"An eight-foot privacy fence should be enough. I glanced up at the back of the gorgeous home. Light shown from some of the windows. "Hey, there's lights on. Are you sure people aren't here?"

Thia Finn

"No, they come off and on by themselves. Part of the security. Crew says it's a fucking ghost that lives here doing it, but I think it's his overactive imagination. Maybe it's his way of getting the women in his lap. Who knows with that one? He can act like a damn weirdo around females. I think growing up around the band warped his thinking." He laughed out loud. "His mom would pop me on the head if she heard me say that. She's still protective of her brood."

"So there's more of them?"

"Oh yeah, two more. And Crew has a little sister and brother, but they're a lot younger than him."

"Sounds like you know these people pretty well." I walked to the edge of the pool and dipped my foot in.

"Yeah, they've treated me great since the boys came to the University. They moved straight into the frat house. Both dads asked me to keep an eye on them and to call if I saw something they needed to know giving me their personal cell phone numbers. I couldn't believe it. I've only had to call them a couple of times the first year. Damn dickheads. Couldn't keep it in their pants to save themselves. Of course, they drank like they expected the reinstatement of prohibition. For boys who grew up around rockers, the adults must have made sure they led sheltered lives."

He opened the ice chest and started setting a picnic out on a patio table. It confused me. How did he get all this lined up when he barely had time between meetings and getting home? I hardly had time to shave the important places. When he said a private hot tub, I wondered if we would be going in sans clothes. Looking around, I'm glad I took the time.

"How did you do all this?"

"I know people, Indy. Perks of being the XOX president for two years."

"When did you have time to arrange it? We've been busy today." I watched him arrange the table as though it was a fine dining restaurant.

"While we were sitting there listening to Coach, I texted my people who texted their people." He laughed as he said it.

"Oh, your people? You must be pretty damn important, Mr. Ex Pres."

"You know it. Now come here and kiss me. I've been working fucking hard since we arrived."

"I can do one better than that." Walking over to him, I untied my bikini top and let it drop to the concrete. The warm night air didn't keep my nipples from hardening, but it could have been the deep brown I saw his eyes change to when he watched me let the top go.

"My kind of woman." He wrapped an arm around me as his hand came up to take my breast. He kneaded the soft mound while his tongue thoroughly assaulted mine.

When we pulled back, I had to ask, "What does that mean? You like exhibitionism?"

"I've been known to have sex in risky places. Hang around the house some, and you'll hear stories. I'm not sure they're all true but, eh, who the fuck cares."

"You seem a little possessive to allow us to be someplace where people might catch us." I leaned down and popped a grape in my mouth. No comment ever came. I looked back from all the food I gazed at. "No comment, Timms?"

"Honestly, I've not been with a woman in a long time that I cared enough about to be worried. I didn't give a shit for the ones in college. Hell, I think most of them came to the house like groupies to fulfill our sexual fantasies so they could say they fucked someone important."

"You used these women?" The shock on my face had to say it all.

"Didn't have to use them. They're like the energizer bunnies. No respect for themselves at all. Hell, I'm surprised there weren't more diseases passed around. Guess safe sex is a thing."

"And you still take advantage of this when you go to the house?"

"Hell no. I haven't been out there this entire semester. I'm through with that. They've invited me plenty of times to their damn parties, but I don't give a flying fuck about going back, especially since we've been seeing each other."

He held me against him tight. "You know it's going to be hard to eat with these babies staring at me looking like they need my attention?"

I smiled. "Maybe you can give them some attention and then we can eat. I'm in need of some stress relief after all the shit we've been through today. What about you?"

"Hell yeah, I do. Want to get in the pool? I'm sure the water's perfect for..." he wiggled his eyebrows at me making me grin. I dropped my shorts and bottoms before I dove into the blue water.

Before I came up, his perfect, naked body caught me underwater wrapping his arms around my middle using his muscular legs to bring us to the surface. We touched and caressed and kissed all the best places on each other before stopping to stand in the middle. The moonlight created crystal- topped ripples to play across the water which had been warmed by the sunlight of the day.

Backing me to the wall, he wrapped my legs around him, and I could feel the hard length of him pressed against the part of me that begged for his attention.

A slow smile barely graced his lips before he picked me up enough to tease me with the smooth head. Sliding it up, he circled my clit causing me to suck in a breath. As he ran it back down to my opening, he barely notched the head inside me before pulling it out and moving back up. This time he tapped the bundle of nerves begging for his attention several times, I almost detonated from the pleasure of it. Before I had time to react, he ran the hard, smooth head back to where I needed him to take me, fast and deep.

"Please. Timms. Please, now."

He surged forward, and I took him all in at once. "Oh, God. That feels so…"

His tongue mimicked the rough pace he set of our coupling. Finally letting my mouth go, he pushed in harder, and my head fell back against the side, the deep surge feeling even better than before. With my neck exposed to him, he nipped at the skin until he reached the swollen nubs that cried for his mouth.

The soft bites he used on the engorged pebbles started my orgasm to build from deep within. When he pulled back tugging the skin with him, I exploded with pleasure causing tremors in my inner walls begging him not to leave my warmth.

"Oh my fucking God, India." I knew he felt my clenching as he pushed deeper and deeper, over and over until he joined me in the euphoria only two lovers feel.

The sensation of him releasing inside me caused my orgasm to continue longer than I'd ever had before or maybe it was another one following behind the first.

He took several deep breaths before speaking. "Damn, that was… don't even know how to describe it.

The way you had me. The way you gripped me tight not letting me go felt fucking fantastic."

TIMMS

"Open up, moon goddess." I held a sugared grape over India's head, the swirling water in the hot tub felt amazing. Heated Texas summer nights always made me want to find a way to cool off. After today with a beautiful woman lying across me while I fed her treats and the water refreshing our skin, life didn't get much better.

"Little cheesy there, Timms, but if you're willing to feed me, I'll take it." She smiled before opening to receive the nibble of goodness.

"Can't help myself. Watching the water flow around a naked woman lounging in my lap makes me want to say cheesy things."

"Awe. Isn't that sweet? Timms giving up that man card one tear at a time. That's okay. I like it. Makes me feel special."

"You should. I seriously doubt I've ever said something so romantic."

"Romantic, huh?" She looked up and glanced around. "Too bad no one's here to hear you."

"The one that counts is here, India. I don't give a shit about anyone else." The light blue of her eyes constricted when I said it.

Something about India pulled me to her. I'd never felt like this about any of the women before her. The way she made me feel like I needed to be with her, to touch her, to protect her—those were all new feelings to me—all the things I knew she'd hate like taking care of her. Her determination to be independent was admirable, but how did I convince her it would be all right to depend on others sometimes, especially me? She could let her guard down sometimes, and no one would think less of her.

"You must be having an entire conversation in your head, Timms."

I glanced down at her. "No, just thinking about how beautiful you are lying here with me. How free you are to be in the buff and not feel like you should be covered up."

"No one's around. Who cares? I know you don't if what's stabbing me in the back is any indication." She smiled. "Kiss me."

I sat her up and put her across my lap. "Convenient position you chose."

"You're the one who demanded a kiss. Can I help it if this is easier to attack those lips?"

"I know some lips you can attack." As soon as she said it, I knew she hadn't meant to say it out loud. I'd never seen this vulnerable side of her, a slight blush creeping up her neck to highlight her face.

"That can be arranged." I spun her around and stood with her in my arms. I stepped to the opposite side of the tub, where I dropped kisses down her back to the top of her perfectly curved ass while squeezing her equally perfect tits. I saw all of her as perfection.

I pushed her forward, not slowly but in a demanding way. She rested her forearms on the side, so her tits were barely suspended in the water where a jet was streaming cool water. I kneeled behind her and kissed across the globes waiting for attention. I bit lightly on one while kneading the other. I wanted her to know I was on the other peachy cheek, so I bit down and sucked the skin certain I left a mark.

"Oww," she squeaked.

"Oww is right. This is my spot. No one will see it but me, and when you sit tomorrow, I want you to remember this moment." I kicked her legs apart under the water and slid my hands up from her knees to the juncture I sought. The wet between her legs was on me not the waters.

"I'm only going to use my tongue and fingers on you this time, India."

She glanced back at me, and I could see her illuminated face. No words were spoken as I gave her what she begged for.

"You're awfully quiet over there." I reached over the console for her hand as we made our way home.

"Just thinking. Tomorrow's practice is the last before the game on Saturday. I have to make a decision and announcement to my squad."

"You don't have to use the same one for each kick. It's a preseason game. Try them all out if it's possible. One might fold under the pressure when he walks into that packed stadium."

"Yeah, I probably will do that, but everything in me says I cannot allow Conner on that field. He expects to start but after all the practices he's missed, I don't think he should be allowed."

"You might not have a say in that. Coach J pretty much announced he wouldn't play when asked about him missing practices."

"With all that's happened, I still think he's going to expect to kick at some point."

"I'm waiting for him to fuck up again. He will, you know it as well as I do." Thinking about him made me angry all over again.

"Let's not ruin the evening talking about him. It's been the worst and best day since I've been in this city. Thank you."

I pulled our hands to my mouth and kissed the back of hers. "Thank you, Indy. It's been special to me, too." She looked at me with eyes that held conflict. I wasn't sure I wanted to know what it was about, so I didn't comment.

On the way to my door, she stared up at the moon that was lower in the sky now. "I doubt I'll ever see a full moon and not think about this night."

"Now who's being cheesy?" We both laughed as we made our way inside. "Come on, I'll use a few more of my lines to see where they'll get me."

"You're terrible."

"Yeah, I'm going to show you how terrible I can be." I shut and locked the door behind us.

Practice started on time with all present and accounted for on the field. Good thing since Coach J started barking orders before we left the locker room. Guess the events had him worried about Saturday's game more than usual.

I knew the practice would be light with tomorrow's game looming ahead. Crew's passes nailed his receivers every time, and he was where he needed to be. The team looked good overall. Minor problems always slipped in during these opening games, but that's what they were designed for. Still, losing was not an option.

India's group continued with all four players practicing and discussing improvements. She knew her squad would be called on probably more than once to advance the score so having her guys ready for anything became her mantra. I hoped it was theirs, too.

Coach motioned for the kicking team to run over their plays a couple of times with the team. That very moment called for a decision, the one she dreaded. Naming the starting kicker might set off a series of events no one wanted to deal with.

India moved over beside Coach J and shared her decision, so he could call the kicking team in for the play. They started with a PAT kick since it would be used the most.

"Ian Brown, you're up. Let's see what you got." Ian latched his chin strap and headed on the field. The grin on his face said it all. His improvements since he'd arrived on campus proved he deserved the spot—that and the fact he'd practiced seven days a week.

Coach J put his hand on the kid's shoulder pad. "Now, son, you've done this little chip a thousand times, so do it right." Without turning his head, he glanced at the remaining people on the sideline. "Forget about your teammates. Forget about the size of this stadium. Forget about the noise. Do your job." With that, he backed away and blew his whistle.

Zac would be the holder since they'd practiced the play this way. The ball snapped on Zac's cadence, he spun it into position, and Ian's foot booted the ball high and straight through the uprights.

"Okay. Do it again from the twenty," Coach J told them. As the team lined up, I watched Conner and Drew walking separately down the sideline to the kicking location. No conversation transpired between them, but they both carried a look of disappointment.

Coach J blew the whistle, and the exact same play ran without a hitch. "Again at the thirty." The scene replayed the same. Everyone clapped for Ian, and I saw a smile on India's face. I knew from here things might fall apart. I hadn't watched Ian kick every time, so I didn't know his limit.

"Again from the forty." The team moved back ten yards, lined up, and the shrill sound of Coach J's whistle signaled the start. The ball split the uprights, but it crossed over barely above the horizontal post.

Coach called 'good enough.' He and India both looked at Ian. "You want to try at the forty-five?"

"Yes, sir. I can do it."

"Line 'em up, boys. Mr. Brown here says he can do it." India held her breath. I knew she needed for Ian to make the kick. If nothing else, so she wouldn't have to involve Conner's skills in the decision-making process. The loud whistle sliced through the quiet on the field. Zac called it, spun it, held it. Ian never missed a beat as he kicked and watched it sail through the uprights. The team clapped again, but I knew if this were a game, I'd hear cheering.

As I glanced to the sideline, Conner kept his anger under control. He'd blown it with missing practice and pulling the other stunts. He'd have to wait his turn to see if he ever played a down of TAU ball for his senior year.

"Huddle up." The entire team made its way to midfield where Coach J gave a short pep talk about earning positions in the upcoming game. He sent them to the locker room on a definite high note.

"I'll see you all in the conference room." Looking at his clipboard, Coach headed inside.

I walked beside India not saying anything. I felt the wheels turning in her head, though. She still had a case of the nerves from the plays. Hell, I was nervous for Ian, when I should be thinking about my QB.

"You okay?"

India looked at me finally. "Did you watch Conner when Ian kicked?"

"Off and on. Why?"

"I didn't. I had to watch Ian's form. Count his steps and the follow-through. I wondered what Conner thought."

"Probably not a hell of a lot since he watched his guaranteed position go to another player."

"Yeah, that's what I thought, too."

The coaching meeting lasted too damn long in my book. We knew what had to be done. I never realized Coach J could be so long winded. The players had been gone at least an hour. How did I not know he put the other coaches through this torture? *Send an email, Coach.*

"Be here in the morning no later than ten. Dismissed."

Thank God.

"You want to stop and get something to eat on the way home? I know the team will be doing stuff they probably shouldn't so I don't want to go anywhere near them." I laughed trying to make light of it, but I knew it to be true. First game of the season meant they'd all be partying at the house. I'd done it for four years and loved every minute of it.

"Yeah. That's fine. I'll follow you."

"What?" I didn't understand.

"I have my car. I'll follow you, and then I can go home when we're done." I grabbed her elbow stopping her.

"What the fuck, India? Why would you go home tonight?"

"Let's see. I pay rent for my apartment, and I've been with you for several nights now. I want to go home. I'm tired."

"Well, okay. I guess." Not how I saw the evening going. "I'd prefer us to be together."

"I know, but I need some time to get my head together for tomorrow. It's been a long day, Timms."

"Okay, I get it. It looks like someone put a flyer on your car. Probably a party somewhere tonight." I reached over to grab it off her car beating her to it. She lunged at the note. "Whoa there, Wonder Woman."

My face changed in a flash. Humor disappeared instantly. This note involved no party plans.

"What the fuck is this, India?" Her eyes flashed in anger.

"I'd have to read it to know, Timms." I thrust it forward for her to read.

"The moment's getting closer."

The cryptic words held a threat to them.

"What's this shit talking about? Did you forget to tell me something?" The clipped words came out too harsh.

"How should I know? I didn't write it." She raised her voice and stood up to me. "Why are you talking to me that way? You'll not speak to me like I'm incapable of taking care of myself."

She took a deep breath before starting in again. "You'll never get by with trying to take the upper hand or talk down to me. I may be hard-headed, but no man will ever run over me. Not now, not ever."

Stepping closer to her, I was afraid she would back away, but she didn't. "I'm sorry. It wasn't directed at you. It scared me. Someone is trying to hurt you or at least scare the shit out of you."

I wrapped my arm around her neck and pulled her in, and again she let me. "Who do you think would leave something like this, or you think they got the wrong car in your parking lot?"

"No, I don't think they did."

I pushed back, confused. "What does that mean, Indy? Have you had others? Why the hell didn't you tell me?" I had to hold my anger back this time, so I used a milder tone.

"Yeah, two."

"Have they been other places?" I had to know.

"Yeah, here at school and my apartment."

"So whoever's doing this knows you're at the University, around the field, and where you live? India, this is fucked up. Do you have the other two?"

"No, I laughed it off and threw the first one away. I didn't take it seriously, but the second one is in my car."

"You might not have taken it seriously, but you should have at least told me about them."

She nodded her head. "Yeah, I probably should have told someone, but I thought I could handle it myself."

"India, this is a fucking threat against you." I tightened the hold I had on her.

"I guess we need to report it," she finally admitted. Thank God she was willing to take this more seriously now.

"Yes, no doubt about that. Someone knows too much about you. Let's start with the campus police since the first one was there, and we'll get them to call Guerrero, too."

"Timms, I know that's true, but no one has done anything so how are they going to move forward?"

"Campus police take threatening students seriously. You're a student, remember?"

"Right. I suppose it's a good plan." She tapped in the number, answered the questioning with the campus police, and hung up.

"Well?" I prayed she'd be honest with me.

"Just like I thought. They want me to come down with the notes. I didn't want to have to get into this tonight." She took a deep breath and let it out slowly.

"I know this is a pain, but India you need to follow through with this. Someone's trying to either scare you or intimidate you. Worse yet, this someone is a psycho and wants to hurt you. People are crazy these days and will do anything."

"I know you're right. It's just I wanted this to be a smooth week, and it's been nothing but hell."

"And I want you to be safe." I hugged her body to me and laid my head over on hers. "You know that, right?"

"I know, and I appreciate everything you've done."

"Let's go down there and get it over with." I pulled her to me, and we climbed in and headed for the campus police station.

The officer who took her call met us at the door and took us straight back to an office. He pulled a glove out and took the note from the ends of India's fingers placing it in an official-looking plastic bag.

"I've got a call into Officer Guerrero since he's who you have been working with, but he's not available until tomorrow morning. We'll get the note to him so his department can see about possibly getting fingerprints from it."

"Thank you, sir," India slowly responded. I knew she was exhausted, but this needed to be dealt with now.

"Until then, you need to be vigilant, Miss Durham. This situation is nothing to take lightly. This person seems to have a vendetta against you for some reason."

"Exactly what I've been trying to make her understand, Officer."

He nodded at the two of us and stood. "I'll be in touch with you as soon as I know something."

"Thank you, Officer," she told him, and we both stood to leave.

"I'm exhausted."

"Yeah, I can tell. Can we go back to my original plan then? Only we can pick up food or have it delivered. I'm good with your place or mine. I only want us to be together."

"Fine. We'll do it your way, but we have to sleep. I mean like the dead sleep. Maybe we should try it with clothes on."

I grinned at her. "You're no fun."

"That's right. Just call me No-Fun Nancy tonight," she offered with a brief smile of her own.

INDIA

"Welcome to Taylor Field, sports fans," blared through the stadium's loudspeaker system. "The season opener for both the TAU Rams and the LGU Cougars will be getting underway shortly."

The locker room roared with energy from the players huddled up while Coach J said his final words before taking the field. I loved these moments—adrenaline pumping, cleats clacking on concrete, positive mantras spoken. It's where minds move to a different head space, and bodies are put on high alert.

My squad stood around on the periphery of the starters. While only two were expected to hit the field today, the possibility of being called on to back this team still existed. I'd had my moment with them before the big man started and gave them my speech about supporting everyone, friend or foe.

Conner acted as though he wanted to be there, and that pleased me. I needed him to be part of the team instead of against it. Maybe a wake-up call brought him back to reality on how teams work. I didn't have time during the game to coddle him.

Taking the field for the first time with thousands of fans filling the stands with both bodies and noise, caused the team to take on the persona of a unit, exactly as it should be. The team worked hard, not just during this season's practice but all their lives to get here—right here—on this field and in front of these fans. They'd endured years of sacrificing their bodies, family time, friends, and living. While most kids grew up using their time to be kids, these guys grew up eating, sleeping, and drinking with a pigskin in their hands. Sacrifice allowed them to end up playing for a Division One school and now for many, it all paid off.

I watched my squad as they stretched waiting for the call to line up across the field. We'd won the toss, and Ian's kick would send the ball down near the goal line, hopefully to the slower receiver.

The whistle blew to let the game begin, and I nodded at him. He gave me a brief grin before snapping his helmet down and jogging to the middle, ball tee in his hand. The ref handed him the game ball that he set up at the seventy-five-degree angle. Ian walked back the required distance and turned. He glanced left and right at his team waiting for the ref to blow the whistle.

Looking back, I saw Conner, Drew, and Zac standing to watch Ian's success, each with a different expression—Zac was excited, and Drew's face read nothing, but Conner was pissed. Did Conner think I would change my mind? Maybe he felt like Coach J would intervene and let him take the field. Conner didn't know Coach J at all if he believed the head coach would undermine my authority in front of the team.

The whistle blew, the team advanced to the line of scrimmage, and Ian put his foot into that ball proving why he'd earned the uniform. It sailed through the air nice and high for plenty of hang time. Our defenders had enough time to sprint down to our opponent's end of the field. The Cougars' player waived them off with a fair catch when he realized there wasn't a chance of running it out. The game would start on their twenty-yard line.

I stood back and watched Timms while I recorded stats on my tablet. He wore his headphones listening to the coaches up top for vital information. The focus he held on each play said all I needed to know about his dedication to this team. He never wavered for a second.

Ian got the call to kick three PATs before the half, and he and Zac had executed them perfectly to tack on the extra points. Unfortunately, the Cougars chalked up the same score on the huge lit sign in the end zone. The clock for half-time ran down, and we all headed for the locker room.

Conner met me at the door. "So what's it going to be, Coach? When do I get my chance to prove I can do this job?"

I tried to keep my face neutral, but the look he returned told me I failed. "Conner, we announced who would kick yesterday."

"No, you announced who would start kicking yesterday. Don't you think the rest of us deserve the opportunity to prove our ability to Coach J?"

I continued to walk down the tunnel preferring not to look at him. Honestly, I questioned if it was safe being beside him. There was no trust on my part with this guy.

"I believe that's what the first two weeks of practice was for, Conner. You remember the practices you felt above attending. I'm surprised he didn't cut you for missing them."

"I had legit excuses for missing, Coach."

"Really? Did you? I don't remember hearing anything from you at all, much less an excuse."

We walked through the locker room door side by side. I spotted Timms watching the doorway as soon as I stepped over the threshold. He looked relieved to see me until Conner walked in. The QB's coaching face changed immediately.

I shot him a quick smile hoping to make him understand all was good. He offered a chin tip and went back to talking to Crew.

Conner continued his argument as soon as we took a step inside. "So, you're saying I'm not getting on the field today at all?"

"The rules for missing practice are firm, Conner. I didn't write them, but I do enforce them because I agree with them. You may have produced lame excuses to someone to keep your eligibility on this team, but you still broke the rules." I began looking through my notes on the tablet attached to my arm. I would not argue with him.

"That sucks." He said it loud enough for only the two players close enough to hear. He leaned closer to me pretending to be looking at my screen. "Of course, I'm sure you'd know all about sucking since you spend your free time with your mouth all over the QB coach's cock."

I spun around facing him. The look on his face told me what he wanted was to goad me into getting into it with him. It might only give him ammunition for later. No way was I playing his game.

"Why, Conner, have you been playing peeping Tom or something? Some people would say that's creepy, but I'm going to go with trespassing, which is illegal." I turned back to my tablet and started walking away.

Calling after me, he let everyone hear him. "Only illegal if you get caught." As soon as he said it, everyone who heard turned in his direction, and he knew he'd made a mistake.

The Rams and Cougars battled score for score until the end. With a minute remaining on the clock, Coach J called me over.

"How close does he need to be, India?" Ian's abilities were about to be tested to their max, but I anticipated this happening.

"The closer the better, but he's gotta have the forty or less."

"Warm him up." The next play gained a first down, and Coach J called a time-out.

The team huddled on the sidelines where he ordered them to get the ball in Ian's range.

I glanced back to Timms and nodded before he spoke to Crew. Their powwow gained me a thumbs-up, and we were ready to rock on putting this game to bed. At least I prayed it would.

"Ian?"

"Yes, Coach." The look on his face spoke volumes to his nerves.

"You got this, Ian. You've done it no less than fifty times in the past week. You worked hard on technique for accuracy and nailed it over and over, so there's no doubt in my mind you can do this today, too."

I turned to Zac. "You ready?" The kid gave me a huge grin immediately before we heard a loud cheer erupt in the stands. I hoped they'd score so we wouldn't have to test Ian's ability but no luck. The ball dropped through our receiver's hands in the end zone, a pass he should have caught without question.

I pulled both of my guys close in. "Do this... right here, right now. Got it?"

"Yes, ma'am," they both told me and took off to the spot exactly on the forty-yard line. I wanted inside, but he could do this. I had faith in him.

As usual, the Cougars called a last-minute time-out to try messing with Ian's head about the kick. We'd discussed it so many times that I knew he and Zac had to be talking about it while waiting.

I felt someone standing behind me without turning around. Conner's hot breath wafted over the skin of my neck causing the fine hairs to rise.

"You know he's gonna fuck this up, right?"

"Don't talk to me like that, Conner." I didn't bother to turn around. He needed to walk away.

"He's not good enough to make the kick. You're kissing your prissy coaching career goodbye letting him even try. Everyone knows it, too. Look at them, India."

His goading didn't change my mind. "Walk away, Conner, before there's trouble."

"Look around, bitch. The team is all staring at you from the field. They know the kid can't do what I can do."

"I don't care what any of you think. You or the team." My anger rose, but I knew in my mind the team would back Ian. His position with his teammates was secure. Conner didn't have one even living in that frat house.

"Keep telling yourself that. When he fucks it up, the team, the fans, the coaching staff, the University Pres, they're all going to come for you. You know 'winning is everything' and all that bullshit. Enjoy the next few seconds of your job."

I refused to turn and acknowledge him. His breathing sped up, and I knew it made him angrier, but I didn't care. Never would I give him ammunition to use against me by creating a scene in front of the stadium. When the ref blew the whistle for play to resume, I took a spot on the sideline where Ian set up the kicking tee. I wanted to see his foot hit the ball. From that vantage point, I would know if the kick was enough to earn the three points we needed.

The center hiked the ball. Zac set it up and spun it as Ian descended on the spot to plant his left foot and hit the pigskin with the perfect amount of force needed to carry it through the uprights. The team, the fans, the coaches all swiveled their heads to watch the ball float through the air and clear the bar by about three feet.

Ian did it, and the wild cheering in the stands only made it sweeter for the kid. He ran to the sideline where I stood still gawking in amazement, picked me up, and turned me around. I couldn't help but laugh when he realized he was holding his coach in the air.

"Sorry, Coach. Guess I got a little carried away." I pushed him on the numbers and laughed hard at him.

"I'm so proud of you, Ian. I knew you could do it all along. You just needed to believe. Now go do the kickoff, and if you let that receiver pass you with the return, I will kick your ass myself. Understood?"

"Yes, ma'am." He grinned and took off to the middle of the field.

As the Cougars lined up on the seven-yard line where we'd stopped the return, I glanced and saw there was only time for one more play. I knew our boys' enthusiasm would carry over and shut down the opponent.

I felt that same hot breath on my neck again. "You've done it now, you bitch. You've ruined it all for me."

This time I couldn't stop myself. I spun on him looking past the face guard at a stare to startle the devil.

"If you'd wanted the position, you should've fought for it. Never take a spot on this team for granted."

"I was told this was my team when I came here." He stepped closer to my face.

"Then you talked to the wrong person."

"No, this is on you, bitch. You've fucked it all up for me. I had this in the bag, and they go and bring in some butch female who thinks because she can kick a ball, she can play in a man's world. Or maybe I'm mistaken about what you've got tucked between your legs there." He looked down at my crotch. "Maybe you are a man. Either way, this ain't over, not by a long shot."

My anger boiled. "You're right. This isn't over. We'll finish it with Coach Jefferies in his office. I don't have time to deal with a piece of trash like you. Head to the locker room now. You don't deserve to celebrate this win."

The deafening crowd noise caused me to raise my voice more than I wanted to. I had to hold back to keep from saying anything more to this kid. No player would talk to me this way and stay on my squad.

He smirked at me over my head when he saw the game was officially over. He called loud enough for the players around us to hear. "See you there, Coach."

I glanced around and realized no one but me had probably heard any of our heated conversation with the crowd noise and watching the final play of the game. It didn't matter, though. Coach J would hear every word from this self-entitled prick's mouth. He wouldn't get away with trying to intimidate me and being crude. Accusing me of being anything other than a woman didn't matter in this field. I'd fought this battle long and hard and won. I'd fight this one, too.

I skirted past the locker room for my changing area to cool off and to celebrate. My cell buzzed inside my bag. I didn't want to talk to anyone, but I knew my family would want to congratulate me on the win.

"Woo hoo, biyotch," Chyna yelled into the phone.

"That's Coach Biyotch." I laughed and answered.

"No really, Indy, congrats on the win. Your guy did a kick-ass job. I'm proud of the little fucker." Yes, definitely Chyna's way of making it her own.

"Thanks, and he's not that young. He's the same age as you," I said it more harshly than I intended.

"Damn, you sound like you're not excited about the win. Aren't you supposed to be like jumping and screaming with the team?"

"Maybe, if I were with the team."

"You're telling me you have the fucking opportunity to go in the locker room where hot bodied, big dicked football players are running around naked or in towels, and you're not taking advantage of it? Indy, you've lost your fucking mind."

"Chyna. Stop. I can't, no I won't, think about my players that way. One, it's unprofessional on my part, and two, they are young."

"God, you find a damn excuse to spoil all the fun. They may be younger than you, but shit, you're not dead. I mean, come on, they still have to look fucking hot with water sluicing down the cuts between those abs and those muscular arms and legs. I bet it drips off those big cocks."

"Stop, Chyna!" I yelled at her. "That's enough. I told you, I can't think of them that way."

"Spoilsport. I gotta stop anyway. I've gotta change my panties just talking about it. The pictures I can create in my mind are enough to have me screaming a big O on."

"Chyna, please. I've had a rough day. I don't need this right now."

"Sorry. What's up? You sound stressed. How can that be when your boy just won the game?"

"One of my squad is unhappy about not getting the starting spot he felt he deserved." I took a deep breath and let it out slowly. "I'm going to have a fight on my hands, probably later today."

"You got this shit, sis. You've never let some guy get in your way of your goals. I know you won't start now." Chyna had witnessed me go against the odds as a female in a male sport all her life. She was right, this shouldn't be any different this time.

"I know you're right, but this fight isn't about my playing. He's questioning my coaching and the choices I make as a coach."

"Paa-lease." She dragged out the word. "That's bullshit, and you know it. If the head coach is that easy to change his mind based on some has-been, then you don't need to be working for him anyway."

"I'm happy you have all this confidence in me, Chyna, but he'll look at my skills from a different angle. He'll want to do what's best for the team. My kicker barely made the kick. He's gotta up his game between now and the next one. This guy who's fighting me says he can do these kicks in his sleep, and maybe he can, but his attitude and cutting practice are keeping him from being the starter."

"Still your boss should listen to you."

"Right." I let it drop.

"Hey, let's talk about something better. How are things with this hottie coach you're with?"

"Timms. They're fine. He's fine."

"Fine? That's the best bone you can throw me? I need some deets. My sex life is lacking over here in Loserville."

"Not now, Chyna. Get out and meet people."

"I know. It's just a lot of work."

"It should be a snap for you."

"Yeah, it should be."

Her comments and tone told me there might be more than she's saying, but I didn't have time to worry about her with all that loomed over my head.

"Listen. Go do some retail therapy. It always gets you excited."

"Yeah, I'll think about it. There're some boutiques on the square I haven't had time to check out." For all her bravado, she sounded depressed, especially if the thought of shopping didn't change her attitude.

"Hey, I gotta go, Indy. Let me know how things are going after your meeting with the coach and the asshole."

"K. Love you."

"Love you, too." She ended the call quickly. Either she was lonely or missing home already. I needed to get back to her soon when I had more time to talk.

TIMMS

The locker room was on fire by the time the coaching staff made its way inside. They'd played their hearts out to win for the home team. Crew executed each play just as we'd practiced. He made a few last-minute decisions to run with the ball as needed to capture a first down. He always had the option, but we didn't like to see him use it needlessly. The danger of being tackled and getting hurt always existed, as I very well knew.

I hit him on the shoulder, and he turned giving me that Cheshire cat smile. "Great job, Crew." I put my hand out to shake, but he hugged me instead.

"Thanks, Coach. I tried my best to remember all the points you made while I was out there. You've shown me so much about playing at this level. Thanks."

I tipped my head to him. "You played a fine game. We've got few things to work on, but I can't find fault in any of the downs you fought through today."

"Thanks again." His grin never faded.

"Time to celebrate. The house tonight?" Crew stepped up as I asked the question.

Tucker wrapped an arm around Crew's shoulder. "Hell yeah, the house. It's the first home game, the first year as starting QB, and it's going to be epic."

Blue joined the two younger players and stuck his hand out to Crew. "Good job, my man. Got your first game nerves out of the way, the rest will be history in no time."

"Right, but you played like a beast out there. How many sacks were you all or part of today?"

"Don't know yet. I ain't keeping count during a game. Just like to take it one play at a time." He turned to me. "Speaking of time, you got a second, Timms?"

"Sure." I turned back to the rookies. "Guys, have fun but not too much fun. We still have shit to work on starting Monday."

"I'm ready," Crew called as he walked off to shower.

Blue and I walked over to his locker area that was already empty. "What's up?"

"You talked to your girl yet?" Blue's cleats hit the floor as he spoke.

"No, not yet. She goes over to the other locker area to get dressed. Why? Did something happen I missed?"

"I heard her have a few words with that Conner kid while Ian kicked the field goal. Didn't sound like he was too happy with her decision."

"He's all talk. She's not worried about his dumb ass. He chose not to come to practice. Should have known he wasn't going to be the starter today." I looked around to make sure Conner wasn't within earshot. "From watching Ian kick, he probably won't ever be the starter."

"Yeah, none of us are too damn happy he's living in the house. I mean, I'm not living there either, so it's not a big fucking deal to me, but the others say he's a complete douche to everyone. Thinks he runs the place because he's an upperclassman. Hell, I'm president, but I don't act like a dickhead to the others."

"Is that so? Well, Mr. President, maybe you need to knock him down a few rungs on the ladder. Make him understand what happens with douchebags when they treat their bros like that." I laughed thinking about others I had to correct a few times last year, like Crew. "But back to India. Did you hear any of it? I mean, I'm sure they argued about his starting."

"I know she sent him to the locker room before time ran out, but it all happened pretty fast, so it looked like he ran in with the rest of us."

"You heard that?"

"Only bits and pieces. It's like he stood behind her so no one would suspect anything was going on until she turned around and got in his face. She said some things and then pointed to the locker room. I figured that's what she was telling him to do."

"Well, shit. That doesn't sound good."

"No, and that whole thing about talking behind her so only she can hear him was a dick move. He did it twice at the end of the game."

"I need to put a stop to that shit. She's not going to like me interfering, though."

"No, probably not. If she's anything like Noelle, she likes to fight her own battles. Damn women."

"Who are damn women?"

Neither of us heard India coming.

"All you damn women," Blue spoke up. "You keep us on a short leash. Can't let us make plans without checking in first." His save needed to be rewarded. She never suspected.

"I don't think I resemble that remark in any way, Blue." She smiled, but I knew it was for show. Something was up.

"Are you about to head home or what?" I asked. She smelled better than anything in that locker room. I wanted to wrap her up in a hug, but the timing wasn't good for any public displays.

"No, not yet." She looked over at the few coaches sitting around in Coach J's office. "I need to talk to the big guy before I leave, but you don't need to wait around. Just some squad stuff I gotta deal with."

"I'll be right here."

INDIA

Coach J welcomed me in with praises of how Ian handled himself on the field. It started the conversation a lot easier than I anticipated.

"Thanks, Coach. I appreciate you taking notice of my guys."

"You don't sound all that enthused, India. What's going on? I told you from the beginning if there were problems to come to me first."

"I know, but I want to handle all I can before I do. Honestly, I think this is just a heads-up for you anyway. I can handle it, but I wanted you to be aware."

"Let me guess, Conner's not happy he didn't get the nod for starting."

"Exactly, and now that Ian's proven he can kick the ball a decent distance, Conner sees his spot being taken away."

"No one ever said it was his spot. We told the kid he could join our program, but that he'd have to earn the position exactly like the rest of the team."

"All he heard you say was it was his spot for the taking."

"We'll set him straight on Monday then. I would never give him the starting position without consulting you first. It's why I hired a special teams coach. I trust your judgment on this."

"Thank you. I appreciate the backing, and I believe I made the right call."

"I believe you did, too. He needed some attitude adjustment anyway. Missing practice is not the way to show what you're good at. He's not some snot-nosed freshman in this either. He should've known better."

"Right. That's what I thought, too. Apparently, he thought differently."

"Monday, first thing, we'll meet." He prepared to stand as if the meeting was over. When I didn't, he looked at me. "Is there something else?"

"Yes, there is. Today on the field, he had some choice words for me over my decision and to be perfectly honest, I'm not happy with him being on my squad at all."

"What's his beef?"

"He feels like I've taken away his opportunity with my decisions. Then, he concluded that I'm either a lesbian or transgender trying to play in a man's world. I'm used to it from playing in a male-dominated sport, but I'm not going to sit idly by and let him or any other player talk down to me."

"I can't say I'm surprised either. It's the easy thing to go to for people like him. I can't understand why men feel threatened by a woman who is good at something they deem male only."

"It's always been a problem for me, Coach, but I was always the player, never the coach."

"Either way, it's wrong. We aren't going to sit by and do nothing. We will address this on Monday as well. You might be down to three players. I'm not above removing him from this team for his poor choices."

"That's good to know. I mean, I hate to see someone lose their scholarship in their senior year, but I'm not going to put up with him treating me with disrespect of any kind."

"As you shouldn't. I won't tolerate any player disrespecting a coach. Sometimes lessons are only learned the hard way, India. This could be one of those times." He looked up at me for a second and then continued. "Has he threatened you?"

"Not exactly." I didn't want him to address all the problems if we could get around them. Coach J hired me to do a job and dealing with my players was part of it.

"What does that mean, India? Did he, or didn't he?"

"He said this wasn't over which could have meant he was coming to you for the final decision."

"Or it could mean he planned to take action himself." He leaned back in the tall-backed chair. "You be careful. Try not to find yourself alone until this is settled. You understand what I'm saying? I don't know what you've got going with Timms and don't care, but it might be a good idea if you planned to stay there the rest of the weekend."

I thought we'd been careful about not outing ourselves to the rest of the team and the coaches.

"Right. I can do that."

"Figured he wouldn't mind playing bodyguard for a few nights." He smiled briefly and then went straight back to business. "You watch yourself, and we'll get this lined out on Monday."

"Okay. Thank you, Coach." I stood and offered my hand which he shook. "I want the rest of the season to flow smoothly."

He rounded his desk. "Don't we all, but wanting and having are two different things."

We made our way out of his office and down the hallway together, and Timms was sitting on a bench inside the doorway.

Coach J spoke before I could get a word out. "Well, Timms. It seems you have another assignment for the weekend." Damn, I wanted to tell him myself. He's going to go all alpha protector with it coming from our boss.

"Your friend here..." he looked at me and winked, "... needs to stay with you until we can hash out the problems with a player on Monday afternoon. Is this a problem for you?"

Timms' lips barely turned up on the ends. "No sir, not a problem at all. I'd be honored to be her bodyguard."

Coach J looked at him hard. "No, I suppose it's not a bother for you at all." He then looked to me, turned shaking his head, and walked through the glass doors of the building.

"Now that that's settled, I know where you'll be staying for at least a couple of days."

"You're enjoying every minute of this, aren't you?"

"Hell yeah. I've been given the keys to the kingdom."

"You're not John Snow, dude."

"Might as well be. And you can be the mother of dragons. Sounds like a kinky game we can play for the next two days. Will you get a blonde wig that reaches your ass? I can tie you up with the locks."

I laughed and shook my head. "Let's see. I will if you'll wear six inches of fur from head to toe and grow your hair long." I stopped with that. "Oh, and you have to speak in an accent all weekend, too."

"I do speak in an accent. It's called Texan. Women love it." He wiggled his eyebrows.

"Which women? I don't I know a single woman who would take a Texas accent over an English one."

"You're listening to the wrong women then, babe, 'cause the ladies love my Texas twang." He was right. I loved his endearing southern drawl. It sounded as though he gave each word a thought before he spoke it. He never rushed, and I was good with it even if I weren't ready to admit it.

TIMMS

"Ah, a relaxing Saturday night at home for a change." The old leather on my couch settled around me as I fell into it. When I started making real money, I might look at buying another one. The thought of throwing this old girl out made me sad. We'd been together all four years of college. She wore the stains of beer, countless crumbs of food, and of course, traces of the real fun and games. I kept her in my bedroom at the frat house for entertaining the ladies who weren't into public displays.

"What are you thinking about? You have the funniest look on your face." India set the chips and a special cheese dip she raved about down on the coffee table. She pushed my feet off and fell back next to me.

"Sweets, this smells delicious." I coated the homemade chip. "Oh, man, did you fry these chips yourself? They're still hot."

"I did. I like them homemade. Don't you?"

"You amaze me with the best things. I do believe I am definitely in love." I popped the goodness in my mouth.

"What plans did you have for the rest of the weekend before your assigned babysitting job?" Her eyes drifted closed as she leaned back. Her head rested comfortably on the cushion.

"Hmm. Let's see. I planned to bring you home from the game, strip you naked, and hide your clothes until Monday morning." I glanced back to see her face about the same time she cracked one eye and gave me 'the look.' "Not good with that idea?"

"Depends."

"On what?" I liked where this was going. "I'm flexible."

Her face broke into a beautiful smile. "I like how you're flexible."

"You didn't answer me."

"Oh yeah. Sorry, I'm exhausted." She yawned. I motioned for her to finish her thought. "Depends on whether you're going to stash your clothes with mine."

"Sweets, if you're naked for the weekend, I'm right there with ya. We should get started on it right now."

"I think you should let me have a nap first." She fell over on the pillow. "Yeah, just a short nap. You watch the football game. Pay attention to the kicker for me, please." The last words whispered past her lips before her eyes stopped fluttering as they fought to stay open.

The blanket I kept for such occasions covered most of her. I left her tits out, though. Easier access for later.

"Guess it's the three of us, guys," I said to the two announcers calling the game. "Good thing it's football season. I can't stand watching soccer on TV." Of course, they didn't answer me back.

Something felt good, better than good. Was it a tongue? It was wet and rough on one side. Wow, could that thing curl around my dick? "Oh." I moaned out loud. "Yeah, babe, take it all. Suck my cock. Make it feel good, sweets. Swallow it, babe. Swallow it down that tight throat. That's right, I fucking love it when you hum and you've got my dick down balls deep. That's right, yeah, babe, don't just lick 'em, put them both in your mouth. Easy, babe. Yeah just like that. Now suck my cock deep again. Oh fuck, sweets. I'm gonna blow, babe. It's coming, you better be ready. Holy shit, fuck, fuck."

I sat straight up. "What the fuck?" Cum shot everywhere.

"Dammit, Timms. I'm going to have a big bruise on my ass."

I looked down where I'd thrown India off the bed. "Sweets, I thought I was having a fucking wet dream about you. Come here." I reached down and pulled her on the bed.

"Remind me never to give you head when you're asleep again." Leaning over, she rubbed her ass cheek.

"I'm sorry, babe. Let me make it up to you." I tried to pull her into my lap, but she wasn't having it.

"I'm hungry now. You can make it up by fixing me breakfast instead."

"You're choosing food over sex?"

"Hell yeah. Go make me pancakes and bacon." She rolled over on her stomach and squished up the pillow under her. "I deserve it after waking you up with a screaming orgasm." She started laughing and put her foot on my thigh. Before I knew it, she was pushing me out of my damn bed. "Go. I'm starving."

"Fuck, woman. You're mean when you're hungry." I studied her lying in my bed. It was the best morning ever. Her hair floated down her body ending midway, but the curved line of the arch in her back stopping at an ass made for spanking or kissing, either one was fine with me, made my dick twitch. My eyes swept up to her face to see a look that spoke of happiness. I always wanted to be able to give her that—Sunday mornings, Friday nights. It didn't matter when, but waking up seeing her lying in my bed and happy, I had to find out how to make that happen as often as possible.

I stood and leaned over kissing her head. "You're beautiful, sweets. You know that, right?"

With closed eyes, a smile graced her face. "Thank you." I kissed her naked ass cheek on my way out the door. "Pancakes, it is but please don't move. I like you just like that in my bed."

Lounging around all day Sunday watching football and then a movie marathon topped most Sundays. Hell, who I was I kidding, it topped most any day having India here. The sounds she added, the conversations we shared, and the arguments we battled through on everyday life events made every moment seem special.

The mid-afternoon rain only added to the day. India pulled out her laptop and opened her email for weekly assignments. I'd put school on the back burner for the first game, but I would have to make time to get it all in. Good thing my profs were flexible on scheduling assignment due dates.

"Don't you have assignments, too?" she asked when I flipped to a different game on the TV.

"Yeah, I'm thinking about looking them up, Mom."

"It's your GPA. I don't want to have to redo any classes to keep mine up." She read down through the mail listing. "Hmm."

"What, hmm?"

"Wonder why this didn't go to spam."

"Damn computers only filter out what you do need, not what you don't want."

She opened the email and started reading it. The color drained from her face. I slid over closer to read her screen.

> *"I unrolled the plastic making sure to cover every inch of the walls and floor. He would be happy with my meticulousness. One spec of blood could ruin everything. I knew that and so did he, so he taught me well. Making my work untraceable was an absolute necessity and being a forensic scientist, I was well trained on how to do that."*—*Dexter, Season One.*

"Who sent you that shit?" I said it louder than necessary.

"I... I don't know, but why... why would they send it?" She was visibly shaken.

"Wrong address maybe?" Even I didn't believe my simple excuse. This was getting too weird. Too many coincidences. We needed to follow up on the reports.

While the excerpt wasn't a direct threat to her, the ominous tone scared her, and that was enough for me.

"Get your note that you magically got out of taking down to the station and bring your laptop. We're getting this straight right now." My words growled out. Whoever's doing this knows too much, and this veiled threat was not going to wait.

We headed out to the station, I'd never dealt with the police so often as I had in this past month. Even with frat shit that attracted the police seemed to take a backseat to this semester, and it was only week two.

Business as usual with people and officers scurrying around the station greeted the two of us. India barely said a word on the way over. Holding her hand, I felt the constant tremble running through her on the drive over. I offered soothing words, but they did nothing to stop her thoughts causing the involuntary movement.

"What can we do for you?" The officer standing at the counter asked.

"We need to see Officer Guerrero, please."

"Let me see if he's around here or out on patrol."

"I called on the way over, and he said he'd be here to see us."

"Wait over there." She pointed to the same bench we'd sat on waiting for Ian.

"Damn, I hate this place." India's big blue eyes seemed washed out. I didn't like the looks of them. Is this what frightened look like on her? If so, I needed to do something.

"Can I help you?" Guerrero asked without looking up from what he was reading.

"Yes, we hope so."

He glanced, and then his head jerked up realizing who spoke to him. Guerrero put his hand out and shook both of ours. "Is there another problem?"

India tipped her head in a nod. "Come on back to my desk, and let's see what you've got."

After a short discussion, I sat back in my chair and crossed my arms over my chest.

"So, let's go over it. You got a note on campus and one at your apartment. Then you received this email that you think are lines from *Dexter*, the serial killer TV show."

"Pretty much covers it," I told him.

"That's not all," India added. She looked at me and then at the officer. "On the field yesterday, Conner spoke to me making it look like it was a coach talking to a player, but what he said was anything but. It was all a threat."

"What did he say, exactly?" Guerrero asked, and I wanted to know, too.

"He said I had ruined his chances at advancing his career, and that I'd stolen his opportunity. His anger over it creeped me out. He whispered it in my ear from behind. I'm sure he was trying to scare me, but I'm not spooked that easily. He tried to be sneaky with the way he did it all. Anything he says out loud in front of the others seems innocent when it's all threatening."

"Have you informed your boss of this situation?" he asked as he continued to take notes. "Also, can the University trace this email?"

I answered for her. "She's given Coach J a rundown, and he agreed it would be addressed on Monday. That was before she got this email, though. I'm not sure it needs to wait until Monday." The idea of him holding something terrorizing over Indy for another day did not sit well with me.

I watched India out of the corner of my eye. She stared straight ahead and finally spoke. "I'm not good with waiting either. He thinks he's going to get by with this."

"Right." Guerrero leaned back in his chair. "Here's the thing. We don't want to jump the gun on this. Let's let the techies tell us what they can about the email, talk to your coach, and then bring this kid in and see what he says. Having our ducks in a row when we get him here will catch him off guard, and that's where we want him."

I glanced in her direction waiting to see how she felt about waiting. Pulling the trigger on bringing him in right now sounded like a good idea to me, but I needed to let the pros do their jobs.

"I guess that's a good idea. I mean, when we confront him, I want it ended. That's all. I want it done with." Her decision didn't exactly mesh with mine, but I needed to be supportive of her wishes and not cause more anguish.

Guerrero looked at me, and I nodded in agreement. "Okay. So, can you contact the IT department or do I need to get involved to expedite the situation?"

"No," she said and then turned to me. "We can get to the right people, can't we?"

"Yes, we can. I'll call the University president if needed."

"Sounds as though we have a plan for tomorrow then." Guerrero offered his hand as he stood. "India, do you feel safe where you're staying?"

I started to speak for her but backed off.

"Yeah, I'm safe." Her eyes cut over to me. Having her trust me to keep her safe caused a strange feeling to run through me. I'd do whatever it took to make sure she was always taken care of. I'd never felt the need to do this with any other woman, but then she wasn't like any other woman.

"See y'all tomorrow then." He turned and walked away as we made our way back out front to leave.

TIMMS

Sunday afternoon wasn't the best time to find someone from IT, but we managed to get their attention when we showed up in person. Being on the staff made it easier.

"Let's see what we have here." The girl pulled up India's email. Whoever sent it made a mistake to use India's university email.

The young blonde worked her magic across the keyboard and then stopped waiting for the answer.

"This will be a problem."

"What?" We both said at once.

"It was sent from a computer at this address." She continued running her fingers across the keyboard at record-breaking speed. "Yeah, just what I thought. It's a coffee shop here in town, a new one that opened about the same time the semester started. Whoever did it tried to cover their tracks, too. They routed it through some other proxy servers."

"What does that mean?" I asked. All the computer jargon flew over my head. It wasn't my strong suit.

"It means the person who did it is sending it to a lot of other places before it came to her email. They wanted to make it harder to locate, but I went around it. It came from Perk Up. I've been over there a couple of times. They have WiFi and computers to use on site."

India spoke up. "Let's go over there."

The computer wizard continued typing as we spoke. "They might have cameras which would help because all we can do is isolate it to where it was sent from. It looks like the person used one of their computers to send it."

"Thanks for all your help," India told the pony-tailed girl.

She looked at me and smiled. "Anytime, Coach Timms." The way she looked me over normally would've been hot, but right now nothing registered beyond her being helpful. I didn't miss the look of disgust on India's face. Jealousy looked hot on my girl.

India looked down at her and barely smiled. "Thanks again."

As soon as the door closed behind me, she turned and glared at me. "Really?"

Thia Finn

"What?"

"You had to flirt with the help?"

"I'm innocent. Hell, I didn't even give her my full-blown smile."

"Heaven forbid you give her the panty-dropper. We might never get to this place."

"What did you expect me to do, go in and scowl at her?" I was innocent here. Why was she trying to make me feel guilty?

"No, you're right. Sorry. I'm irritated is all. This asswipe is getting on my last nerve with all if this. Why can't people do the right thing?" Opening the door for her, she sat down in the car. I leaned in and took her chin in one hand.

"Sweets, people always want what they can't have."

"I know. I shouldn't take it out on you." I ghosted her lips with mine before she reached up and put her hand on the back of my neck pulling me in for a full-blown, heated kiss.

I smiled at her when I pulled back. "It's going to be fine. We'll get Conner."

We made our way over to the small shop and walked through the door. The best aroma floated around inside, and I knew I'd have to buy a cup before we left.

"What can I get for y'all?" the tall barista asked from behind the counter.

India held up a pic of Conner she had on her phone. "You ever seen this guy?"

The guy leaned over to see the small screen up close. "No, he doesn't look familiar, but I'm only here ten hours a week."

"Okay." She jumped into her interrogation. "Does the store have security cameras? Who has access to view them? When does the manager come in?"

I put my hand on her hip and pulled her to me some. "One at a time, Indy."

She looked at me and then at the worker again. "Sorry."

"No problem." He leaned back down and spoke quietly. "Yeah, there's cameras, but I'm not sure if they're hooked up yet. You know, being a new shop and all." He looked around to see who might have heard his comment. Since there was only one group of giggling high school girls in a corner playing on their phones, I felt like his secret was safe.

"The manager will be here in the morning, and I'm pretty sure he's the only one with access to anything like that." The door opened, and two guys with backpacks walked in looking for a table.

"Okay, can I leave my number for him to call me? It's very important." Then she added, "Please." She topped it off with her own killer smile.

"Uh, sure. If you want, I'll tape it to the office door."

"That's great. Thank you," she added and rattled off her number. "Please tell him how important this information is to me."

"Sure thing." He wrote the number, pulled out a piece of tape from under the counter and affixed it to the closed door at the end of the counter.

"Thanks again, I appreciate your help." India hit him with another smile before we walked out to the car.

"That was a fucking bust." She buckled her seatbelt with a huff.

"You don't know that. As soon as the manager sees it, he might call with what we're looking for."

"Yeah, maybe." She took in a deep breath and let it out slowly. "Why can't anything in my life be simple?"

"Sweets, life would be boring if it were simple." I reached for her hand and kissed the back of it.

"I'm ready for simple. I'm ready to live a normal semester. You know, get up, go to class, coach some kickers, go home to study, watch mindless TV, and go to bed."

"Boring," I said loudly.

"Yeah, I need some boring. Why can't coaching just be easy?"

"It'll get there. The end of the whole damn season will roll around faster than you think."

"Good. I think I'm ready for it."

"The hell you say. We've got a fucking championship to win."

"Right. I forgot." Her lips turned up in a brief smile, but her heart wasn't in it. "Stop by my apartment, so I can get some clothes, please."

"Sure. You can get enough for the week if you want to be safe." Her head whipped around to look at me.

"I think one day will be enough."

"It might be for you, but I'm happy having you at my house all the time." The idea of her not sleeping in my bed didn't sit well with me.

"Timms, I'm not ready to live in your space."

"I didn't say live... I said stay." I grinned at her knowing it was all semantics.

"Right. How about we take it one day at a time and see what's going to happen?"

I huffed out a breath trying to sound mad. "Okay, if you insist. But damn, it's nice waking up with a sweet, hot body wrapped around me."

"If you'd sleep under covers and not just a sheet, I wouldn't need your body heat to stay warm."

"The hell you say, woman. You cannot replace this..." I pointed up and down to myself, "... with a comforter."

"Woman? Okay, caveman." We both laughed. I hoped to lighten the mood before we got home.

We pulled up and walked into my apartment with her packed bag over my shoulder. "I'm sure as hell glad you didn't pack for a week or anything. I could last a month on this much shit."

"It's not all clothes, you know. There're shoes and makeup and coaching clothes."

"Uh, huh. If you say so." I looked down at the unmade bed then turned and grabbed her around the waist. "As long as we're in here..."

"Just looking at the bed makes you think of sex?"

"Hell yeah, it does. All I see in my mind is what we did when we were in it." I pushed her until she fell backward taking me down with her.

She wrapped her arms around my neck and pulled my face down to hers. "Kiss me."

"You don't have to ask, babe." I kissed her nose, then her cheek before I nibbled my way along her jaw working my way toward her lips. After nibbling on each end of her mouth, I ran my tongue over the lips that were barely making a smile.

"Make me forget about this, please, if only for tonight?"

"I tell you what. How about I run you a bubble bath and let you soak with a big glass of wine while I get us some dinner together, and then we'll go from there?"

"Sounds wonderful to me."

I got up and walked to the bathroom, starting the hot water—lucky this apartment came with a whirlpool tub. She walked in and stood watching the water. After adding relaxing crystals to the water that someone left under my sink, I turned to her.

Her shirt slipped over her head easily before I unhooked the lacy bra she wore. Sliding it down her arms allowed her beautiful tits to be released. They called to me to show them some love, but right now Indy needed to get in the hot water.

I reached down and pushed the button starting the jets causing the bubbles to build and the floral fragrance to take over the bathroom. Turning back to her, I unhooked the button of her shorts and pulled them down with her panties all at once. Kneeling before her and looking up, she looked like a goddess standing before me. Her smooth, soft skin still had a summer glow of warm golden brown. I couldn't resist leaving one kiss on her bare lips that had a siren's call to my ears.

She ran her fingers through my hair and sucked in a breath. When she refused to release me, I knew she needed more than one kiss to her sweet spot. My hands wrapped around her ankles and slid up the calves slowly. All her time spent demonstrating her kicks kept them tight and toned, but the skin had a silky feel.

Leaning down, I kissed the inside of her knees with my hands cupping the backs of her thighs as my tongue traced a line up her smooth leg to the spot begging for attention. When I skipped over it and started up the opposite leg, she made a pouting sound. It didn't last long, and my tongue inched along at a slow, agonizing pace.

My right hand bumped her legs further apart as my left one wrapped around her below her hip bones leaving my thumbs to manipulate the lips that hid what I sought. My flattened tongue slowly licked up her barely parted lips just getting the tip of the hardened nub as it peaked through. The slight moan that escaped from India caused my lips to turn up at the ends knowing the teasing caused it.

Before swiping down the same path, I parted her with my thumbs gaining full access to the bundle of swollen nerves. The tip of my tongue lingered over them, circled them, flicked them to the point that the moans she gave me were loud and needy.

"Timms." Her breathy sound told me she was close to cumming on my tongue alone, so I sucked the nub into my mouth and tantalized it until she bucked against me and cried out a low, long wail all while holding my head to her body.

As she came down from the pure pleasure, I eased off and looked up. The stormy look in her eyes made me want to stand and take her against the counter, but this was about making her feel good. I picked her up and lowered her limp body in the swirling hot water. I kneeled next to the tub to put a rolled towel behind her head to rest against.

"Relax, babe. I'll go make dinner."

A soft, "uh, huh" was all I got.

INDIA

"Hurry up, Timms," I yelled down the hallway toward the bedroom.

"That's not what you said last night." A high-pitched voice mimicked me, "Go slow honey. Yeah, now move your tongue just like this. Slurp, slurp, slurp."

"You're nasty. You know it?" I looked at him walking through the doorway making the slurping noises.

"You love it, and you know it." Again with the female tone. "Yes baby, your dick's the perfect size," followed by more disgusting noises while he made a humping motion.

"Stop. Stop, please," I asked nicely.

He laughed at me. "Okay, but you know I speak the truth." This time it was more of a Darth Vader voice.

"Thank you. I want to be sitting in Coach J's office when he calls Conner. I need to be prepared.

"Sweets, we'll be there in plenty of time. Calm down."

"This is important, and you're making it all into a big joke." I didn't want to sound like a pouty girl, but this was serious.

He walked up and put his arms around me. "India, it's going to be all right. Today, we'll get this figured out. He's going to have to come clean, and then Coach J can kick him off the team, and you can be done with him. I have confidence in Coach and you to get this settled, and if that doesn't work, we'll get Guerrero involved. He'll scare the kid back home."

I rested my forehead on his chest and wrapped my arms around his waist. "I hope you're right. I want it behind me so I can move on, and do the job I was hired to do."

"And you will. After today, we'll be done. Now put your big girl coach shorts on, and let's go kick some ass."

I nodded and let him go.

For some reason, I felt like my feet slugged through wet cement as we made our way up to the steps of the athletic building. A thousand possible scenarios ran through my brain. What if Coach J didn't get it settled?

What if the police were no help? What would I do then?

Timms knocked on the door before opening it. "Morning, Coach," he greeted the older man sitting behind his desk.

"Both of you come on in, and let's get this taken care of." He had his no-nonsense voice working this morning. "We'll call Conner and tell him to come here first thing this morning. Are you good with that, India?"

"Yes, sir. I want it done and behind me."

"Good. We've got a new team and a new week to prepare for." He picked up his desk phone and called the number he had on a card in front of him.

"Conner, this is Coach Jefferies. I need to see you in my office this morning. What time can you be here without missing a class?"

"Uh, huh. Okay. I'll see you then. Be prompt. I don't have time to waste today waiting around on you, understand?"

"Right." He hung the phone up and looked up at me. "He'll be here after his eight o'clock class lets out at 8:50."

Timms stood. "Good, that'll give us time to get some more coffee."

Coach nodded at him. "Y'all be back here by 8:45." Timms gave him a salute.

The coffee shop on campus had the same vibe as the one I frequented as an undergrad. Students were rushing, studying, and surfing the net all inside a twenty by twenty room with aromas made to perk up anyone. Compared to the one we visited over the weekend, it was alive.

"Coffee and muffin?" Timms asked, and I nodded.

I took a seat to see the doorway. People-watching always interested me, and Monday morning on a college campus offered lots of subjects to observe.

"Here ya go." Timms set down a tray loaded with breakfast goodies.

"You must be hungry. Did you buy one of everything on the counter?" I smiled at him.

"It's too damn hard to decide with that many choices." He popped a mini muffin in his mouth.

As I opened my coffee, I saw Drew walk in and waved at him. He returned the gesture and got in line with barely a glance. Hmm, he must still be asleep. He glanced our direction and grinned at the two of us when he headed out the door.

"I'm surprised he didn't stop by and say hi," I said before sipping the mocha latte.

"Probably late for class already."

Looking down at my phone. "Yeah, we better go, too. I want to be there in plenty of time."

The doorway to the athletics building had a few people standing around waiting when we started up the steps. "Have you thought about what you were going to say to Conner when we meet?"

"Yeah, a lot. I want him to own up to his actions before I consider allowing him to return to the team, including the notes and the email. I don't think I can trust him at all if he's not willing to admit his mistakes."

"I'll be surprised if he comes clean. He's probably not all that fucking excited about owning his shit. People like him rarely are."

"I know you're right, but how can I even think about trusting him on the field if I can't believe a damn thing he says off the field." I threw my cup away and turned back to the hot guy watching me. "Come on, Coach Sexy. Let's get this over with."

"Coach Sexy, huh?" He smiled at me. "I like it."

"Figured you would and don't let it go to your head." I leaned closer to him. "Either head."

"Awww, sweets. You know us too well."

I glanced down to his junk. "Hell yeah, you got that right."

Coach J sat behind his desk looking at the playbook as we walked in and sat down.

"Working on something new, Coach?"

"Always, Timms. Always." He looked up from the book. "You planning on sitting in on this meeting?"

"I'd like to, but if you think it's not right, I'll wait in the locker room or the hall."

"It's up to India. I don't care."

I shrugged a shoulder. I wanted him there since he knew all the different things that were going on. I only expected Coach J to deal with Conner's problems on the field.

A knock on the door startled me.

"India?" Coach asked, still waiting on the call with Timms.

"I'm good with him being here."

"Fine." He looked at the door and yelled, "Come in."

Conner walked in and looked at the three of us. "Hey, Coach. Didn't know we were having a big meeting. What's going on?"

His innocent act made me want to gag. Who did this little shit think he was dealing with? I told him his actions wouldn't fly, and now he was going to know why.

Coach J stood up and came around the desk, so we sat in a square. "Conner, we seem to have a problem that needs to be settled if you plan to stay on this team."

With complete innocence in his voice, Conner responded, "For reals, Coach J? I thought things were going well. I know I didn't get to start because I'd missed practice, and I apologized several times to Coach Durham. I thought she understood."

If it were possible, I could shove the steam out my ears, and it wouldn't be the first time over something this kid said or did. Losing my shit over something he said or did would be so simple right now. I took another deep breath. If he kept this up, I might hyperventilate trying to stay calm.

"Is that so, son, because I have several players who observed you trying to pull some tactics that appeared to put your coach on edge."

"Really? I'd never intentionally try to intimidate you, Coach D." He turned and gave me a look of pure innocence. This kid deserved an Oscar. "I'm so sorry you feel this way. I'd never do anything to make you feel uncomfortable." His voice grated on my last nerve.

"Is that right, Conner? What about when you purposely spoke into my ear on the sidelines when Ian prepared to kick the first kick?" I drilled him with a hard stare.

"Oh, I thought you understood. The crowd's yelling topped anything I could do, so I had to speak in your ear. I meant no disrespect, ma'am, but I wanted you to hear what I had to say."

Ugh. The lying shit frustrated the hell out of me. He twisted things, so it was always going to be his word against mine. I dropped my eyes to the floor in front of me intent on remaining calm and professional.

He was staring at me when I raised my head. "So this is how you're going to play it?"

"Coach, I know I've not given you a good reason to trust me with missing practice and all, but I had some issues I needed to deal with when I came to this campus. They were personal, but I'm trying to outgrow them and deal in my own way."

The deep breath I held whooshed out. As much as I wanted to believe him, there was still the matter of him getting Ian arrested and then the notes and email. How could I possibly overlook his actions? Each act needed addressing.

"Let's start at the beginning and talk about each event you took part in. Shall we?"

He nodded. "Yes, please. That's a great idea. So shoot." Now he was teasing, and unlike him steering me down the path to pass over admitting his guilt, I needed him to confess it.

Timms spoke up. "Let's talk about the notes being left on Coach D's car."

"Notes? I haven't left any notes, Coach. I've only spoken to you in person. Where were the notes?" He knew I would have no way of connecting him to the notes. I'd even thrown the first away, so how could I use it against him?

Coach J cut his eyes over to me. Notes were news to him, and I hated he'd been kept in the dark, but this all needed to be brought to light now.

"So you're saying you don't know anything about notes?"

"No, ma'am. I don't." This guy's innocent act was outstanding.

"Okay. What do you know about Ian's arrest?" Timms asked what I thought.

"Only that you guys all thought I did it. That officer was on a fishing expedition when he brought me in. He had nothing on me. I've been brought in before by the cops. I knew the game he played trying to get me to admit to something I had nothing to do with." His eyes never left mine. If he lied, he didn't exhibit any of the signs, but I couldn't forget the actual words he'd used with me when others couldn't hear. He wasn't completely innocent in all this.

I stood and walked over to the window and leaned against it. "Well, let's talk about what you said to me about not getting to kick on Saturday. You can't deny what you said to me was meant to intimidate me not to mention sexist. I could file charges for sexual harassment on you today."

Conner shook his head. "Okay, you've got me on that, Coach." He stood and faced me, but didn't get close because Timms' face told him he better not even try. "I'm sorry, Coach Durham. Truly sorry for all I've said that offended you. I do have issues with working for a woman. If you knew the wrongs that had been done to me in the past by women, you'd understand why I don't have the kind of respect I should have for them."

"Why are you just now telling us about this problem, Conner?" Coach J asked in a calm voice.

His head swiveled quickly to look at the older man. "Do you think I like admitting this to people? Do any of you think I like talking about my mom working for a pimp most of my life? Men coming in and out of our shack of an apartment? Me listening to her and her friends talk about sex like it was just another day on the block?" His voice got higher with each question.

"Every day of my life, my mom had johns on top of her. Every damn day. She didn't care if I watched or not when she kneeled before strange men and sucked them off. As long as she got paid for her work, she didn't give a shit about me. She loved those other hos more than me, and they were no different from her. Hell, I'd seen orgies happen so many times, I thought group sex was normal.

"Then I found football. I was pretty good at playing the game, but one coach told me with my muscular legs, I should try kicking. He taught me how and kicking came naturally to me. I didn't need other people around to practice. That man gave me a ball and a kicking tee of my own. When those men came in, I picked up my stuff and left for the empty lot behind our apartment, and I kicked. I kicked until my toes bled. I kicked until the muscles in my right leg hurt so bad, I'd almost have to crawl home. I kicked until I knew my bedroom would be empty and then I'd go home and sleep.

"I'd known that coach a week. One damn week. He made more of an impact on me than my mom, and her friends had done all my life. He praised me when I did it right and showed me the right way when I didn't. For once in my life, I was told I had worth in this world, something no female had ever done... still hadn't ever done. Do I have a problem with women? Hell yeah, I do, and then I show up here and am expected to work for one who once again thinks I'm not good enough for the job."

He turned to me. "Yeah, you told me when I did it right, but if I didn't do it your way, you'd tell me I did it wrong. I couldn't handle it, so I did what I know how to do. I tried to put you in your place through intimidation. It's the only way I know to deal with women like you."

The three of us listening to the story stared at that kid. The words I wanted to say when I walked in the coaching office were stuck in my throat. Processing Conner's story felt impossible.

Coach J walked over to Conner and put his arms around the big kid and hugged him for a minute and then stepped back. The shock on the player's face shined red. "Conner, I see we have some things we need to work on with you. You've been dealt a shit hand in life, but a lot of us have. Life isn't always good, son. We have to separate the bad from the good and keep working on the good. That coach you had, saw your good. He set you on the right path to work on it and look where it's gotten you. You can't lose sight of it, though, son. You've got to continue moving in the right direction, and eventually, you'll get there. Right now, you're so close you can taste it, too. Let's not stray from that path.

Coach J turned to me. "If Coach Durham thinks you have the skills, we can all work together to get you on the field." Conner's lips turned upward but not in a full smile.

"Are we going to overlook what you've done? No, we aren't, but we are going to deal with your mistakes, call it even, and move on. Can you accept that, if Coach Durham is willing to?"

The kid looked at me waiting to see my reaction to my boss' plan. I looked at Timms to see how he took the idea, and he gave me a quick nod. I felt like I could live with it if Conner were willing to work for the position.

"I'm willing to try, Conner, but you have to give me one hundred percent and no attitude. I'm not going to sacrifice the rest of the team's hard work to hand you the position. They've worked from day one, especially Ian." I paused and continued, "The first thing we have to have is complete honesty."

"Yes, ma'am. I know that."

"Then start with Ian's incident. Did you have anything to do with it?"

"No, ma'am, I did not. I might not be happy that he took what I felt was mine, but I didn't sabotage him to get it back. I promise you."

"Why did you come into the police station with such an attitude?"

"Because I've been in trouble before, and I know how they work. You show any weakness and those cops are all over you blaming you for something you didn't do." The hard look told me he'd been in situations that cost him.

"Okay." There was nothing left to say. "If Conner is willing to accept the punishment for his mistakes, then I can move on and coach him. We'll let Coach J levy the sentence."

The head coach stepped up and said he'd take care of it. Timms and I shook my redeemed player's hand. "We'll see you at practice today."

"Yes, ma'am. Thank you. Thank you all."

For the first time, I believed I saw the kid for who he could be instead of what he tried to be. I prayed he lived up to our expectations and his own.

The door closed behind the smiling player, and Coach J turned me. "Now, India, I believe you have some things to tell me to get me up to speed on all your problems. Let's start with why I'm just now hearing them, please."

TIMMS

Practice buzzed all week with excitement after last Saturday's win, but one win did not make a season. By the time the second game rolled around, changes had been made, new players fought and won a try for spots, and the team was meshing as it should. Conner stepped up and joined the other four with a renewed desire to be part of the team. He proved over and over his worth to both India and the three underclassmen.

On Friday, when Coach J called for special teams to run through the kick, they each had an opportunity to try. It was decided that Ian would handle kickoffs while Conner would take the field goals and extra points. Zac held the ball each time it was needed. It looked like we would be red-shirting Drew. He'd come a long way, but we needed to keep working with him. Since he hadn't played a down of football, the eligibility to tag him for four more years remained.

The team gelled as it should by the time the game came to an end with the Rams beating the opponents by thirty-five points.

The roar in the locker room could be heard for miles. Everyone's excitement and enthusiasm spelled winners. Our season looked locked and loaded for champions.

"I can't believe the players are so excited." India walked in with the rest of the coaching staff. "It's only the last preseason game. We've got a shitload of great teams to beat to get to the championships."

"Okay, Debbie Downer." I laughed at her. "Let's at least enjoy the fucking win before we start thinking regular season."

"Sorry. I don't like making assumptions about anything this soon."

"Hell, Coach. It's a win. Enjoy it." The bright smile broke over her face followed by a sultry hooded look that told me she was excited about more than celebrating a win.

I watched her as Coach J spoke to the team. She kept her thrill of the win contained. Walking over to her, I leaned down and whispered, "What's going on in that crazy head of yours. You look like something's up."

She cut her eyes over at me and turned to whisper, "Something's going to be up all right in about thirty minutes, give or take." She wiggled her eyebrows at me.

Holy hell. This girl could make me hard with only a look and a few words. "Standing in a locker room with half-dressed guys is no place for a boner, India." I kissed her earlobe before I backed away. "Good thing we are standing behind everyone else."

The little minx stepped behind me and moved far enough forward that her tits rubbed against my back. Hard nipples slowly moved from one side to the other a few times making my dick want to stand at attention. Glancing over my shoulder, I whispered, "Stop." It only seemed to spur her on more.

She'd only heard stories of the college fun and games with sex in public places, but we couldn't do that now. We both had too much at stake.

India stepped beside me and slid in front this time. "What are you up to, sweets?"

Grinning over her shoulder, she backed as close to me as she could get while watching the others standing in front of us listen to Coach J's congratulatory speech. Damn, I hoped he didn't go on and on.

The arm hanging by her side slowly inched around her hip until her hand lined up with my semi-hard erection. I'd managed to keep it somewhat in check until she closed her hands around what she could over my coaching shorts. As her hand outlined my dick, it continued to get harder with each move up and down the shaft.

"India, you have to stop," I said directly into her ear and sharply bit the lobe this time.

"Oww!" she squealed, and everyone turned to look at her.

"Sorry, I broke a nail." Her lie gained her eye rolls from the team.

"What a girlie thing to say, sweets."

Once everyone turned back to Coach J, she grabbed my dick with both hands behind her back. Her legs began to bounce her back and forth as though she was rocking to an internal beat based on the great words the coach spoke.

I wanted to throw her over my shoulder and run out the door to find the nearest private location and fuck her senseless for pulling this stunt by the time he finished his speech. When he spoke the last word, I grabbed her upper arm and dragged her down the hallway to the women's locker area where she dressed. I knew it would be empty.

"What are you doing, Timms?"

"No, the question is, where am I doing it, you devil in disguise. Does winning a game make you horny?"

As soon as the locker door shut, she pulled out of my hold and ran off to the coach's private restroom. I walked through the doorway, and she pushed it closed with a bang before locking it.

"You're mine now." Her voice oozed sex as she backed away dropping one piece of clothing at a time until she stood before me naked and unafraid.

"Damn, sweets. You look good enough to eat."

"I'm game, but you have too many clothes on. Let me help you with that." She pulled my shirttail up, and I jerked it over my head.

"Mmm. I like it," she whispered as she dropped wet and hot kisses down between the muscles of my pecs. She continued down until she reached the top of my shorts before kneeling. "These need to go. They're blocking all my senses. I want to see your hot cock and taste it between my lips and feel it with my tongue and touch the long shaft and smooth head and smell the sex we are going to have."

"Son of a bitch, India." I pulled her sweet body up and turned her around, pushing her hot body against the cold white subway tile causing her tits to mash against it.

"Oh. That makes them hurt, Timms."

"Good. You made me hurt the whole time your hand clutched around my hard cock in the meeting. You're going to pay for that."

I lined my dick up against her crack and wrapped it between the two cheeks. I moved rubbing the head across her tight opening each time I went up and down making sure to push against it.

"Timms," she yelled my name. "I can't decide if it hurts or feels good."

"I'll only do what feels good, sweets." I backed away and moved her over to the sink before bending her forward. "Grab the sink, babe. This is going to be one hard fucking. You'll think it's a punishment until I make you cum in so many good ways, you'll know it's all a gift."

I reached around and took both nipples with my thumbs and first fingers, pinching and rolling them with some pressure. "I want you to feel me here, India. I want it to almost hurt, but not. Tell me when I'm there." I squeezed a little harder and pulled the swollen nubs outward, shaking them back and forth.

"Is it enough? Do you feel it, Indy? Is it barely hurting?" I shook them again, and I knew from the way her breath sucked in she was there.

"Yes, Timms, yes." I let go to line my dick up with her opening knowing she would be wet for me from the nipple play and her reaction to it. "No, Timms, no. Don't stop."

"Oh babe, I'm not stopping. I'm getting ready to go harder and deeper than ever before." I slid the head up and down gathering all the liquid she held waiting for my entrance.

"Do it, Timms." I pushed only the head in as I reached around and took the lonely nipple waiting for the pain and pleasure to go together.

When I pinched the pebbles, and she started to scream, I pushed in hard and fast to the hilt, stopping both actions when I was fully seated inside her warmth. "You ready, sweets?"

"I'm sooo ready." I rolled the nipples and squeezed as I fucked her hard and fast while she used the sink as leverage to deepen the motion with each push and pull.

"Damn, India. It feels so fucking good. I'm not going to last long at this pace."

"Me either, but I love it hot and hard like this, so don't stop." She reached down between her legs and scissored her fingers to each side of my dick as I moved in and out, then took the cum to trace around her clit. Watching this in the mirrors to our side and in front of us made it even hotter.

"Watch yourself, babe. Look in the mirror and watch us both cum." I caught her eyes and saw them move between our fucking and my face. It only took a few seconds before I felt ripples against my dick from her walls, and I knew she was as close as me.

"Cum for me, babe. Cum now. Cum now with me." I yelled, "Cum now, India," as I shot hot lines into her while her slick walls spasmed on me, wringing out every drop as I strung out her orgasm as long as possible.

"Shiiittt," she said in a moaning voice. I leaned over covering her back and held her as our bodies slowly descended back to normal breathing. "That was some good shit, Timms, and I needed it just like that."

"Anytime, anywhere, babe. All you gotta do is tell me." I leaned down over her and kissed up her spine before laying my head against her soft skin.

A little while later, I stood up bringing her with me, and we both looked in the mirror. Her beauty glowed with a fresh fucked face and sex hair. "God, you're beautiful, Indy."

She returned it with a sexy smile and turned toward me. "Thank you."

"Let's go home now."

"I'm good with that. My home or yours?"

"I don't care. I just want to be where you are."

She looked up at me and kissed me slowly running her tongue over my bottom lip and sucked it into her mouth. "I feel the same."

"Why don't we go get your stuff and move it in with mine?"

She pinched her eyebrows together. "You want us to move in together already? Don't you think it's a little soon, Timms?"

"No, I don't. I want to wake up looking at your beautiful face and go to sleep doing the same."

"I'm not sure, Timms. It's been such a short amount of time for us. I mean, my heart says go with it, but my mind is asking is it a wise decision." I looked and saw the sincerity of his offer and the question still fresh on his drop-dead gorgeous face. He gave me that panty-dropping smile. "Well, when you put it that way, how can I say no?"

"Would it be too soon to tell you I love you?" I wanted to test it out on her, but I meant every word.

She cocked her head to one side and stared at me as though she were trying to come up with a reply. Finally, opening her mouth, she started to speak and then stopped. On her second try, she said, "I don't know. If I said I loved you back, would it be too soon?"

"Hell no, it wouldn't."

"Good. I love you, Theo Timms."

"That sounds perfect coming from your sweet lips. I love you, too, India Durham."

She let out a breath. "Shew, glad you said that. It would have been awkward if you decided it was too soon."

I smiled at her. "Let's go home, babe."

The day couldn't have been more perfect. We won with plenty of extra points. We had awesome sex in an unusual place. My girl said she loved me. What more could we ask for? That was an easy answer until she saw the white paper under the wiper blade.

"What the fuck?" her voice strained. She pulled it out from the rubber strip.

It read, *"Watch closely, it's not over."*

"Dammit, I'm going to kill someone," she said as she looked over at me.

INDIA

"Holy shit, how the hell can this be still happening?" I screamed it when I walked in the door to my apartment.

"I don't know, but we're getting to the fucking bottom of this. I'm ready to kill whoever's doing it."

"Dude, you're standing in the damn line behind me. I was upset and worried before. Now, I'm beyond pissed."

"How do you want to handle this?" The look on Timms' face told me his worrying was intense.

"I'm calling Guerrero, and then I'm getting a fucking gun. I'm gonna shoot someone's dick off."

"If you're going to shoot, you better aim to kill and shooting his dick won't do it."

"That's not funny, Timms." The force in my voice told him I was not amused one single bit.

"I know. This is serious, sweets."

After calling Guerrero to meet us at the police station, we drove over and walked in. I'd picked up the paper but then used a rubber glove on it in case he could get some prints off it.

"At it again, huh?" Guerrero greeted us.

"Yeah, but maybe we can get something off this, this time." I handed him a baggie holding the latest note.

His skeptical look told me he didn't hold much hope with the evidence. "We might get some prints, but you know unless they've been fingerprinted before, we won't be able to identify them. I want you to sit down and tell me everyone you've had an interaction with since you've been on campus. There shouldn't be too many since you're new to the University. Do you know anyone from your undergrad days that followed you to TAU?"

"No, no one."

"Right." He pushed a yellow pad over to me. "Start thinking, and I'll see what I can pull off this."

"Babe, how many enemies can you have made so soon? Who else do you know besides the team? Have you met anyone from your classes?"

"I've only been to class once. There's no way it was someone outside the football program. All the notes seemed football related."

After an exhausting evening at the station, we made our way back home to Timms' apartment. People stood around the doorway waiting for us.

"Why are they here?" I didn't want company. I wanted to veg out and not think for a while with this guy who loved me.

"It's a tradition to celebrate, sweets. I'll make them leave if you want."

"No, it's fine. Maybe they'll distract me from thinking about bad things."

"You mean like killing people?"

"Exactly."

Blue called out to us, "Well, fucking finally. Where y'all been?"

"Long story," Timms greeted them and bumped shoulders in a man hug. "Great fucking game today, dude."

"Thanks, man. Appreciate it." Blue's proud grin stretched across his face. Wrapped around his middle was Noelle. I'd met her once before.

She let go and stepped forward and hugged me. "Great job to you, too, Coach Durham. Your team did awesome work."

"Thanks, Noelle."

"I know you probably are the least commended on the team."

"Yeah, it's the nature of the squad. They only like us when we score under pressure in the last three seconds." We both laughed. "Y'all come in."

"Quinn's coming by, too. She's pouting because Gerrod couldn't be here this week so watch out."

"I've only met her once. She seemed great then." Timms and Blue looked at me.

Timms laughed. "You haven't met the real Quinn. She and your sister could be BFF's from what you've said about Chyna."

I looked at Noelle. "So her mouth's rated X?"

"Yeah like the X on a pirate map."

"Cut from the same cloth then. Chyna's terrible."

"So is Quinn. Just wait till she gets some alcohol and gets started on Gerrod not being here," Blue added.

We all grabbed a beer and went to the back patio to relax. The evening colored skies were starting to appear sooner with fall coming upon us.

"Where y'all been, anyway? First, you disappear immediately after Coach J talks, and then you're gone when we get here," Blue asked in all innocence.

Timms started laughing. "We had a little meeting of our own in the women's locker room after the victory speech."

"Timms!" We didn't need to tell that."

Blue held up his hand to congratulate Timms. "Good job, dude. Never made it happen in that room of the athletics building. Hell, you two probably christened it."

"Blue, you're embarrassing India."

"Oops, sorry, Coach D."

"I think India is fine here in our home, Blue."

His head jerked up. "What's this shit, *our home*?" he asked.

Timms spoke before I could. "Yeah, she's moving in with me."

"Congrats, man, or I should say congrats to India. The woman who finally captured Theo Timms. Do you know how many women spent four long, sad years trying to do that?"

"That's enough, Blue," Timms said with a growl in his voice. "We don't need to talk about frat days."

"Oh remember that time—"

"Shut up, Blue," we all said in unison.

We sat around enjoying the evening, and it would have been perfect if the note hadn't destroyed the idea of celebrating a win. While the group laughed and talked, my thoughts centered around who could still be trying to harass me. I wanted to believe Conner didn't do it, but who else could it be?

"Earth to India." Noelle snapped her fingers. "Let's get some more beer," she suggested.

I looked around coming back to earth and the conversation. "Oh yeah, sure." Standing up, I followed her into the kitchen.

She stopped and spun on me when we made it through the doorway away from the guys. "What's going on, India? I mean, we don't know each other all that well, but I can tell you're worried about something or not happy we're here. We can go if y'all want to be alone. I mean, I understand completely.

Deciding to move in is a huge step, and you might want to celebrate."

"Oh, no. It's not that at all. I'm glad you're here. We're happy to have company."

"Then what's going on?" She wasn't letting it go.

"There's a problem with something on the team. It's been causing me a lot of stress."

"Do Blue and Timms need to kick some ass?" She grinned.

"Uh, no. Not at all. I'm the one who needs to kick some ass."

"A girl is causing you a problem? I know Timms is hot and all, and I know the football groupies can be a pain." She waited for an answer.

"No. Well, I'm not sure. Maybe?" Evasive much?

"And you don't want to talk about it?"

"I can't. We've had to get the police involved, and we were told not to say anything." I tried to be as honest as I could.

"Okay, but please know I'm here for you. You don't have time to make girlfriends around here, and I know we could be great friends." She glanced out the patio doors where the guys all sat laughing and talking. "After all, look at who we chose as partners."

I turned my head in the same direction and thought about what Noelle said while she rummaged around in the refrigerator for a beer. Her comment made sense. I didn't have time to make female friends when I spent all day with guys. Other than the ones Timms had introduced me to, I hadn't even met another woman. With our guys being great friends, we would be spending time together.

Her second comment made me think about this relationship I suddenly found myself living in. I'd never been in real love before. My gaze moved to Timms sitting there with the others. He enjoyed spending time with these people.

They all seemed to be the kind of guys I enjoyed hanging out with. The loyalty they shared with one another surprised me. I guess I never had girlfriends long enough to have that kind of relationship.

I turned to Noelle. "Thank you. I'd like that. Other than my sister, I don't have any female friends."

A beautiful smile lit up her face. "Just wait until we can get your sister and Quinn together. They are going to be so much fun."

I rolled my eyes. "Sometimes my sister embarrasses me to death, but I love her all the same."

"And you'll learn to love Quinn, too. I promise," she added as we made our way back to the patio.

As the last two walked out the door, I put my arms around Timms' waist. "That was so fun having friends over. Thank you for making me take the time to socialize. I'd have probably just gone home and wallowed in my misery over that damn note."

"Shhh. I don't want to think about that."

"Yeah, me neither."

He locked the door and turned out the lights while I waited at the hallway door. Holding out my hand to him, he clasped his to mine. I looked up at him and back to our joined hands. "I think I'm going to like this arrangement. What about you?" We took steps down the hall together.

"Sweets, it's the best decision I've made in a long time." I stopped after passing through the doorway, and his body nestled up against my back as he wrapped his arms around me.

"Yeah, I think so for me, too."

"I'm in the mood for celebrating. What about you?" He moved my hair over to one side and left a line of kisses across my shoulder and up the curve of my neck. "I want us to get the rest of your stuff moved in tomorrow." More soft kisses were left under my ear. "Are you good with that?"

I moaned as he nibbled on my earlobe. "Uh, huh. I'm very good with that."

"I like doing things that make you moan. Let's see what else I can do." He scooped me up and kicked the bedroom door shut.

Walking down the sidewalk, I knew we were both anxious to see if a note waited on my windshield.

"Let's take both cars over to the apartment. I have a lot of stuff, but I think we can get it all in one load with two." I spoke with my eyes trained on my car which sat beside his. I let out the breath I held when I saw nothing under the wiper.

"Sweets, take it easy. I know what you were expecting because I was, too. But we can't let this asshole dictate our lives. We'll get whoever it is, I promise."

He shut my door, and I backed out hearing him revving up the engine causing the loud motor to attract attention. He pulled in behind me on the road. We only lived a few blocks apart, so the trip took minutes. I turned down the row of parking places when I saw someone running from my front doorway.

I sped up to get a better look at the tall person, but he rounded the corner going to another set of buildings before I could catch up with him. I turned into a spot and jumped out determined to see who it was. If he hadn't run, I wouldn't have been suspicious but watching a tall man running away from my front door caused every hair on my neck to stand on end.

"India? What the fuck are you doing? Stop!" Timms yelled getting out of his car.

"Come on. Someone was coming out from my apartment and took off running when he saw me." We both turned the corner between the buildings and nothing. Early Sunday morning the courtyard resembled a ghost town.

"The guy must live here or have a friend who does." Timms walked in a large circle looking at each patio area of the bottom-floor apartments. "Do you know anyone else living here?"

"No, I haven't had time to meet anyone. I don't even know my neighbors."

"All the more reason for you to move in with me. This shit's not gonna fly having you here alone."

"I know. Let's go back and get packing."

Backing our cars into the slots, we found my front door lock hanging from a hole in the wooden door.

"Damn, whoever did this wanted in bad enough to risk making noise." Timms stopped me from touching anything. "Call the police. This person's getting out of control, Indy. They need to step up this investigation."

A little while later, Officer Guerrero found us sitting on the steps to the second floor. "Looks like the situation is escalating, Ms. Durham. Still no idea who it is?"

"No, not really but we're pretty sure it's not Conner." We explained the meeting to him.

"Yeah, sounds like it's probably not him. We'll still check in with him, though. Some people are very good at covering up." A couple of people walked in and started looking around the apartment.

"I didn't go in there to see if anything was missing."

"Smart move, but now we need you to go in and look around. Tell us what you don't find, but I'll be surprised if anything's missing. This person isn't out to rob you."

The three of us made our way through the small group of rooms. I pushed open the jarred door to my bedroom with my foot, afraid to touch anything. We found what we were looking for—bright red spray paint above my bed.

"You've made your bed" marked the wall with a big arrow pointing down to my bed.

"What the hell does that mean?" I didn't understand the message.

"India, have you made some important decisions since the last note?"

"She decided to move into my apartment yesterday, but only our close friends know that."

"No one could have heard you discussing this?" The cop wrote something in his notebook.

"No." I thought back to where we had sex in the women's locker room bathroom. Could someone have been outside the door listening to us? That creeped me out. My eyes met Timms, and I knew he thought the same thing I did.

Timms turned to Guerrero. "Yes, someone could have heard it. We made the decision yesterday and talked about it."

"Where were you?"

I dropped my head, and Timms continued to talk, "We were in the bathroom of the women's locker area after the game." The policeman looked up from where he was writing as if he needed clarification to process what Timms had told him. Neither of us said another word, but Timms did nod his head once.

"Okay. Well, let's say someone was outside the door of the restroom. Did either of you hear anything unusual?"

"We weren't paying attention to anyone else. We were kinda busy celebrating the win."

I glared at Timms. This was no time for bragging about having locker-room sex.

"I understand." Guerrero wrote some more.

"Did you discuss this anywhere else?" He looked between the two of us.

"I told our friends who came over to Timms' apartment later."

"Right. Well, let us do our job, and we'll see if we can find any evidence from inside here that's useful to us. Come back later and pick up what you need for the week. I don't need to tell you to be careful. This person has proven he has access to you and can strike anytime so be vigilant."

"Not a problem. She's not going anywhere without me until this shit's over," Timms offered his solution.

"I'll be vigilant as you suggested, Officer. Thank you."

I looked around my bedroom.

I felt violated.

Someone had invaded my world. They'd touched objects I touched. I wanted to throw it all away and buy new everything.

"I don't want to take these things to your apartment."

"Then don't. We'll go buy new stuff."

"That's crazy, though, and expensive. I'll just wash it all." Using my thumb and index finger, I picked up a tainted bra hanging out of my lingerie drawer.

"Indy, let it go." He pulled it out of my fingers and dropped it on the floor. "We'll go buy new things. You obviously won't ever wear any of this after he's touched it. I'll buy it for you. It'll be fun shopping for you in that *Secret* store. It'll take your mind off all this shit anyway. Don't all females love retail therapy?"

"I guess."

My mind continued to mull over what this person looked like wandering around my bedroom.

TIMMS

"I know you didn't want to buy new scraps of material, but damn, I think this is the best shopping trip I've ever been on." I held up a tiny piece of lace and silk. "Are these underwear?"

"I'm not in the mood, Timms." My anger flared. He laughed at me. "There isn't a fucking thing funny about having to buy all new panties and bras."

"I don't recall saying anything about it being funny. Sexy, hell yeah. Funny, not so much. Fun? Abso-fucking-lutely. Best shopping ever. Now, what color do you like?"

"Beige."

"Beige is boring. I like this one." I held up hot pink with some feather looking strings on the edges."

222222alral Moves

"No. Hell no. I'm not wasting money on that."

"Sweets, there's nothing about this that says wasted money. It makes my dick hard rubbing the feathers on my hand."

"You're too easy, like most men."

"Don't care. I'm buying it."

"No, you're not." She picked up a lacy black thong.

"Okay, now we're getting somewhere. Get that in every color."

"No, I like other styles as well."

"I like you in other styles, too." I leaned forward and whispered, "Maybe we are wasting money. Go commando. Makes getting to your best spots easier."

"Eww, that's gross." She picked up several pairs in her two favorite styles.

"What about one of these, Indy?" I held up a silky garter belt.

"No. Waste of money."

"In whose book? I like it."

"You want me to wear this? Under my coach shorts?"

"Fuck yeah." I stopped and ran my palm down the back of my head and neck. "Well, maybe not a good plan. I'd have a permanent boner on the side of the field while trying to coach Crew. Who knows what that little prick would say."

"Exactly." She continued around the store and picked up frilly bras and little sleep shorts. "Okay. I'm done."

"But most of that black bag is beige and black."

"That's what I need."

"Uh, no. Let's get some things you don't need, but you want."

"I have what I want."

"Then let's get things I want." I wandered through the store with my own black shopping bag picking up pieces I thought she'd look beautiful wearing.

In the end, we compromised on some of each. "See, we are so compatible. We know how to compromise. That's important for all good relationships."

"Have you been reading my *Cosmos*?" Her intense look made me realize she was serious.

"Maybe. You left them on the coffee table at your house and mine. I'm learning a lot about what women like." I gave her my best panty-dropping smile.

She rolled her eyes and leaned over to talk softly. "Good. You can practice those things on me sometime. Now, pay your bill." She decided we'd split that, too. I'd volunteered to buy it all, but she wouldn't have it. See... another compromise.

My apartment bulged at the seams with the items she agreed to move. "We might need to get a two bedroom when the lease runs out. You've got a lot of shit, Indy."

"Sorry. I can get my own place if you want?" She grinned at me knowing I would never agree now that I had her here.

For the rest of the day, we unboxed her items and made it look more like a home. She chose pictures to hang and arranged breakable objects. "Are you sure you want to leave shit like that lying around? They could get broken."

"You'll need to be careful then. This 'shit' makes a house more homely. Don't you want it looking nice in here?"

I looked around. Maybe she had a point. "Yeah. It looks better but what's going to happen when we have a real party, and guys are making a fucking mess everywhere?"

"Guys will need to be careful or better yet, stay on the patio." She laughed when I gave her a hard look. "I'm kidding. If we're going to share this home, it needs to be both of ours. Do you have something you want to hang?"

I thought about her offer. "Yeah, I do." I went into the bedroom closet and brought out my framed Rams' team photo which was taken after we won the championship last year. "This. I might not have played in that damn game, but I helped win that trophy. This was my fucking team."

She looked at the huge picture. "Great. Where we going to put it?"

"Some place where everyone can see it." I looked at the spaces available. Not many were left after she hung something on almost every surface.

"How about in the hallway?"

"No. People can't see it." I moved to a spot by the door and took down a picture that I didn't have a clue about it. It looked hung upside down to me.

"But that's my Alfredon painting. I got it in Italy."

"The Alfredon needs to be in the hallway so it can brighten it up." I could play her game as well as she could. I turned and looked at her. I thought she would pout or something, but she was still smiling.

"Great idea." I hung my photo on the hook. "I love it." She nodded as she said it.

"Me, too. I love this compromising thing. We're good at it." Backing away, I moved behind her to admire my picture. My arms automatically encircled her. I kissed below her ear. "I know something else we're good at. Want to go to the bedroom, and I'll remind you?" I spun her around and kissed her lightly, but she wasn't having it. She hung on and deepened the kiss which I was more than happy to get on board with.

I slipped my tongue into her minty mouth and ran it along the sides of her. A slow moan came from deep down inside her as I cupped her ass and pulled her against my hardening dick.

Pushing her back against the wall beside the picture, I lifted her legs and wrapped them around my waist continuing the assault on her lips. I moved down her jaw and bit slow nips down her neck before running my tongue from her ear to the beautiful curve of her neck.

"As good as this is, our bed is a whole lot better, Indy."

"I agree."

I lifted her and carried her down the hall to our bedroom.

"Mmm. Our bed, Timms. Make love to me in our bed."

"Sounds perfect, sweets." I laid her down and came down over her. "I love you being here, India. I love your clothes in my drawers, your flowery pictures on my walls, your bottles of sweet-smelling things in the shower. I love everything about you." My lips came down on hers in a kiss hot enough to burn us both.

I inched her shirt up her body and pulled it over her head. She unhooked her shorts, and I raised up on my knees pulling them down her legs throwing them over my shoulders. "God, India. I could stare at you like this all day."

"But don't." She sat up and took my shirt hem lifting it over my head before unhooking her bra letting the straps fall down her arms. The heaviness of her beautiful tits caused it to fall away revealing the soft pink nipples that hardened to peaks from my heated look.

I stood, and she came up on her knees pushing the button through the eye on my shorts. She tugged them down leaving me standing in my black boxer briefs. "I thought you favored commando." Her eyes cut down to my hard length straining the underwear material.

"I've been told women like tight black underwear, especially with a big dick hiding behind it."

"Oh really? Were you told this or did you read it in my *Cosmo*, too?" Her lips ghosted across the skin below my navel and then her tongue snaked out and started up my abs causing me to flex from the sheer pleasure of it. "Whoa. Look at those." She continued tracing the valleys between the muscles as her fingers snaked their way in my underwear pulling them down. I dropped them and stepped out as she made her way upward until she was looking at me.

I wrapped my arms around her and kissed her again as we lay back together on the bed. "You're making it hard to make love to you, sweets. I might need to do that the second time around because right now, I want to fuck you hard and fast. Why do you do that to me?"

"No, stop."

"Stop?"

"Yes, stop. Take a deep breath. Calm down. I want it to be nice and slow this time." The look on her face told me she needed it this way, and I always aimed to please my girl.

She spread her legs and moved them around me lining my hard length on her sweet pussy. I stroked my length up and down her, scraping across her clit feeling it swell to a hard nub with each pass. I bent and kissed each pink tip before running my tongue slowly around the nipple. Sucking the pebble in my mouth, I lavished each one with my lips and tongue until she started writhing under me rubbing her clit even harder against me.

"I'm going to cum, Timms. It feels so good." She moved harder against me pushing down on her clit with each pass. I sucked her nipple in and bit down pushing her over the edge like I knew it would.

I grabbed my dick and slid it down to her opening knowing I would find it leaking her sweet juices waiting for me to use them for something even better. Around and around her opening I slipped the coated head of my dick until she was on edge from need.

"Please, Timms. Please. I need to feel you inside me."

"Anything for you, sweets." I slid home slowly. It almost killed me to go this slow. I wanted to plunge balls deep in one stroke, but I held back giving it to her inch by inch. I finally felt her sweet cheeks against my balls. I moved in and out of her alluring channel making sure to rub against her clit all the way in and all the way out.

A moan started from deep within her. She squeezed down with her legs holding me to her. "God,

Timms. It feels so fucking good, but I need more. I need to feel it harder."

"But you wanted slow."

"Changed my mind, babe. Fuck me."

I flipped us over, and she rose up leaning her hands on my chest. "You fuck me, Indy. Take all you want."

She began to move up and down my dick. The more times she did it, the more frantic she became. "Help me, Timms."

"Yes, ma'am." I took her hips in my hands and began pumping her up and down, slow at first and then harder and faster.

"Oh, it feels so good." I leaned her back still taking her at a fast pace. "Oh my God. That feels different. It's hitting something good. Oh yes. Do that. Do that." She began pumping on me harder than I was moving her, rubbing the rough patch inside her. "Timms, Timms, yes, oh my God, yes. Right there." She screamed and pumped and screamed some more until we drained every ounce of orgasm out of her.

She collapsed down on my chest. "That was the best ever. I mean it's always good, but something about that was different. It hit a new spot, and I fucking loved it."

"Good to know, sweets." I flipped us back over and took it slow and easy again moving in and out of her warmth. My own orgasm began building inside me, and I felt a tingle moving down my spine. She must have felt it too because she pulled her knees up, and I put them over my forearms so I could go deeper making her feel every move.

"Yes, sweets. Oh yeah." She began squeezing down on my cock and capturing it as her walls clenched around it in another heated orgasm for her.

"Oh, fuck, Indy, fuck yes, fuck... *yes.*" I pumped into her over and over, each time leaving a long rope of my cum until I was drained dry.

When I finally could move, I unfolded her legs and laid them down on the bed. Crawling off the bed, I retrieved a warm washcloth from the bath and cleaned both of us up. Then tucked her body in next to mine with my arm wrapped around her back and her head on my chest.

"I love you, India. More than I ever thought possible."

She barely spoke loud enough for me to hear, sleep trying to drag her under. "I love you, too, Theo. I do love you."

TIMMS

Waking early for some strange reason, I made my way to the kitchen to start some coffee. I slipped out of the bedroom as quietly as I could not wanting to wake my sleeping beauty.

The sun's rays barely shown over the horizon providing just enough light to make out the new objects in the den area so I didn't trip over them. I wanted to make coffee and enjoy the quiet before we hit the field for the day's practice.

Having an awesome patio was the reason I rented this place. My friends and I could drink beer and enjoy it in the evenings, and I could sit out in the mornings and chill before I had to face reality.

Apparently, we forgot to close the blinds from the night before because some extra light filtered in enough for me to almost see outside.

What I saw was movement.

Someone was on our patio.

"What the fuck?" I cleared the top of the couch to get to the patio doors. Slinging the blinds back, I pulled them out of the wall, getting myself mixed in the vertical plastic. I jerked on the handle and remembered the bar automatically falls into place. I kept my eye on the person as I tried to get it opened.

He jumped the wall when he saw me and took off. I watched as he ran, his long legs covering a great deal of ground fast. Finally, sliding the door back, I ran out and jumped over the wall, too. I looked in all directions but saw nothing.

Dammit, how could that be? How did he evade us twice?

This was too much. I ran around in all directions hoping to catch sight of him but came up empty-handed.

As I walked back to the apartment, I tried to think of what I did see of this guy. He had height on him as Indy said. I think he had dark hair, but under the cover of the patio, it was hard to be sure. I couldn't say what he wore—shorts and a t-shirt maybe. I didn't see his face.

India stood in the doorway of the patio when I jumped back over the wall. "Timms, what are you doing? You tore down the blinds."

"He was here, India." I pointed back out. "Right on the patio looking in."

"No. Please, no."

I pulled her in my arms. "Yes, Indy. He was out there."

"That's it. I'm getting a gun."

"No, you're not getting a gun. If you killed that guy, it would haunt you the rest of your life."

"I don't care. I'm not going to allow him to dictate my life."

"We need to get him. I agree with that, but we need to be smart about it."

"I'm tired of being smart. I want it over with."

"So do I, but we've got to catch him in the act, so there'll be no reason to doubt what's been going on."

"How, though? I'm so sick of it happening. What does he want? Why is he doing this?" She laid her face on my bare chest and then looked up at me. "Are you part of the problem now? Have I drawn you into my mess?"

"Indy, the day you became mine, I was in it. You didn't draw me in. You didn't make me part of it. He did."

"I don't want something to happen to you, Timms. I love you. If something happened to you, I couldn't handle it. I know what we have is new but still, I would be lost without you."

"Sweets, I know. But we need to get this settled together." I kissed the top of her head. I had no idea how to solve this problem until this guy was brazen enough to do something we could catch him at, but I was determined to stop this once and for all.

Guerrero came to the apartment as soon as we called him. After he left, we went to TAU. Indie had class, and I wanted to talk to Coach J. I planned to also talk to my guys. Surely we could come up with something to catch this fucking psycho.

Blue walked out of the locker room as I made my way down the hall to Coach's office.

"Hey, Half sac. What's up?" I hardly ever called him by his nickname anymore, but sometimes I liked to catch him off guard.

He gave me a grin. "What's up, dude?" We shook and did a man hug like always.

"Coming to talk to Coach about some shit going on."

"Something I need to help you with?" Blue was a forever friend, and I knew he would help me however he could.

"Maybe. India's got a fucking stalker that's getting too close, but I need to talk to Coach and her before I say anymore."

"I'm here if you need me. Don't hesitate to ask, man."

"Thanks, and I won't."

Walking off I made my way to Coach's office, I didn't know where to start on how to get help for this problem. Everyone was willing to do whatever necessary, but we didn't know where to start, and so far, the police didn't have any leads.

"Morning, Coach." He looked up from his papers.

"Oh... morning, Timms. What's got you here so early?"

"I'll get right to it. That dickhead that left notes on India's car has gotten more aggressive. He broke into her apartment leaving a message spray-painted on her wall, and this morning, I chased him off my damn patio. That's too close for comfort in my book."

"Hell yeah, it is. We can't have one of our coaches being stalked. Was all this noted in the police report?"

I nodded.

Coach J took a breath and let it out rubbing his hand down his face. "I've never had this problem before hiring a woman."

"This isn't her fault, Coach. It could be a crazy woman stalking any of the male coaches, but I'm beginning to wonder if this is a player."

His head jerked up. "What? You thinking Conner is still trying to harass her?"

"No, but it's possible. We need to look at others, too, though. This guy knows a lot about India, like where she goes and who she's with."

"She's not exactly trying to hide what she does, though."

"No, the girl's a damn hard-head. She refuses to stop her life for this guy."

"Son, all women are hard-heads. Didn't you know that?"

I had to smile because I knew he was devoted to his wife. "If I didn't know it before, I sure as hell know it now. She's talking about getting a gun to keep on her."

"That might be a good idea. Can she shoot?"

"Oh, hell no. She's not getting a gun. What if she got mad and shot me?"

A skeptical look crossed his face. "There's nothing wrong with protecting herself, Timms."

"No, but I'm going to step up and make sure she doesn't need a gun."

"You can't be with her twenty-four-seven, Timms. You smother an independent woman like India, and she's going to run the other way."

I thought about what he said. He knows a shit ton more about women than I do, so maybe he was right. That didn't mean I didn't want to take care of her and see to her safety, though.

"I know you're probably right, Coach, but I don't want her ever to feel like I'm not there for her."

"Then talk to her about it. Including her in decisions will make your life a whole lot easier down the road."

"I can do that." I stood stretching my arms above my head. "Guess I'll heed your advice. I just wanted to keep you in the loop on the problem and tell you my thoughts on who it is."

"If it's a teammate, we need to catch him. The sooner, the better."

Standing, I leaned against the doorframe. "Right. See ya at practice."

A beautiful woman leaned against the side of my car. With her long, dark blonde hair hanging in loose curls around her, she stood out more than any of the others making their way down the sidewalk to class. She looked up, and those glacier blue eyes met mine. How did I get so fucking lucky for a woman that perfect to love me?

"Hey, gorgeous," I called from the steps, and she immediately looked around to see who might have heard me. I didn't give a fuck who heard me. I'd shout it to the damn mountaintops. If people didn't see her beauty, they were blind.

I stopped in front of her and grabbed her around the waist, picking her up and swinging her around then kissed her hard. Let the damn masses see this shit. They'd all know she was mine, and I didn't give a shit what they thought.

She looked down at me and finally wove her hands across the back of my neck. "Hey, my hot-stuff boyfriend." She glanced around. "Guess you're doing a caveman act to inform everyone about us?"

"Hell yeah, I am. They all need to know who's got you now."

"Got me, huh?"

"Yeah, you're mine, and they better understand I take care of what's mine. Bring it on, piece-of-shit stalker. I'll take you down here and now."

"What the hell are you shouting about?" Blue walked up beside us.

"Just informing the world that she's mine, and I don't give a fuck who knows it." I looked at India and raised an eyebrow.

"Did you tell him?"

"Did he tell me what?" Blue asked her.

"Sweets, I wanted to make sure you were okay with it. I think the more who know, the better."

"Tell me what, Coach Durham?" I liked he addressed her with the respect she deserved.

"Let me down, Timms, and I'll tell him." I purposely slid her down my body creating some sexual friction for both of us. I grinned at her when her feet touched the ground, and she slapped my chest.

She turned to Blue. "I have a stalker, and he's getting more and more aggressive with the deeds."

"Damn, Timms, can't take care of your woman here?" He turned to India. "You don't have to worry about that another minute. Blue here will make sure you're safe. Hell, the whole team will."

"No, that's part of the problem. Timms and I both think this person is either on the team or associated with it."

"For real?" He looked at me. "Who would do that?"

"That's what the fuck we need to figure out and soon. The cocksucker was standing on my patio this morning but got away."

"You had him that close and can't say who the hell it is?"

"No, dude. It was still dark outside. He made sure to keep himself hidden in the shadows." I went on the defense immediately.

"Fuck that. We're going to get to the bottom of this."

"Wait, caveman one and two." India got between us. "We aren't going off half-cocked. This is serious."

"Sure as fuck is, India, and I'm tired of waiting around to see what he'll do next. Let's get it out in the open and be done with it." I needed her to be proactive to solve this problem.

"What's the plan?" Blue chimed in. I knew he'd have my back on this shit.

I turned to India. "Any ideas, Indy?"

"I've been thinking about it while I waited for you. Since he's obviously after me, we need to set up a sting using me for bait."

I stood straight up. "Oh, hell no. That's not happening."

"It's the only way, Timms. He's made it clear he plans to do some harm to me, so let's set him up."

"No, we aren't doing that. We don't know if he wants to hurt you."

"That's why I need a gun." She glared at me.

"Nope, no gun. I've already told you this. It's too damn dangerous."

"And this guy hurting me isn't dangerous?" she fired back.

Blue stepped up. "Yeah, I'm not in favor of you having a gun either. Besides, you can't carry it on campus even with a permit."

"Yeah, that's right. We know he's been here on campus from the notes."

"Timms, he's been in my personal space. I want him caught."

"Let me ask around at practice today."

"This needs to be discreet, Blue." India's skeptical look said she doubted his ability to do so.

"Hey, I can be discreet. I'll find out if anyone knows anything."

I looked at India and nodded. She needed to be the one to make the call, but I wanted her to know I was in agreement.

"Well, okay. I guess it'll be a good way to find out, but please keep the talk to a minimum. I don't like the idea of the players thinking I'm incapable of taking care of myself."

"I'm trying to tell you, sweets. You don't have to take it on alone. I'm here. My guys are here. We've got you." How did I convince her of this?

"Yeah, sweets, we got you," Blue repeated my phrase.

I gave him a go-to-hell look, and he laughed. "But seriously, Coach. We do have you. Let us do what we can."

She finally nodded her head. "Remember, though, be discreet."

"You know it." Blue jogged off catching up with a few of the players who walked down the sidewalk.

I turned back to her. "It's going to be fine, Indy. You'll see. We'll get this bastard."

"I hope so. I want it done."

"I know, sweets. Me, too."

INDIA

Practice started with a bang when one of the tight ends got hurt. It put everyone in a mood including my guys. Coach J ended up calling us all into a midfield huddle after the player's ambulance sirens died down as they moved further from the field.

I watched Blue off and on making his way around the team talking to various players here and there. His eyes met mine occasionally, but he tried to question them as I would.

We returned to practice, and my guys worked on distance. I knew sooner or later we would be called on to win another game, and a long field goal could do it. We took a break for water after an hour of kicking.

"Hey guys, we haven't had much time to talk. How are things going for all of you off the field?" I got some grumbling but nothing specific. "Zac, are your classes going okay?"

"Yes, ma'am. I got a pretty easy load this semester knowing football would take all my extra time. My grades are good, so I'm happy." He gave me a huge grin.

"Sounds great. What about you, Drew?" He looked down at me.

"I'm good." His face gave away nothing.

"How are your classes going? Anything we need to be worried about?"

"Nope, got it covered. Zac and I have the same classes."

"Great. Y'all can study together come finals."

"Conner? Don't tell me you have the same classes as these freshmen. I know better." I smiled at him, and he returned it.

"Nah, I've got nothing but kinesiology classes left. Simple. I saved all my easy ones for this last year, so I could skate for a change."

"Skate?" I hadn't heard this term.

"Yeah, you know. Skate by on easy street. Nothing to worry about. Roll into graduation."

"Oh, right. I get it now. Sounds like a plan."

"Ian, what about you?"

"Yeah, my parents helped me make my schedule. Major mistake. They wanted me to get started on everything, so I have a full load. I've been busting my ass since day one studying."

"You need help? I'm always around if you need me. I don't want you struggling while trying to play ball."

"No, ma'am. I'm good. I've found a few helpers on campus already." His face turned red, and the smile stretched from ear to ear.

"Helpers, huh?"

"You know how it is when you're a member of the Rams' football team. The women naturally flock to us, and when you say you need help, they come running."

The others laughed and made comments about him not knowing what to do with a woman anyway. The camaraderie between the teammates reminded me of why I loved being part of a team. In a way, each member became your family. I learned to depend on my team in college for everything, and it looked like I would eventually feel the same way about the coaching staff and players on this team.

"It sounds like you guys are set for now. Please remember I'm here to help you, too, for whatever you need." I glanced at Ian. "Not to find you new helpers, though. You're on your own for that."

"Not a problem for me, Coach. I got that taken care of the first few days." We all laughed at this kid.

The doorbell rang a few hours after practice, and I opened it to four big guys, Noelle, and Quinn. "Hey. Come on in." I stepped back allowing them to enter.

"Sorry to barge in," Noelle said and hugged me. "You remember Quinn, right?"

"Sure, come in. How are you?" The petite redhead stepped inside.

"I hear some kid's trying to fuck you over."

Yes, she's every bit like Chyna.

"I don't know about all that, but yes, I am having some problems with one."

"That shit's gotta stop. That's why we're here. We'll fix his dumb ass."

I couldn't help but laugh. "Okay. I'm all about that."

"Great. Now do we have beer or is it wine tonight?"

I walked to the kitchen. I have a big bottle of Moscato. You game?"

"Hell yeah. What's a planning party without booze?" I handed her a glass and opened the bottle. "Noelle? Some for you?"

"Sure. I love Moscato."

After pouring, we joined the guys on the patio.

Timms pulled me into his lap and whispered into my ear, "You okay with this?"

"Absolutely. Power in numbers, right?" I kissed his cheek. "Thanks for this."

He turned to Blue. "Did you learn anything today?"

"Nada. No one seemed to know shit about anyone being angry or wanting to get revenge on a coach. Whoever it is wants to keep it to himself."

"I spoke to all four of my guys, and they seemed okay. No one acted strangely."

"You mean stranger than usual?" Blue asked. "Kickers are a fucking breed all their own, you know."

"Hey, I was a kicker for four years." I tried sounding angry.

"Yeah, and look at you now, all over Timms. That takes a strange woman to want this asshat."

Everyone laughed at Blue's comment while Timms ran his middle finger up his forehead and then spoke. "Seriously guys. We joke about this shit, but really, there's nothing funny about it. We need to keep watch for someone who seems wrong or out of place. If you see my girl here, walk her to the next spot she's going to on campus, please. I don't want her to be alone."

"I told him I'd carry a gun, but he nixed it."

"No open carry on campus, sweets. I told you this already."

The group got involved in a heated conversation about guns on campus, and before long, I found myself drifting off on Timms' shoulder. The stress was starting to get to me and coupled with the amount of wine we'd downed, I couldn't prevent the sleepiness taking over.

I felt movement, and Timms stood carrying me with him. "I could've walked. I need to tell them all bye," I mumbled as I wrapped my arms around his neck.

"They're gone already. They didn't want me to wake you."

He laid me down and pulled my shorts off. The tank had a built-in bra.

"Hmm. I think I like this tank. No bra needed. Pretty good trick, sweets. Instant tit access." He gave a soft laugh before kissing my forehead. "Sleep, Indy." I'll be right back.

He pulled the covers up and kissed me again.

The bed dipped, and I rolled over to a dark room.

"I'm home," he said.

"I must have been extra tired to fall asleep with our company still here," I mumbled still half asleep.

"Maybe it was that second glass of wine you had."

I felt something wrap around my ankles. "What are you doing? I'm too tired tonight for fun and games with ropes, Timms."

"You're never too tired for this." He cinched the rough rope.

"That's too tight. You'll leave a bruise."

"I plan to." My eyes shot open wide, but with the room shrouded in black, I couldn't see much.

"What the fuck?" The outline of a tall man moved around me and grabbed my wrists.

"No, I don't plan on fucking you."

I realized then it wasn't Timms' voice talking to me.

"Who are you?" The sardonic laugh sent a chill up my spine. I twisted and turned trying to get away, but he laid across me keeping me from moving at all.

"I'm your judge, jury, and executioner."

"Why are you doing this?"

"Because you've caused me problems."

"What kind of problems? We can fix whatever it is." Keeping him talking might give Timms time to get back here.

"You can't because you've made up your mind." With my hands tied to the headboard, I wasn't going anywhere.

"About what?"

Where did Timms go? Surely, he'll be back soon.

The light flipped on, and I was now looking at a black mask.

"You picked your favorite, and I wasn't it."

"My favorite what?" I pulled and twisted, but nothing budged.

"Fuck it. You'll know soon enough." He ripped the mask off. "There, I can see you better now."

"Drew? What are you doing or why? I don't understand." This took me by complete surprise.

"Surprised, Coach Durham? I figured you would be."

"Why Drew? You're part of my squad."

"Shut the fuck up, bitch. I'm not part of your damn squad." He screamed into my face. He pulled my wrists checking them. "You chose your squad, and I'm not part of it. I'm the loser. I'm the bastard with no future on the team. Come next year you'll get someone better than me again. I'll still be the odd fucker out."

"No, you won't. You'll be the one to replace Conner. Don't you see? We planned to red-shirt you. I know you've got skills we aren't utilizing right now. We need to continue your training to take his place with four years of eligibility to play. You're ruining your life by doing this, Drew. Stop now. It'll be our secret. You'll still be able to play."

"Right. You're going to forget about this? That's a line of shit, and you know it."

"It's been you all along? You let us believe it was Conner." I twisted in trying to get loose.

"Yeah, badass Conner fed right into my plan with his stupidity. Him keeping that key became a huge stroke of luck. Then you and your fuck buddy talked the police out of it."

I heard a noise I recognized, but I didn't think Drew would. Timms' loud car rumbled to a stop outside our apartment. I didn't know where Timms had taken off to, but it didn't matter now, he was back. I prayed to God he wouldn't hang around outside listening to a song or his motor. If Drew didn't know the sound, Timms had the advantage of surprise.

"Dammit. That's his loud fucking car. Why couldn't he stay gone five more minutes? The son of a bitch is always in the wrong place. How can you let him keep you under his thumb that way and then be such a bossy bitch on the football field, or are you one of those kinky women who likes being told what to do? Is he like your Dom or something? That's it, isn't it? Does he spank you? Do you let him tell you when to cum? Maybe you like what I'm doing to you with the ropes."

"Timms will kill you when he finds you." I kicked my feet up.

"I said shut the fuck up, bitch. He's not going to find me."

He pulled back the curtains and opened the window pushing the screen to the ground below.

I'd had enough. "Timms!" I screamed and screamed over and over.

The front door rattled. "Open the door, India."

Drew must have locked it.

I screamed again. "He's here. Hurry, Timms, hurry."

Drew climbed through the window.

"India?" Timms started busting down the door with his shoulder.

"I'm tied up. He's out the window. Get him," I screamed as loud as I could. "He's going to get away again."

Timms rammed through the front door. "India?"

"I'm in here. Hurry." The bedroom door splintered into pieces as Timms broke his way through it.

"Go, he went out the window." I nodded toward the open window. "Get him. It's Drew from my squad." He might have heard me on his way through the opening.

I couldn't move. Lying here thinking about what might be happening made me crazy.

Drew could be killing Timms.

Did he have a weapon?

Worst case scenarios ran through my mind as I laid tied on the bed.

TIMMS

I bolted out the front door and around the corner hoping to catch him. As I rounded the end of my building, I barely made out a tall figure running in the dark. It might not be Drew, but it was someone running, and that's all I needed. The fucker would not get away from me this time.

In and out of buildings, the culprit zig-zagged his way back to the parking lot. He cut between cars weaving back and forth trying to lose me, but that wasn't happening. I'd been working out with my guys since being released, and I kept up with the best of them now.

"Stop, motherfucker, stop," I yelled as loud as I could. If anyone came out to see what I made noise about, maybe they would slow him down.

He continued onto Watters Avenue, which I knew like the back of my hand. The obscenities I yelled caught the attention of some driving by, but no one I knew.

I realized I was gaining on him when he crossed Gates Street. He had to slow because of traffic, but he did his best to weave through the stopped cars. "Stop him. Stop him."

Only one person had to be willing to step up.

A man stepped out of his car he'd paralleled parked and heard my noise. He looked up in time to see Drew running his way. There wasn't time for him to think, but he stepped to the side, and as the player ran past, he stuck out his foot and tripped him.

Drew sprawled on the sidewalk and tumbled over several times. The break in his stride was all I needed to catch him. Jumping on him while he was still down, I punched him hard. My adrenaline pumped heavily through me and came out with harder hits than I usually throw.

The man came up behind me and grabbed my arm before I could kill him. That's not what I intended to do, so the fight drained from me when the good Samaritan held my arm back.

A siren wailed in the distance. "I called 911 as soon as I stopped him."

My breaths came fast and heavy. "Thanks for that."

"What'd he do, anyway?"

"He's been stalking my girlfriend, and he broke in our home tonight."

"Then I'm glad I stopped him. After he tumbled over, I thought what if you were the bad guy and he was trying to escape you."

I stood up and put out my hand to shake his. "Thanks for your help. Theo…"

"Timms." He finished my name with me. "You were the quarterback here at TAU. I'm a huge fan. Sure hated to see you go down with the injury like that. Coach Jefferies bringing you on to help that new young man was brilliant on his part. I'm glad you agreed to join the staff." He shook my hand as long as he spoke.

"Thank you. I'm proud to be part of the Rams team now."

"You have every reason to be proud of the three-and-a-half seasons you played."

My chest puffed out some at his praise, my performance as a player was my only claim to fame.

"Looks like you're off to a great start this season, too. What's that new QB's name?" I was more than happy to answer his questions, but I wasn't sure now was the right time.

"Crew Devillier. You watch for this kid because he's going to do great things for the Rams." We heard a moan at the same time. I put my foot on Drew's chest determined to keep him down until the police arrived.

"Let me go," Drew said with a groan.

"The only place you're going is to jail." The sirens blasted down the street. Red lights flashed as the cars came to a stop. Police jumped from cars and ran to where we stood. I still didn't move my foot. No way would Drew get away this time.

The first officer kneeled and then spoke into his radio. "We need an ambulance at 575 Watters Ave." He stood and looked at me.

"Want to tell me why you gave this guy a good beating?" I looked at my new friend beside me and smiled.

"Be happy to, Officer." I gave him the rundown of tonight's events, and he wrote lengthy notes.

"Call Officer Guerrero. He can verify everything I'm telling you. He's been working this case trying to catch this dude." I glared down at a whining kid.

"Right. I'll be in touch with him." The cop looked at Drew as the EMTs loaded him on the gurney. "You do realize he might file assault charges against you?"

"Don't care. He deserved everything he got for the stunts he's pulled." I stopped and looked at the cop. "God. I've got to get home. He tied up India. She's still tied to the bed." I turned to run.

Thia Finn

"Stop, Mr. Timms. I'll give you a ride. I'll see if we can get Guerrero over there, too. We'll need to question Miss Durham."

With red lights swirling, we arrived in no time. The front door stood wide open where I'd left it running out. "India? Sweets?" I called from the doorway. In two long strides, I stood in the bedroom, the officer right on my heels.

"Timms, thank you, Lord. I've been trying my best to get these ropes off."

"Indy." I dragged out her name. "You're bleeding. Why did you try that hard? You knew I'd be back."

She looked past me to the young cop.

"Hello, miss."

Her eyes cut back to me. "Did you catch him? Why are the police here?" She expected answers from the look on her face.

"Yes, sweets, I caught the sorry bastard. They carted him off in an ambulance." I stopped realizing I probably didn't need to explain how I beat the hell out him with the police standing there listening to every word.

"Timms, did you hurt him?" I looked at her beautiful face.

"No, Indy. I only let him know he picked the wrong woman to tie up in my bed." My face broke into a smile hoping she would see some humor in this.

"You didn't say why the police brought you home." She sat up on the bed wearing only a tank and underwear. I saw the officer's eyes widen. I pulled up the comforter. He'd seen enough.

"We called the cops when I stopped him."

"How far did he get?"

"Down Watters, past Gates." I knew there would be an interrogation to follow.

"You ran all that way on your knee? How? You shouldn't have done that. You could blow it out again."

I sat down on the edge. "Indy, stop. This guy wanted to hurt you." I took her hands and turned them over examining her wrists. "Look what he did to you? I had to stop this madness and running him down got the job done faster." I continued untying the rough ropes from her bloodied skin. "I might have lost him if I'd stopped to get in my car."

I pulled her to me. "It's over, and that's all that matters to me."

"True." She turned her face up and kissed my cheek." "Thank you for everything."

A throaty noise interrupted our moment.

"Oh yeah, sorry. I forgot you were there, Officer."

He nodded. A loud banging hit the front door before I heard it hit the wall. Several large bodies filled our bedroom doorway.

"Dude. We came as soon as we heard. Did you get the fucker?" Blue huffed and puffed.

I stood. "Hell yeah, I did." I stopped again with the cop still listening.

"Gentlemen, I need in there, please." Another voice sounded from the back of the pack of muscle.

"Officer Guerrero. Dude, I'm glad you came so fast." I stood and shook his hand. "We got him this time, but I hate to say it, not before he hurt India."

"You're injured, Miss Durham?"

"Hell yeah, she is. He tied her up, and my girl here fought to get away." I pulled India's hands up so he could see the bloody wrists. She turned a bright shade of red, so I tucked them back under the comforter. She wrapped her hands at the end of the covers and pulled them up under her chin, looking at me.

"Uh, guys. Can you give her a few minutes with Officer Guerrero, please?"

"Oh yeah, sure thing. Sorry, India. We'll be right out here." Blue shot a look between the two officers and then at me. "Come on, guys. Let's give them a little privacy."

Office Guerrero stepped forward and looked down at the bed. "May I?" She nodded. I'd never seen a shy act out of this strong woman before.

"Can you tell me exactly what happened?"

I had to sit and listen to her retell the story of him coming in the room as she slept. The longer I listened, the angrier I became—mad at the culprit and myself. Here my beautiful woman slept without me in the bed. I failed to do the one thing I could do, protect her. What kind of man am I, thinking I can be the one she needs in her life? What a dumbass I was to put her in danger knowing something like this could happen at any time.

She didn't need someone like me. India needed a man she could depend on, someone who would always put her first. Did I need to run to the store for some pain reliever for her and more beer for me? Anyone of the guys would have gone for me. Why didn't I ask one of them to go? I should have been here for her knowing everything that had already happened.

Those expressive blue eyes answered questions from behind the covers. Was I capable of being the man she needed? Hell, was I the kind man any woman could ever depend on? She deserved the best, and I doubted I qualified.

INDIA

With my wrists healed and my testimony recorded, I wanted to move on with my life. My job waited for me. I appreciated the other coaches stepping up to cover for me. My squad knew what needed to be done, and I knew Coach J saw that my position could be eliminated with every practice I missed.

I stepped into his office and sat down. "Morning, India. Glad to see the bandages are gone." He glanced down at my wrists. "How are you feeling overall?"

"I'm fine, Coach. I'm ready to get back to work."

"What did the doctor say? Did she release you?"

"Yes, she feels like the sooner I get my life back, the better I'll be for recouping mentally."

"And what about the nightmares? Timms told me you wake up often yelling. Said it scares the hell out of him."

"I know it does, and I hate he's having to put up with it, but he refuses to let me go home. He's stuck to my side like glue except to come to practice."

I hated how he smothered me. I got that he felt responsible for not being there, but he can't be with me twenty-four-seven. We'd be sick of each other in no time. I tried to convince him to do other things, but he wouldn't have it.

"Have you met with your squad yet?"

I shook my head. "I was hoping to show up at practice today. I wanted to come to the game but decided it might create a scene, and games need to be about winning and not about me."

"India, no one feels that way. You got hurt because of being a part of this team. We're ready for you to return when you are."

"I'm ready. Today." I smiled at him. "I need to be there. Let's have a normal week of practice and then kick ass on Saturday."

Fortunately, Coach J returned my smile. "Then we'll see you this afternoon. Come ready to work those guys hard. I think they've been slipping without full-time supervision to push them."

I knew he exaggerated some for my benefit, but I would take it. "Thanks, Coach J."

"Yeah," he looked back down at his papers. "We'll see you on the field then."

I slipped out on the empty field. I felt like I was coming home after a long vacation. The quiet on the field calmed me. A few footballs lay on the sidelines so I picked one up and the tee one of my guys must have left behind. *Do guys ever pick up after themselves?*

Balancing the ball on the tee, I stepped off the marks needed to kick it from the thirty. It'd been a long time since I kicked to make it over the goal. Mostly, I kicked to demonstrate form these days, but today, I wanted to feel my foot hit the ball and watch it sail between the uprights. It used to be second nature to me. Now, I needed to concentrate and focus so the ball would do what I wanted.

I stood and stared at the goal posts for a while remembering every step necessary to complete the task. My mind cleared of everything clouding it for the past week. Counting off, I stepped into the motions and did a practice run at the ball without hitting it. The stretching of those muscles felt right.

On my second pass, my foot met the leather in the exact location, and my leg followed through after it flew off the tee. I watched the ball float with force and clear the horizontal bar of the upright but only by a few inches—*not good enough.*

I kicked ball after ball. Tomorrow my legs and foot would hurt. I didn't care. It felt good to work them out, do what they knew how to do, and repeat the action they felt made for.

My mind cleared of the turmoil as the balls flew through the air. My concentration on the task stopped all the dark clutter from taking up space. I felt right for the first time in so long.

I kicked the last ball from the four I'd gathered over and over, and it hit the bar and bounced over one last time. My leg was spent. My foot burned. My mind emptied. I sat down, and tears started down my cheeks for no reason I could explain. I knelt down beside the tee and bowed my head letting them flow.

"You know, you don't have to kneel and pray to the football gods, sweets. They'll hear you standing up." I knew Timms stood behind me.

"Yeah, but if you kneel, they understand you better. You're closer to the turf."

"Is that right? I guess I always wanted to be off the grass more than on it." He walked around and knelt down in front of me. "I wondered where you'd gone off to. I asked Coach if you'd been by, and he said you had. He said I might find you out here."

"I only know this place." I gestured with my arm around the stadium. "It's the one place I know I can feel at home."

"I get it."

"Drew's stunt almost took this from me, almost made me afraid to come back. If he could get to me to hurt me, others can, too."

"No, Indy. That's only true if you allow him to."

"Part of me says that's right, but then I see the marks still on me, and I question it all over again. Will I ever truly be safe wherever I am?"

He wrapped his arms around my middle and pulled my body into him. His chin moved over my shoulder so our bodies could touch from knee to head.

"I'm so sorry, India. I failed you in every way. I promised to keep you safe, and I didn't."

"You didn't. Our lives can't be put on hold to guard me, Timms. I won't allow it."

"Won't allow it? Indy, you have no idea what went through my mind when I heard you screaming. I couldn't get to you fast enough. When I chased that dickwad down the street, I berated myself for every wrong thing I've ever done because leaving you alone was like the straw breaking."

"Timms, I wouldn't want someone who's going to hover over me. I need us to be partners in this relationship, not you taking over my life. I want us to live our lives side by side."

"I want that, India, but if I can't protect you, how can I be the man you need me to be?"

"What I need you to be is yourself. I don't want you any other way. I love the person you are, Theo Timms.

I've spent the afternoon kicking balls so I could clear my mind and think about my life. Never once did you question the idea that I was a female on the man's football team. Never once did you doubt my ability to be a good coach. Never once did you suggest someone else would be better suited for this job. You supported me at every turn, you helped me make friends, you brought me into the fold of your group without hesitation, and you understood my need to be here.

"I love you, Theo Timms."

He just stared at me. He never took his eyes off mine. I expected him to at least comment on my profession of love, but he stared instead.

Slowly, a smile started at the end of his lips. It curled up his mouth until it spread across his face from side to side. "You still love me, right?"

"Yes, I love you. Did you not hear what I said?" I couldn't believe his question.

"You're telling me that even though I'm a big fuck-up when it comes to always doing the right thing, you still love me?"

"Yes, Timms. I love you."

"No, call me by my name."

I laughed. "Yes, Theo, I love you."

"Oh my fucking God." He stood taking me with him. "You hear that, football gods?" he shouted to the blue sky above us. "This beautiful, smart, talented football goddess loves me!" He swung us around and around laughing all the way.

"And..." I questioned with a raised eyebrow.

"And I love you, too, India Durham. I love you." He lowered his lips and kissed me. It started sweet with the barest of brushes over my lips, but then he pressed me harder to him and deepened the kiss as he ran his tongue over my lips seeking entrance. He slipped inside and ran his warm tongue around mine before I slowly edged up the side of his and entered his mouth. He sucked my tongue in and pulsed it in and out as though we were making love.

"If you two are through checking out each other's tonsils, I'd like to get the team practicing on this field instead of using it as your personal make-out spot. We used to go parking in a car in my day, not standing in the middle of a wide-open field for anyone to come along and watch."

We pulled apart and looked around as the whole team stood behind Coach J and the other coaches.

The team raised their helmets and started cheering for us.

He let me go but kept his arm around my waist. "Now Coach J, come on. What better place in the whole world for a beautiful woman to tell you she loves you than standing on a football field?"

"Is this true, Coach Durham?"

India looked at me and then at the team. "Yes sir, it is."

"Say it, sweets."

"I love Theo Timms."

We could hear the catcalls and wolf whistles for a mile as the team jokingly harassed about me using his real name. I could only laugh.

"Okay, that's enough. I'm not paying them to entertain you bunch of knuckleheads, let's get to work." He turned to us. "And you two, get back to your jobs and no more love birding on the field. Keep it in the bedroom, please."

We both grinned at Coach J. "Sure thing, Coach," Timms called as he gave me a peck on the lips for Coach's benefit and ran off leaving me to face the older man.

"Should have known he would do something like that." The boss shook his head and blew his whistle. "Let's get to work, men...." he turned to me, "... and woman."

EPILOGUE

TIMMS

"Pick up the couch, Blue."

"It's too damn heavy. Why did y'all get this big monstrosity, so I'd have a place to stay when Noelle kicked my sorry ass out?"

"Hell no, boy. Get your own couch to sleep on."

We walked in and set it in the spot India indicated. "It looks perfect there. I love it looking at the fireplace." She smiled as she ran her hand over the buttery leather.

"I love it looking at the big screen TV above the fireplace." Blue and I high-fived. "Sports for the win."

"Hell yeah, it is," he added.

"Stop congratulating each other and go get more furniture. We'd like to get this done before dark,"

Noelle berated the two. "You guys have such one-track minds."

Blue wrapped her from behind. "Oh no, babe. I can think of several other things always on my mind, and they all involve your body, preferably naked."

"Shut the fuck up, Blue. No one wants to think about the two of you getting down and dirty," Quinn said coming out of the kitchen. "The last thing I want on my mind is your naked half sac running around this apartment."

That garnered a laugh from all of us, especially when Blue grabbed his junk and shook it behind his hands while staring at Quinn.

"You two are nasty," India told them. "I can't believe you talk to each other like that."

"Always have. She knows I love her." Blue wrapped his arm around her neck and kissed the top of her head.

"Eww. Now that shit right there's nasty. Keep your mouth to yourself. Who knows where it's been." Quinn pushed him off her.

"My mouth has been in places you'll never go, sweet thing." Blue laughingly told her. "And don't be talking bad about my woman like that."

"Bllluuueee," Noelle yelled at him. "Too far."

I watched India during all of their verbal sparrings. She took it all in stride and continued to work unpacking. She fit in with my gang of friends without missing a beat as I knew she would. They accepted her into the fold easily, too. She was part of my family now.

"Let's hook up the TV first so we can watch the Orange Bowl," I suggested to change the subject, or before Blue got himself in trouble with all the women.

"That's a great idea. I'll be glad when we finally get to play in the Championship Bowl next week," Blue added. "I'm ready to get this massacre over with and hold that huge trophy up for all the world to see."

Quinn rolled her eyes. "Good plan on the TV. It'll shut the twat-waffle up faster," Quinn added. This gained her a laugh from the ladies.

Blue whispered to me, "What the hell's a twat-waffle?"

"Who knows, but coming out of her mouth it could be the worst." We both smiled knowing what I said was the truth.

A knock on the door caught all our attention. Tucker and Crew walked through the door with Tucker holding a bottle of wine.

"Dude, wine?" I snickered.

"Yeah, my mom sent it. Said it was an appropriate housewarming gift." Tucker walked in the kitchen and stored it in the fridge.

"That was very nice of her or you or everyone," India told the two. "Are you even old enough to buy booze?"

"No, so my mom sent it back with me after Christmas so I wouldn't have to. Made me ride with it wrapped in the trunk so I wouldn't get a ticket, too."

"Smart mom," the three women said.

India stopped what she was doing and questioned the two players about their holidays. "So did you both have a great holiday with your families?"

"Oh yeah, the band always takes a break until New Years," Tucker added. "They play a small venue on New Year's Eve so we can all come along. The bigger venues get too rowdy according to my mom."

Crew spoke up. "Our moms think every venue's too rowdy to bring us. Sometimes I think they believe we're still playing ball for the middle school and are twelve-year-olds."

India laughed. "I'm sure they don't want your younger brothers and sisters exposed to the wildness."

"We weren't allowed to go to a big show until we were eighteen," Crew added.

"Right and then the little kids had to stay with the sitter. His mom would say twenty-one, but our dads finally overruled her. Said we were going off to college and needed to see what life was really like, and we did, didn't we, Tuck?" The two kids bumped knuckles.

Quinn listened to this. "You see that right there is the reason I doubt I'll ever have kids. Mine will be exposed to too much way too early."

Blue looked at her. "Your kids will be exposed to bad language in the womb. They'll probably come out with a pirate patch and cussing like sailors."

"Hell yeah, they will, and it'll be fucking funny, too." Quinn bent over with laughter. The other two women shook their heads.

I caught what the boys said when they high-fived. "Wait, back up. What exactly did you guys see when your dads took you to your first big show?"

Blue joined in. "Yeah, maybe Timms and I need to go to one of these shows. We might be missing out."

"Dude, you don't even know what those groupies will do. My dad made me take a condom in each pocket. Said, 'always wrap before tap.'"

"That's disgusting," Noelle commented with a turned-up nose. "You are not going to one of those shows if that's what it's like."

"It's not disgusting if it means some skanky ho keeps her germs to herself," Quinn added.

"If they are skanky ho's, why do they let them backstage?" India asked with innocence.

Tucker turned a little red but looked her straight in the eyes and said, "Because some of the band members like being watched when they have sex, and those women will do anything to have it with a rock star. Crew and I were treated like rock stars when we were backstage, and our dads threatened us all the way home. Told us if we let it slip to our mothers, they would take us out of their wills."

"And we believed them, too. My mom would probably beat my dad with her frying pan if she ever found out the things we did with those women."

"Oh, really?" Quinn egged them on. "Tell us, oh wee ones, what kind of kinky things did you do with the women?"

"Stop," I yelled. "We are not discussing their sex lives. India and I don't need to know that much about our players." I looked at both guys. "Save it for another time." I glanced at India and Noelle knowing this would never fly.

"Right," Blue spoke up. I think we should get this furniture finished up, and these two wild children can help us out. "Come on guys." We led them out the door.

INDIA

I looked around our bedroom. It held each piece of furniture I picked out in the perfect location. Our townhouse looked like a home now with pictures hung, boxes unpacked, and beds made. I loved our little home.

"Theo, are you almost ready?" He walked in with his suit on, and my heart skipped a beat. I'd never seen him look so hot. "You've been keeping the hot businessman look from me. I think I like it better than the football uniform look."

"You like it, huh? I'm not too fond of a tie, but I can handle it sometimes." He pulled at his collar a little.

I stepped up and adjusted the knot. "I think you look good enough to peel this off you and have my way."

He pulled me in for a kiss. "Good, turn around, and I'll unzip you."

"No, we have a New Year's party to go to. It was so nice for Crew and Tucker's dads' band to invite us to their private party."

"Besides that, you look too beautiful not to take out and show off." He pulled down on his cuffs. "Yeah, good to have friends in high places, huh?"

"Why thank you for the compliment." I kissed his cheek. "Assured Distraction is a big deal in high places, too. I just hope we don't see the kinds of things that the guys were talking about over here."

"No, it's not that kind of party. This is a formal party. I bet groupies aren't invited, especially since the wives will all be there."

"Honestly, I don't know how the wives handle those women around their husbands. I wouldn't want you around them, and you're not even my husband. That's too much temptation."

"You're all the woman I need. No skanks in my bed." We both laughed knowing the frat house had its fair share when he lived there.

After we gathered our things, we took the drive over, and the valet took the keys to my car as we stepped out.

Timms looked at me as the kid drove it away. "I don't know why we couldn't bring my car. These kids would like driving mine a hell of a lot more."

"Because yours is too loud. When are you going to give that muscle car up?"

"Never, woman." He pulled me into his side, and we walked under the awning into the ballroom.

"Wow. This place is beautiful." I looked around at the decorations. "Someone did an awesome job making it look perfect for the party."

"Not as gorgeous as you look tonight." He winked at me.

We snagged some champagne from the tray as the waiter passed. I took a sip. "Mmm, it's the good stuff, too."

"I'd rather have a beer." We both laughed. "Not too much on these damn bubbles."

We stepped over and joined our table with Blue, Noelle, Quinn, and Gerrod, who made it in today for the holidays after his big game the past week. The group talked and laughed. I enjoyed listening to the stories the guys told on each other. They had all enjoyed their time on the team together in college and the fraternity.

I heard some noise at the main doorway to the venue and glanced over to see Chyna arguing with the guards. My head whipped around at Timms.

"What? How? Did you do this?"

"Yeah, but I think we better get over there and rescue the guards before we discuss it. She looks like she's ready to castrate them in one smooth move." I couldn't help but laugh knowing it was a distinct possibility.

We made our way over to Chyna as quickly as we could in the crowd, but not before they managed to subdue her in a body hold from behind. She kicked everything she could get her legs to touch. The poor guy holding her might never have children.

"Chyna," I yelled. "Calm down."

"It's about time, India. These jerkoffs weren't going to let me in since I don't have a ticket. I assured them I was invited."

Timms spoke up, "Guys, she's here with us so let her go, but only if she promises to play nice." He smiled at her, and she nodded her head.

As the guard let her down on her two feet, I yelled again, "No kicking, Chyna."

"Well, dammit, you take away all the fun." She turned and snarled at the bewildered guard who raised his hands in defense.

I noticed Tucker and Crew stood behind me now. I guess everyone in the venue caught some of her captivity.

I stepped forward and hugged her. "I'm so excited to see you, but what are you doing here, Chyna?" I asked as I hugged her close.

"I got an invitation from your man there." She ran her eyes up and down Timms like she was going to eat him alive. "I can see now why you're here, though. Woo. That's a lot of hotness in a suit."

"Chyna." I used my *keep your hands to yourself* voice.

"All right, I get it." She looked over my shoulder at the two younger players standing there staring at her.

"And these two? You keeping something on the side, sis?"

"Oh my God, Chyna. You're the worst, but I still love you." I hugged her again. I pulled back but kept an arm around her shoulders. "This is Theo Timms, and you know already this is my sister, Chyna, since apparently the two of you have talked behind my back."

"Great to meet you in person, Chyna." He kissed her cheek. I feared she would climb him like a tree, so I kept my arm firmly planted around her shoulders.

"Nice to meet you, too, Timms. I can see what's keeping my sister here in Texas." He looked at me baffled as to what to say to her blatant comments.

"Damn, guys, you are both too serious. It's only a fucking joke. Calm down."

"Chyna," I admonished. "We're guests in an important party."

Quinn piped up. "Hell yeah, I think I found the younger version of me. I fucking love her already." We all laughed.

"This is Quinn and Gerrod." They shook hands.

"And who are the two guys with their eyeballs on the ends of their noses?"

I looked around and knew she referred to Tucker and Crew. The usually talkative two stood staring. Hmm. I'd need to keep an eye on them. She might have them for dinner.

"This is…" Before I could get the names out, the two younger guys were standing in front of her talking at the same time and trying to be first to shake her hand.

"At the risk of being rude, let me introduce you. This is Tucker Powell and Crew Devillier."

Chyna seemed to be stunned for a second, not typical behavior for her.

"You mean like, Powell and Devillier from Assured Distraction? Are you two related to the band?"

Crew stepped up and offered his arm. "Why yes, we are. Come with us. We'll introduce you as soon as they walk in." Not to be outdone, Tucker took her other arm in his, and the three headed to the front of the room.

A short time later Assured Distraction came in from their big concert and played a few songs for us to enjoy. These men were smoking hot even if they were a good twenty years older than me. They performed songs we all loved and sang along to.

When they finished, Tucker and Crew brought their parents over to the table to introduce us to them. Noelle, Quinn, and I totally fangirled when it came time to speak to these gorgeous men and their beautiful wives. They were all dressed in formal wear making them seem even hotter. I caught myself before I fanned my face.

We all laughed and talked. Even though they were important people, they treated us like family and thanked us for keeping an eye on their sons. Tucker and Crew didn't like that their moms asked us to do it. We got a good laugh at that.

They said their goodbyes and started to leave, but Timms walked away with Tuck, Crew, and the two dads still talking about football. He came back to the table shortly after.

"Let's dance, sweets. I like this music." Timms took my hand and kissed it.

"How can I turn that down, girls?" I smiled at Quinn and Noelle.

"No fu—" Quinn stopped herself and looked around. "No way. Old Timms here cleans up nicely."

The entire table laughed at Quinn's attempt to watch her language for a change. "I can do it if I have to. I just try not to go places where I have to very often." This brought on more laughter because we all doubted her still.

He pulled me close, and we swayed slowly to James Arthur's 'Say You Won't Let Go.'

"I love this song," I softly spoke into his ear before I left a kiss on it.

"I love you more."

I leaned back and looked at him. "You are certainly romantic tonight."

"Can't I tell my best girl I love her and how beautiful she is?"

"Anytime you want. Who wouldn't like hearing it from a hot guy like you?"

This made him chuckle a little. I laid my forehead on his chest, and he kissed the top of my head. New Years' Eve magic seemed to float around the room with the decorations, beautiful people, and gold and silver tables fully dressed.

The song came to a stop, and I stopped moving my feet, stepping back. I looked around, and we were the only ones still left on the dance floor. My face turned red because I thought we'd stayed too long on the floor. Did they clear the floor for a reason?

Tucker stepped up with a microphone and clipped it on Timms' lapel.

I looked between both guys. "What's going on?" My face had to look puzzled.

"India." Theo took a deep breath. "I've been thinking about this for a while now… I guess since the day I knew I was in love with you and now I'm kinda nervous." He glanced around the room. My face started burning. What was he doing?

"I never expected to find a woman who loved football and loved me, too." This caused the audience to quietly laugh and me to get redder. "I knew when I found you, I had someone special, though. Someone I could share my goals with, my wins with, my losses with, and you'd understand because you get me. You get my need to have someone who can walk beside me in all ways even when I want to try to be the caveman." More laughter. He looked around. "Man, am I messing this up." He took another deep breath.

"Anyway, what I'm trying to say is I love you, and you've told me you love me, too." He glanced around at the onlookers. "She's crazy, huh?" More laughter.

"I think that two people who are in love like us and enjoy so many of the same things as we do should be together for all times." He got down on his knee and pulled a vintage ring from his pocket. "So for all the right reasons to be married, I wanted to ask you," he cut his eyes to our table and then back to me. "I wanted to ask you if you'd do me the honor of being my wife for now and forever?"

With tears breaking over my lower eyelids, I put my left hand out and nodded yes. I knew for a fact I could speak after the proposal he'd made. My other hand covered my mouth as I continued to nod while he put the perfect ring for me on my ring finger.

He stood, and I wrapped my arms around his neck and his went around my waist as he picked me up and kissed me for all to see. The audience clapped and shouted words of congratulations before joining us on the floor.

"I love you, India," he whispered in my ear before lowering me down.

"I love you, too, Theo Timms."

Assured Distraction Boxed Set

Coming soon with a brand new Novella included. You asked for it, so I'm including Ryder Steel's story from when he leaves Laina, unsure if he's going to be a dad.

Be sure to watch for the announcements on my social media pages.

ACKNOWLEDGMENTS

It's been said it takes a village to raise a child. I feel the same way about a novel. My village consists of people from various parts of my life.

To the readers. Only through your encouragement do I continue this journey of storytelling. I've met so many people online who send me messages, ask me questions that make me think and extend stories, offer suggestions about characters, and generally keep me grounded.

To the friends I've made at signings. Meeting you at parties or meet and greets allows me to hear what you have to say. I listen when you're talking to me, to the models, to other authors, and to each other. These nuggets I gain are stored for future use. Sometimes they are positive and sometimes not, but everything comes back at some point to mold and shape my future books.

To the authors and all the peripheral people in the book world I've met online. Your comments mean the world to me. Your acknowledgment offers me hope. Your positive outlook makes me want to work harder. Your negativeness makes me re-evaluate my outlook. I feel fortunate to interact with all of you.

To the authors I've met at signings. Your words shape and mold my writing and my friendships. Your genuine words and behaviors change me. Seeing who you are, how you interact, and why you react to situations makes all the difference to me. I learnt to trust your opinions and question the motives through your eyes.

With all that being said, there are many I need to personally thank for making this book a reality. **Sharon Johnson**, you make me feel like I can take on life. **Michele Mankin**, your kindness and willingness to offer your expertise makes me hopeful. **Hilary Storm**, you show me that I need to be strong and not let little things get in my way. **Sharon Johnson** for believing in me and pushing me to try new things.

The **Wander Team—Wander Aguiar, Andrey Bahia**, and **Jenny Flores**. Y'all are the best. You make me feel like I'm able to do whatever I want. I love each one of you in your own way. Wander captures beauty like no other. Andrey makes sure I've got all the best pics. Jenny, my road-trip warrior, keeps me young.

My beta readers—**Mayas Sanders, Julie Lafrance, Theresa Talbot**, and **Cynthia McGowen**. I need you all to make my books the best. Without a perfect story, they would be nothing. Thank you all for listening, suggesting, correcting, and loving my guys as much as I do.

To **Finn's Freaks**. Wow, you people are so fun. Your support of my books, my takeovers, and my games is amazing. The kind words and encouragement goes further than you know. We need more time together!

To the ladies at **Swish Design and Editing—Kay, Kim,** and **Nicki**. Thank you for working with a crazy lady who cannot meet a deadline, EVER. They make my books look beautiful and read professionally.

To **Julie Lafrance**. She stepped in and took over when I wanted to walk away. She allows me to spring things on her at the last minute and never complains. She boosts my spirits when I'm down and laughs with me when I'm in the clouds. I love the friendship we've developed and pray we continue to have it for years to come.

My family. **Mary LeFebvre**, my sister, reads all my books and never complains at some of the crazy things I include. I love her support because it often shows up when I need it the most. My girls, who won't read my work but understand my need to write, thanks for not complaining when I'm not available to do your bidding. To my husband, **Steve**, thanks for agreeing to hold down the fort while I run around the nation even when I get in a little 'fix' and need saving. (NOLA could be the death of me.)

These people fall under several different categories, so I want to say thank you! **David Scott, Jamie Walker (model extraordinaire), Dale Gardiner, Mayas Sanders, Tre Talbot, Kim Ginsberg,** and **Elaine Marie**. Thank you all for talking and helping me, believing in me, and working with my craziness!

Goodreads Links
Check out the books below and add to your TBR list.

Assured Distraction Series
Assure Her (Assured Distraction Book One) –
Keeton's Story
His Distraction Assurance Distraction Book Two) –
Ryan's Story
His Assurance (Assured Distraction Book Three) –
Gunner's Story
Distracted No More (Assured Distraction Book Four) –
Carter's Story
Hayden's Timbre (Companion Book to Assured Distraction
Series) Hayden's Story

Fat Boys Series
Half sac
Lateral Moves

Website
http://www.thiafinn.com

Email
author@thiafinn.com

Facebook
https://www.facebook.com/ThiaFinn/?fref=ts

Goodreads
https://www.goodreads.com/author/show/
14206242.Thia_Finn

BookBub
https://www.bookbub.com/profile/thia-finn

ABOUT THE AUTHOR

Growing up in small town Texas, **Thia Finn** discovered life outside of it by attending The University of Texas, only to return home and marry her high school sweetheart. They raised two successful and beautiful daughters while she taught middle school Language Arts and eventually became a middle school librarian. After thirty-four years, she retired to do her favorite things, like travel, spend time off-roading with family and friends, hanging out at the Frio River, reading, and writing.

She currently lives in the same small town where she grew up, with her husband and the boss, Titan, the Chihuahua. She can often be found stalking on social media, watching Outlanders, Vikings or Game of Thrones to name a few on Netflix.